WOLFSBANE

MIA CASE FILES 1

KC BURN

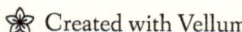 Created with Vellum

PROLOGUE

One Year Ago

CARMICHAEL HOISTED his duffel bag on his shoulder and strode out into the sunlight. He stood out on the base in his brand-new black jeans and black t-shirt, but as of today he was no longer part of the military. After nine years, the standard combat uniform was no longer part of his wardrobe and would never be again.

The sun was every bit as bright as in Afghanistan but nothing else from smells, to sounds, to the thick humid South Carolina air, was the same. After that one patrol, that one *incident*, he'd never been happier to be stateside, knowing he'd never have go back to that arid, war-torn country.

Never again.

Despite being closer to evening than high noon, a fine sheen of sweat popped up on his skin that could only be banished by finding some air conditioning. *Best get going, then.* All of his belongings fit in his duffel bag and he had a brand-new life to start. One that would hopefully keep the nightmares at bay and let him forget the terrible things he'd seen, the worst of which had happened over two months ago.

Carmichael walked toward the guard house at the base's entrance. He'd have to think about getting a car, but his first concern was getting the fuck away from here.

Probably he should be thankful. He was alive. Most of the men who he considered to be friends hadn't made it out of the desert, three of them perishing during the *incident*. The knee injury he sustained that night had been enough to get him a medical discharge. He'd originally intended to be a career soldier, and the military police suited him perfectly.

Until that night. Until he and his partner, Martin, had tracked down who—what—they'd thought was a serial killer. That night had changed him, irrevocably.

The memory of flashing eyes in the dark and the clack of teeth—fangs—sent a shiver down his spine.

No. Just no. Bad enough that unnatural, inhuman teeth and claws haunted his dreams. He refused to think about the *incident* during daylight. Because there was no way he'd seen what he thought he'd seen.

He had no idea how that particular delusion had come about, but he'd been sane enough to know he had to keep that shit out of his after-action report, or he wouldn't have had the luxury of an honorable discharge. If he was truly losing his fucking mind, his position of authority would only result in innocents getting hurt or killed.

He walked past the guard station and continued on down the road. Around a bend the base and guardhouse disappeared from view behind him.

Another couple of miles and a gallon of sweat later, he was on the main road, well off government property. He appreciated the lush greenery because it looked nothing like the desert, but that wasn't enough for him to want to stay in South Carolina. He pulled out his phone and ordered a rideshare. Only a fifteen-minute wait. Not too bad.

It looked like he was totally in the sticks, but the base wasn't far from a couple of towns. One of them would have a bus into Charleston where he'd head to the airport and take the next flight heading somewhere north, as long as it wasn't Cincinnati. Someplace that would have snow in a couple of months might be a novelty.

He'd never really planned what he'd do after he left the army, since he hadn't intended to leave this soon. One city or town was probably much like another, but there was no way he was heading back to the shitty memories of Cincy.

He'd find a job, find an apartment, then he could plan for the rest of his life. He had enough savings after nine frugal years in the military that he could probably buy a small place just about anywhere he decided to hang his hat, as long as he got a halfway decent job.

Ten minutes later, a large, pearly white SUV pulled off to the side of the road in front of him.

Not his ride, though. He'd opted for the cheapest version, not an executive ride. Also, the app had told him to expect a blue sedan. Unless he'd imagined that too. Just to reassure himself, he opened the app. Yup, a blue sedan. This guy must be lost or need to take a leak.

Then the image on his screen...fritzed. Like when he was a kid and his granddad's old television needed the antenna on the roof to be adjusted. Carmichael had never seen his phone do that. He tapped at the screen. Scrolling didn't work, and he couldn't flip to another screen or open another app.

Fuck. He did *not* love the idea of having his phone die out here. In desperation, he rebooted the whole damn thing, and a few seconds later, his rideshare app was back.

Now, though, the car was listed as a white SUV. A quick comparison confirmed the license plates matched.

Carmichael frowned at the vehicle, idling on the shoulder. Weird. He'd feel a lot better if he had a sidearm, but he'd never bothered wasting his money on a personal weapon. He'd never seen the point. He didn't particularly want to figure out how to deal with one on a commercial flight, either, but buying one was going near the top of his mental to-do list when he landed in whatever his new hometown would be.

Top of the list, naturally, was figuring out if he was sane and safe enough to be trusted with a weapon, and at this point he only gave himself fifty-fifty odds. Hallucinations and weapons were a lethal combination.

A trickle of sweat slid down his spine into the crack of his ass. Fuck it. He was getting in that SUV.

Between his build and his training, he had an advantage over the average Joe Q Public, so he wasn't too worried. Walking another fifteen miles or so in this heat was definitely not on his agenda today.

He opened the passenger side back door. The driver, a well built, older dark-haired man twisted in his seat.

"Carmichael? Toss your bag in the back and come sit in the front."

With the restraint born of nine years listening to asshole commanding officers, Carmichael avoided rolling his eyes. Front seat meant dude wanted to talk. He hated chatting, he hated small talk, and he hated telling complete strangers about himself.

But the driver would soon figure out that conversational attempts with Carmichael would be less than rewarding.

To Carmichael's surprise, they rode for several miles without even a radio to break the silence.

Then the driver cleared his throat, and Carmichael cringed inside.

"I'm Oliver."

Carmichael grunted. Dude already knew his name from the app, and there wasn't a good reason to say it again.

"Got a job lined up?"

Every muscle in his body tensed for a second. "What?"

"Got a job lined up? Security, maybe? Or law enforcement?"

"Why do you think I need a job?" Because he did but it wasn't like he was wearing a sticker on his chest: Hello, my name is Homeless and Unemployed.

Oliver lifted a shoulder in a half-shrug but didn't take his eyes off the road. "You're wearing civvies, your bag is army issue, and the only thing down that sideroad is a military base."

Carmichael narrowed his eyes. "And that means nothing. I could be on leave."

"But you're not, are you." The words should have formed a question but Oliver made them into a statement.

It wasn't a question and Carmichael wasn't going to volunteer any information. He did, however, inspect his driver a little more thoroughly. He had an oddly official air about him, not like any driver he'd come across over the years, unless this was a side gig for him.

But something about this didn't sit right and the renewed silence was maddening. An effective interrogation tactic, but fucking maddening nevertheless.

A few minutes later, they drove past the exit for the nearest bus station and Carmichael had had enough.

"Turn around, you're going the wrong way."

"I've got a job for you."

"What the fuck does that mean?"

"I have a job for you. I think you'd be perfect for it."

This was some serial killer level shit, or this was the end game for Carmichael's scrambled brains.

"Turn this fucking car around."

"Just do this one job. It's... sort of fugitive recovery. It might suit you. If it doesn't, after we're done I'll not only drive you directly to the airport, but I'll pay for your ticket. Anywhere in the world you want to go."

Anywhere in the world? Maybe there were two insane people inside this vehicle.

"I want to go to the bus station."

"Look, this is a bit of an emergency. I was hoping to ease you into this, but we don't have the time."

"Your emergency isn't my concern." If there even was an emergency. If his buddy Chris hadn't died in the desert a year ago, he'd suspect this was a prank Chris had dreamed up. But he didn't know anyone else who'd even bother setting up something this elaborate.

"No, not until you're employed by our agency. But I think you'll find this is a good fit for you."

"I have no intention of living in the South." For a number of reasons, but right now, the temperature was number one.

"No problem. Being this far south is an anomaly for us. We're based in the Northeast."

Carmichael huffed and clenched his hands into fists. "I haven't had many job interviews in my life, but I don't think this is how they're supposed to go."

"That's fair. But our agency is not exactly... standard."

"This is a sex thing, isn't it? I'm not interested."

"No, it's not a sex thing."

Right. Carmichael curled his lip. "Just turn the car around, okay? I have a bus to catch."

Oliver gave that half-shrug again. "But we're heading into Charleston anyway. And that's where you were heading, right? You might as well let me drive you there."

"Oh, hell no, I'm not paying for that." Then Carmichael noticed the one thing, the one glaring thing he should have noticed before he even got into the SUV.

There was no phone or tablet contraption with the driver's part of the rideshare app. There was nothing that would tally the cost of his ride, either. And Oliver—if that was his real name—was also wearing a navy sports coat. In South Carolina. Sure, it was the week before Thanksgiving, but it was also ninety-eight degrees out, not factoring in the humidex. They were swimming in moisture the same temperature as normal body heat and it was fucking awful.

"Who are you? You know what, never mind. Just let me out of the car right now."

Oliver reached into his jacket pocket and Carmichael tensed until he saw the slim leather wallet. With a flick of Oliver's wrist, the wallet landed neatly on Carmichael's lap.

Propelled into hyperawareness mode, Carmichael lifted the wallet up so he could continue to keep an eye on Oliver while he opened it.

The only thing inside was a government issue ID card for Oliver Cardoso. Looked legit, and Carmichael had had some experience over the years assessing forged documents.

"What's MIA?" The letters were a faint holographic watermark in the plastic.

"You know the government and their alphabet soup, right?"

The non-answer made Carmichael grit his teeth. "What does MIA stand for?"

"Classified. If you accept the job offer, you'll find out."

Fuck. What the hell had he gotten into?

"And when will you tell me what this job entails? What it pays?"

"Later."

The traffic got heavier as they approached Charleston, hitting rush hour, and Carmichael fiddled with the air vents to direct more cold air his way. He had to admit, he'd half expected Oliver to take him someplace even more off the beaten path than the road outside the base. Traffic sucked, and a whole city full of people couldn't dissuade a person bent on criminal or violent activity—obviously—but the sight of civilization eased a bit of his worry. Only a bit, though. He'd thought he was done serving his country.

But he did like the idea of a ready-made job falling in his lap, even if Oliver's secrecy and attitude sucked. He'd met a couple CIA guys over his years as an MP and they'd been total assholes. The jury was still out on Oliver. Maybe MIA was related to the CIA? But fugitive recovery sounded more like the Marshals.

There was a destination set up in the vehicle's GPS but Oliver hadn't seemed to need the directions as he exited the highway and made several turns along surface streets.

"Why aren't you driving a regular government black SUV?"

"Because whenever anyone sees them, they immediately think government."

"But you are the government, right?" Carmichael could still be convinced that this was all some weird scam. If this "job" entailed anything illegal, he was punching Oliver in the face and getting the fuck away.

"But we're extra secret this way."

Carmichael grimaced. *Extra secret?* What the fuck ever. Oliver was definitely an asshole. The lack of standard government license plates probably helped too. He would have noticed those.

A few minutes later, as the sun finally dropped below the horizon, they pulled into a neighborhood that was economically depressed in a severe way. Reminded him of the neighborhood he'd grown up in. He hated it but there wasn't anything here he was afraid of. Not even extra-secret Oliver.

Windows were barred over, or boarded up. Grass along the boulevards was scraggly, patchy, and losing a battle against weeds. Balconies sagged alarmingly, concrete had cracks or missing chunks, and cars parked along the curbs were older, rusted models not worth the effort of jacking.

There were almost no people to speak of, not even the homeless. But they had to be around somewhere. There was an odd feeling in the pit of his stomach that might be anxiety but he wasn't nervous or afraid. He was, however, on high alert.

They pulled up behind another shiny white SUV that had, amazingly, not been stripped down to the bones. Might be interesting to meet some more MIA agents. Could this be an elaborate reality TV show? If so, they were going to a lot of trouble to make a fool of him. Or to get his hopes up for a job that didn't exist.

Oliver got out and Carmichael did the same. He met Oliver by the trunk.

"What's going on?"

Oliver used a fob to open the back of the SUV and pressed his thumb to a biometric scanner on military grade footlocker. It flipped open to reveal far more guns and boxes of what appeared to be custom ammo than Carmichael would have wanted to leave in an undefended vehicle, but not enough to suggest Oliver was an arms dealer.

Oliver loaded clips into two Glocks, slid one into an underarm holster, then offered the other one to Carmichael.

"Uh. No." Carmichael took a step back. Since the incident, he'd been counting the days until his discharge took effect, petrified he was losing his mind and was going to end up hurting someone innocent. He really couldn't be trusted around firearms until he'd had a chance to find a therapist he trusted.

"Take it."

"I can't." Carmichael shook his head. "I really can't. I... it's not safe."

Oliver put the other gun in his waistband and handed Carmichael a couple of extra clips before shutting the locker and trunk. When Oliver made no move to take them back, he shoved them in his pockets. Instead, Oliver picked up a few small metallic canisters that looked like next generation tear gas or flash bang grenades. He placed those in custom loops on his holster strap then grabbed two small Maglites. Carmichael readily took one of those when offered—night had fallen and there were no working street-lights on the block.

"C'mon. We're heading to the church." Oliver tilted a head at the spire visible behind a old tenement house on the corner.

"Where are the other... agents?" Carmichael waved a hand at the second SUV.

"I lost contact with the team a couple of hours ago. I was already planning to approach you, but I need back up now."

"You mean me? That's crazy. Surely SWAT or something. Local law enforcement would be better."

Oliver sighed. "Unfortunately, that's not possible."

Carmichael took a deep breath. Not calling in back up supported his new theory that this was a new reality TV show. That custom ammo was probably blanks or paint balls. But he'd go along with this for now, pretend Oliver and his "agency" was for real. If nothing else, he'd probably get paid for his time. Not like he had any other commitments in his social calendar.

Oliver took the lead and Carmichael followed, because why not? When the church came fully into view, Carmichael shivered. The producers had chosen their location well. The church was creepy as fuck. And their equipment was great because he hadn't spotted one camera so far. Overhead drones, maybe?

One of the worn wooden doors hung partially open, and Oliver climbed the full flight of stairs, heading straight for it, Carmichael only a few steps behind.

Before he opened the door, he turned back to Carmichael, and grabbed his hand. It took a great deal of effort suppress his instincts to take Oliver down, but he didn't want to overreact on camera.

Oliver pressed one of the guns into Carmichael's hand. If those were blanks, there was no real reason to not take it.

"Listen, before we go in there, I have to tell you something."

"Okay." Carmichael pulled back, Glock at the ready. It didn't feel like a prop gun, which meant he still had to be careful. Even blanks at close range could be deadly.

"You weren't hallucinating."

Icy dread swept through him from head to toe. "What are you talking about?"

"Out there in the desert. The night so many of your fellow soldiers died. You've been telling yourself for weeks you didn't see what you thought you saw."

Carmichael's stomach twisted and his heart kicked into his throat. Another layer of sweat, cold and clammy and sourced from fear, dampened his shirt.

"That isn't funny."

Oliver shook his head. "No, it's not." Then he turned and slipped into the church.

For a few seconds, Carmichael was frozen, unable to feel the fingers wrapped around the grip, unable to force his feet to move in any direction. Oliver's words were madness. Pure and utter madness.

As he stood there, immobile, he realized how still and quiet his surroundings were. How wrong and empty everything felt. If there was even a slight chance he hadn't imagined those... creatures in the desert, if there was a slight chance those creatures were, against all odds, inside this church, in the middle of a city, for fuck's sake, he couldn't stay out here. He might no longer officially be a soldier but the mindset wasn't going to disappear in a matter of hours.

Every bit the professional, he held the gun ready and slipped inside the church. Oliver was already halfway down the aisle. The inside was in worse shape than the outside, riding the edge of being condemned.

The area behind the altar was dimly lit with tall, sputtering candles. Oliver paused ten or fifteen feet shy of the altar and Carmichael easily caught up. As soon as he did, an all-too-familiar scent hit his nose. Blood.

Unless reality television had changed substantially since he'd last watched an episode of *Survivor*, this was not a fucking game.

"What the fuck, Oliver?" Carmichael spoke quietly, although there didn't seem to be anyone visible, aside from the body—well beyond saving—draped over the alter. "Is that one of your team?"

"No. We need to search the rest of the church. Probably downstairs."

The church was bigger than it looked from the outside and it was a lot of ground to cover for two guys. Especially when they had no idea how many people were inside. Were churches even open on Wednesday evenings?

"Split up?"

Oliver sighed. "I hate the idea, but I don't think we have a choice." He turned to face Carmichael full on.

There were two doors leading out of the church on either side of the altar and Oliver gestured to the one on the left. "I'll go west, and search, heading downstairs as soon as I can."

Carmichael pulled out his phone. "What's your number? We can keep in contact via text."

"Don't bother."

Carmichael frowned and stared down at his phone. The display flashed $34:97$ *p.m. Wednesday DclM* 54th.

"What the fuck is wrong with my phone?"

"I'll explain later, but we can't rely on electronics this close to the nexus. Old school all the way herein. If you need help, yell. And if you get a chance, go for a head shot."

Carmichael wanted to shake Oliver, get a full explanation, but Oliver's urgency was visible, despite his efforts to hide it. Instead, he wrapped all his experience and training around him and took the east door.

BY THE TIME he'd cleared the area between the nave of the church and the back stairs, he'd found a few more butchered corpses, likely homeless, but no sign of the perpetrators. Or of the clergy. But as the church had no living quarters attached, there may not be any clergy present in the evening midweek. Carmichael was not a religious man, and had only dim memories of infrequent childhood attendance at church to basis that knowledge on.

The scent of blood and death hung thick and cloying in the still air, and when he finally descended the steps to the lower level, the smell only got stronger.

This was not going to be pretty.

By this point, he had no idea where Oliver was, or if he'd even found another way down to this level. His only goal was to find anyone alive, and make a determination if they were potential victims or people he'd need to shoot. And if he had to shoot, Oliver's "secret agency" better keep him the fuck out of jail.

He'd cleared a couple of rooms, with more corpses, that might have functioned as classrooms, before coming to a small institution style kitchen. The counter tops were cheap, peeling Formica, and the appliances were practically antique.

A flicker of movement outside the circle of light cast by his flashlight had him spinning wildly, looking for an enemy, but there was nothing.

The industrial fridge caught his eye, also of advanced age, but big enough it needed to be cleared also. Carmichael opened it up and found a man and a woman alive inside, tied up and bloody, both wearing suits similar to Oliver's.

He grabbed a nearby cooking implement. It was metal and sturdy, but he had no inkling of its true purpose. But the thing suited Carmichael's purposes just fine and he jammed it into the door frame to keep the heavy door from accidentally closing.

"Are you both okay?" Carmichael knelt beside them and whipped out his Swiss Army knife to work on their bonds.

As soon as the guy had a hand free he pulled out his makeshift gag and coughed. "Who are you?"

"I'm with Oliver." More detailed introductions could wait until later.

"Shit. Behind you."

Carmichael didn't question, didn't hesitate, but swiveled bring his firearm up, and aimed. He got a glimpse of orange eyes, horns and claws before he pulled the trigger.

An unholy shriek spilled out of the creature's gaping maw as the hole between its eyes caught fire and burned for a second or two before the... thing collapsed like its bones had dissolved.

Carmichael kept his weapon trained on the beast, ears ringing from the shot in such enclosed quarters. If it so much as twitched he was emptying the clip into it.

"Don't worry, it's gone." The female agent put a hand on his shoulder, and he let his arm relax. He had to have been standing over the beast for several minutes, because both agents were now standing free from their bonds.

"What the flying fuck was that thing?" He nudged it with his foot. It had similar elements to the glimpses he'd seen out in the desert, but the grenade he'd used in desperation that night hadn't left enough to confirm his initial impression.

Adrenaline still raced through his bloodstream, and this wasn't a hallucination.

"I thought you said you were with Oliver." The male agent had gone from thankful to suspicious.

"Yeah, but I just met him today. He offered me a job. Would it be killing those things?"

"Umbrae." The female agent elbowed the male in rebuke, and he sputtered.

"You realize that tells me jack shit, right? Are there any more of them around here?" Because he was ready to mow them down. Knowing he hadn't lost his damned mind was such a relief.

"It's classified," the woman said.

"Of course it is. Looks like a demon." He'd watched *Supernatural* but he'd never have thought he'd ever use any of that in a real-world situation.

"We can neither confirm nor deny," the woman said primly.

"What about that ammo? What kind of ammo does that kind of damage?"

The agents looked at each other before the woman answered. "It's a silver iron alloy."

Silver and iron? Weird, but he suspected any further information about it would also be classified.

"Let's go find Oliver and make sure these demons are all dead. Are you both okay to walk?"

They nodded, but they'd been stripped of their weapons so as Carmichael led them back through the kitchen, they each grabbed a large knife from a wooden block on the counter.

An enormous boom shook the building. It felt like an explosion but the sound was different and ripped into his brain like weaponized glass shards. Carmichael dropped the gun and sank to his knees, hands pressed to his ears. Unable to catch a breath, tears slid down his face as sound waves reverberated in his skull.

An eternity later, the sound stopped but his head felt raw and tender like his skin had been sandpapered. His injured knee throbbed at the unexpected contact with the floor and that counter-point was the only thing that kept him from passing right the fuck out.

Moisture tickled his upper lip and he swiped at it with the back of his hand. Bright red streaks decorated his hand.

"It's just a nose bleed." He didn't know which agent spoke because his ears were not working right. Crumbly white bits rained down on them from above, and the two agents had to work hard to get him on his feet with his knee working against the idea.

"We have to get out of here. The ceiling is ready to collapse. That blast means Oliver's taken care of any other creatures." This time, it was definitely the guy who spoke because his lips moved along with the words.

The three of them shuffled back toward the stairs, the woman taking charge of Carmichael's gun. No way he'd be able to fire it right now anyway.

Several agonizing minutes later, they were out in the moderately cooler night air, and they guided him back to the SUVs where Oliver was already waiting. Carmichael opened the door and sat down. He didn't give one solitary shit if he was getting dirt and blood all over the pristine interior. He tried to glare at Oliver but the adrenaline had completely deserted him, and he was about to crash hard.

"You did great, Carmichael."

"Does this mean I'm hired?" If nothing else, he wanted the job so they'd explain everything.

"The job is yours."

"I'm not wearing a fucking suit."

Oliver nodded, and Carmichael blacked out.

ONE

Present Day

"DOESN'T LOOK like a hotbed of satanic activity, does it?" Agent Lachlan Carmichael asked his partner as he put the SUV in park. In fact Rothburg resembled the complete opposite of evil. Agent Oliver Cardoso gave him a blank look, which, after a year working together, Carmichael had no problems interpreting. And the interpretation wasn't flattering.

"You should know better by now," Oliver replied.

"Yeah, yeah, I know. Things aren't always as they seem."

Carmichael wasn't sure he'd ever used the word *quaint* before, but it repeated in his mind over and over since they drove into town. The bed-and-breakfast was almost terrifying in its storybook perfection—two-story white farmhouse, lacy crap edging the roof like a gingerbread house, and complete with a stereotypical white picket fence. The sight of the place gave him hives.

"But are you sure your mystic antenna isn't on the fritz?"

Carmichael peered through the windshield at the only lodging the town had to offer.

"Mystic antenna?" Sarcasm infused Oliver's tone.

Carmichael didn't bother looking at his partner. He still wasn't used to all this paranormal shit he'd been recruited for. No matter how often he'd tried to convince both his partner and his superiors at the agency that he had no particular skills in this area, they hadn't believed him. Hell, he'd spent nine years in the military, six of that as an MP and never heard a whisper of a government agency dealing with weirdness like this. Despite that, it had only taken one case with the agency to convince him that the unbelievable wasn't. And his continued derisive remarks about both of their livelihoods only pissed off Cardoso.

"C'mon, look at this place." Carmichael gestured in front of them. "This is where rich folk go to escape the big bad city. This is where they wallow in their bland, orderly existence. There's no way anyone here would tolerate something as chaotic as satanic rituals." Every other case they'd investigated delved into tenement houses, the projects, the slums. Places just like where Carmichael grew up. Places he'd been determined to escape by joining the army.

"Stop with the 'satanic' already, Carmichael," Oliver drawled. "We've been over this. People into satanic rituals are like children playing dress-up. Satanism wouldn't create a blip on the agency's radar, and you know it."

"So what is going on here? How come you never know?"

"Carmichael..." There was an edge to Oliver's voice, the one that told him he'd almost gone too far. But he couldn't help it. Why couldn't they tune their paranormal receivers, or whatever the hell they used, properly? Cardoso could talk all day about the effect of open portals on electronics, but Carmichael had trouble under-standing why detecting and tracing those portals was so inefficient, considering all the gadgets and shit they'd lugged along in the trunk.

With a sigh, Carmichael opened the door and got out. Disappear-ances. When it wasn't straight-out dead bodies, it was people disappearing. Trouble was, they rarely reappeared. Well, alive. The deaths were always ugly, sordid.

"Don't they have a normal motel here? What about back on the highway?" With the white paint, cutesy frills, and pink trim, if Barbie needed to hook up for a night with dickless Ken, this was where she'd do it. G.I. Joe would take her to the Motel 8 back on the highway, which was where Carmichael would much rather be.

"Agent Carmichael." Oliver's exasperated voice was reminiscent of mothers everywhere, or at least Carmichael imagined, especially if one's mother were a six-foot-tall Latino baritone.

"Yeah, I know." Protocol dictated they stay as close to the center of disturbance as possible for monitoring purposes. But damn, he hadn't been so out of his element in a long time.

"Trust me, it could be worse. Go check us in. I'll get our stuff out."

Carmichael did as ordered, hoping the interior would be less... quaint. Seriously, he'd need a damned thesaurus if he was stuck in Rothburg for more than a couple of days.

A prim older woman, the name *Gladys* printed on her name tag, looked up over her glasses as Carmichael walked in.

"Can I help you?" Derision, faint but present, colored Gladys's voice.

Not that he blamed her. Much. He'd been told he looked sinister dressed all in black, despite his blond hair. Had something to do with his size, he imagined. But black, camo green, and sometimes blue were the only colors he was comfortable wearing. The clothes were similar in design to the army combat uniform he'd worn most of his adult life, but he couldn't bring himself to wear desert colors anymore.

Even so, if it weren't for his black trench coat, most would peg him as military right away. Oliver also dressed in dark, subdued colors. But suits like Oliver wore all the time only made Carmichael look like an idiot and he'd rather be sinister than laughable.

"Checking in, ma'am. Two rooms under the name Cardoso."

"Oh, yes. It's kind of late in the year for visitors," she speculated as she fiddled with her paperwork. He had no intention of responding to the hidden question in her comment. Deflecting questions as prettily as Oliver could was not a particular skill of his, but he was adept at ignoring them.

"Uh-huh." Carmichael plucked the generic corporate credit card out of his wallet and placed it on the counter. With a minimum of discussion, he managed to get keys to the two rooms as Oliver brought their suitcases inside.

God, this place gave him the creeps. It was so perfect. Too perfect. Now he found he could imagine this place as the site of the ugly paranormal activity they suspected had been happening for some time. Rothburg had a very *Stepford Wives* vibe to it, although only torture would make him admit that he'd watched that movie. Either version.

Carmichael traded a key for his bag and preceded Oliver up the stairs to the second floor.

"Breakfast at seven, downstairs." Carmichael repeated the information Gladys had given him.

Oliver nodded and unlocked the door to his room. "Get settled. I'll meet you downstairs in half an hour, and we'll take a look around. Maybe get a coffee."

"Yeah, no problem." Coffee would be good. They'd left at the ass crack of dawn this morning, on what was supposed to have been the first day of Carmichael's weeklong leave. Er...vacation. Not like he'd had any plans. Carmichael unlocked his door, situated right next to Oliver's, maneuvered his bag inside, then let the door close behind him.

And felt like he was going to start itching. He wasn't allergic to cats. He liked cats. These weren't even real cats. But there were an alarming number pictured here. On the walls, in framed photos. Ceramic ones, in various poses on every available horizontal surface. Plush ones on the bed and on each chair. Woven into the pattern on the drapes and bedspread.

Oh, he hadn't blinked an eye when that diabolical woman told him that he'd be staying in the Manx Room. He hadn't known what prompted naming a room after the Isle of Man and hadn't cared. Cats hadn't crossed his mind for a second, for Christ's sake. Carmichael imagined his manhood shriveling in direct proportion to the length of time he stayed in this town—and in this room. He also had a sudden desire to adopt a large, growly dog.

He made short work of unpacking, gave his face a quick splash in the thankfully unshared, though equally cat-infested, bathroom, and was downstairs in less than twenty minutes, trying desperately not to glare at the woman behind the counter. He collapsed into an over-stuffed chair, releasing a cloud of rose scent. Yep. Shriveling manhood. It was official.

What had the charming Gladys called Oliver's room? It started with an *M* too. He hoped Oliver's room was every bit as offensively cute.

Five minutes later, when Oliver strode downstairs with a stunned yet amused look on his face, Carmichael assumed it was as bad as his own.

He struggled out of the cocooning chair to join Oliver. The minute they were out the door, Oliver turned to him and said, "Ducks."

Right. The Mallard Room. "Cats," Carmichael replied with a snort. Okay, it was kind of funny. "Drive or walk?" It was getting on toward winter, the fall colors in the trees more or less over as they shed their leaves in preparation for the oncoming season, but it was a sunny day and more than warm enough.

"Drive," Oliver said as he unlocked the car. He tossed the keys across the roof to Carmichael. "Don't know how much ground we'll need to cover in the prelim survey."

"SEE ANYTHING SUSPICIOUS?" Oliver asked as Carmichael guided the car through midtown.

Carmichael turned to gape at him. Uh, yeah. It was suspicious that there weren't any bums. It was suspicious that there wasn't any garbage or graffiti. But that might be a paranormality that he could get behind. Did they even *have* crime in this place?

"Turn here. We'll park and walk a bit."

Carmichael turned the wheel in the direction of Oliver's pointing finger.

"Look out!" Oliver yelled.

Carmichael whipped his attention forward and jammed his foot onto the brake. Adrenaline twisted his throat shut, and his chest heaved in an attempt to draw in some air.

Damn, that was close. The kid he'd almost hit looked as pale as Carmichael felt. He flipped his skateboard up into a shaky hand and looked through the windshield, wide-eyed, at Carmichael. And oh damn. He was young, but not a kid, not really.

Those eyes, in that face, acted like a fist in Carmichael's diaphragm. The kid was gorgeous. Stunning. The clear green of his eyes was visible even through the windshield and past the length of the car hood. Eyes the color of old glass Coke bottles, surrounded by thick, dark lashes. Below, a narrow nose, a pointed chin, all framed in blunt-cut, near-black hair.

Carmichael couldn't have designed a more beautiful man. The faint hint of dark stubble on his sculpted jaw saved him from appearing completely like jailbait. He was probably legal, despite the story the skateboard told. Carmichael's dick flexed in his pants as a flame of lust swept his frame.

Adrenaline reaction. Had to be, because damn it, he was here to work. Missing people. The Umbrae. Mortal danger. Getting laid could wait. God knew it had waited long enough already. Used to hiding in the military, he was never open about his desires. But now he was virtually panting for a different reason than fear.

Oliver rolled down his window and called out, "You okay?"

He got a nod in response, but the kid never took his eyes off Carmichael. The gaze was so intense, it was like the kid had run a finger up Carmichael's partial erection.

"Sorry 'bout that," Oliver continued. The kid nodded again and seemed to realize that he still stood in front of their vehicle. He shook himself and flipped his skateboard back down to continue along the sidewalk.

Carmichael shifted in his seat, uncomfortable and far too aware his gaze was glued to the fine, round, bitable ass boarding away.

"Carmichael, can we go now?" Oliver asked gently.

"Oh. Yeah. Sorry." Carmichael started driving again, looking for a parking spot. He didn't know if Oliver had any idea which way Carmichael bent. Although Carmichael found his partner attractive, he knew he'd concealed it far better than his intense, lustful attraction to the green-eyed kid, who must be close to a decade his junior. Shit. Hidden? Yeah, right. He'd practically waved a rainbow flag and drooled. After so many years in the military, he wasn't sure he'd ever be comfortable being open and out, but this was the closest he'd come in, well, ever.

Casting a couple of surreptitious glances at Oliver, he didn't notice his partner giving him any weird looks. Or any more weird than usual. Oliver wasn't the most normal guy Carmichael had ever met. How could he be? He'd been dealing with this supernatural shit since Carmichael had been in high school, trying to pretend that his teammates on the football team didn't turn him on way more than the cheerleaders.

ADAM FARELLI HUMMED to himself as he walked into the coffee shop. He grinned at Susie, the girl with whom he shared his shift today. He didn't have any true friends left in Rothburg, but Susie was a decent person. They got along rather well, and she didn't treat him like the village idiot, the way most of the townspeople did.

"Hey, you're in a good mood." Susie smiled back as she lifted the counter to let him into the back room.

"Yeah, doing okay." Adam set his skateboard out of the way. He had a few minutes before his shift started, and he wanted to contemplate his elated mood. Technically there wasn't a good reason for it. After all, he'd come close to being squished. Not for the first time, by any stretch, but this was the first time he'd been buoyant, excited. The guy behind the wheel—the reason for his euphoria—couldn't have been as good-looking as he'd seemed through the tinted windshield. Probably wasn't gay, anyway.

If anyone who lived or visited this parochial, hidebound little town was gay, they'd hidden it well. Better than Adam did. Of course, Adam hadn't tried to hide at all after high school.

It was one of the reasons he'd left and why a number of the inhabitants treated him like a leper. Like the gayness would rub off or something. They tolerated him for the sake of his parents, but Adam knew damn well that some of them had entertained the notion that his parents' affliction was somehow his fault, that he'd brought it on them by being a deviant.

Even if the sexy yet shitty driver lived up to the promise of good looks, live and in person, it wouldn't matter. Adam would be left to gape from afar. If he didn't want to get beaten up, that was.

Adam slipped his apron over his head and smoothed it down. Good thing he was wearing jeans today, because he was still half hard from his encounter. He'd heard adrenaline sometimes did that, but having his dick *sproing* after his near-death experience was unexpected.

Since it would be an hour or more before the rush began, Adam took his time in the back room, hoping that his erection would subside more before he had to go out and face the public. What he needed was a distraction. Otherwise he'd never stop thinking about that guy long enough to deflate.

The bell above the door tinkled as he emerged from the back room, but he didn't pay any attention. Susie could handle whoever walked in. Or so he thought until he heard Susie gasp. Had her ex showed up again?

Adam looked up, and he couldn't even get a gasp out.

Him. The guy from the SUV. The guy who'd almost run him over. The most heartbreakingly gorgeous man he'd ever seen. If anything, the windshield had protected Adam from that devastating sight. Sexier and better-looking than anything Adam could have imagined, Susie's reaction was no surprise.

Tall, much taller than he'd expected, and muscular. Six-two, at least. Black cotton encased a sculpted torso like a second skin. Bright blond hair, a touch too long to be military, topped the square face.

Oh. Oh my. Adam's breath came back. He bit his lower lip to hold in the whimper wanting to escape. Desperate to take a peek at the package surrounded by black jeans, but given the disparity in their sizes, Adam didn't dare. The blond could kick his ass without spilling his latte if he caught Adam checking him out. Instead he glanced at the other man. The sharp suit gave the older man an offi-cial air, but an official of what, Adam couldn't quite guess.

However, neither man was from Rothburg—he hadn't been away from town long enough to lose that innate sense.

"I'll take this one, Susie," Adam said, unable to help himself.

"You don't say." Susie smirked. "They're kind of out of place here. Friends of yours?"

Oh, if only.

"Nope," Adam replied. But that didn't stop a guy from hoping. His cock twitched as he watched the two men scan the interior of the coffee shop and its patrons as they casually made their way to the counter. Neither of them had looked his way yet, and Adam prepared to paste on his most gracious customer-service smile, all the while telling his overeager prick to ease off. He *really* didn't want to be sporting wood at work.

Who were these two, anyway? The blond hunk's demeanor screamed military, but his companion's didn't. Yet they both had the same indefinable quality that told Adam they were there for a common purpose. Which wasn't to get a coffee.

Adam didn't much care why they were there. He'd get the sexy bastard coffee and whatever else he wanted. As his cock leaped up to agree, Adam clutched the counter. A raging hard-on might be considered too friendly for good customer service. His smile tightened and he hoped Susie hadn't noticed his reaction. His stupid reaction. He wasn't a teenager anymore.

The other patrons eyed the two strangers as well. Anyone would think they'd never seen a stranger before. Unless lust punched everyone here in the gut like it had Adam. Somehow he couldn't quite see old Mrs. Jenkins overcome by lust. If he ever did see that, he'd have to scrub his eyes out with acid, because yuck.

Okay, good. That horrific thought made his jeans less constricting.

Finally the two men completed their lazy approach to the counter.

"Good afternoon. What can I get you today?"

The good-looking, older man ignored Adam while perusing the menu overhead, but the gorgeous blond dropped his gaze down to Adam and opened his mouth to order. Adam was able to pinpoint the exact moment when recognition struck in those...oh, God...stunning blue eyes, the exact shade of lapis lazuli, Adam's new favorite color.

An adorable flush stained prominent cheekbones, and kissable, mobile lips worked around words that wouldn't come out. Adam stared, mesmerized. *Am I drooling?* His unintentional yet self-imposed celibacy had now lasted about a year and might account for his lust. Or it had just been too damned long since he'd gotten laid.

"Large coffee," the blond stuttered.

"Anything in it?"

"Like what?"

Oh, nice. Adam had flustered him. He hoped it was for the same reason he flustered Adam. Could he—should he—hit on this guy in front of his companion?

"Cream, sugar?" Adam made sure his tone was devoid of sarcasm, tempting as it would have been with anyone else. Wasn't enough to save the blond from further embarrassment, as the blush heating his cheeks got stronger.

"Oh, sorry. No. Black is fine. And, uh...I'm sorry about earlier." Big-and-Sexy was having difficulty meeting Adam's eyes.

"No problem. It's forgotten. Anything else?" Jesus. Had that sounded as suggestive to anyone else as it had to Adam's ears? Maybe it had, given that the blush somehow intensified. Apparently his mouth had already decided to try a gentle come-on, without his brain's consent. While Adam wondered if he should be more overt, the blond's friend broke the moment.

"A medium latte, please." The older man gave him a pleasant smile and a nod. He'd clearly recognized Adam, but then, he'd already apologized for the near mishap and undoubtedly didn't feel the need for any further discussion of the matter.

"I'll go get a seat." the blond slipped away, still unable to look at Adam.

"I can bring you your drinks to you." Adam made change for the older man.

"Thanks. That would be great."

The older man followed his companion to a table in the corner. Both appeared relaxed, but Adam was sure that wasn't the case.

Curiosity stabbed at him. This was just too odd.

Susie returned from busing a few tables. "Serving them too?" She winked. "Find out what they're doing here. Or, better yet, how long they're staying in town."

"They're staying in town?" Adam strove for nonchalance but feared he'd failed miserably. "How do you know?"

"The bed-and-breakfast was expecting two visitors today, staying for an unspecified length of time. Maybe they're businessmen looking to invest or something."

Just a week ago, Rothburg had been crawling with strangers, and the only accommodation within the town proper, the Sleepytime

Bed-and-Breakfast, had been filled to capacity. Most of the surrounding area motels, as well as the campground of the nearby park, were too. The sensational riot of color during the autumn turning of the leaves brought tourists flocking every year. But the season was over, and the town was bracing itself for winter's onslaught.

Summer and fall might be busy tourist seasons, but they meant more money for Adam. The slowdown in work would be nice if it didn't mean tightening his belt. Grateful as he was for the job in the café, it could never make up for the hours he worked in the park and campground. In the off-season, even the hours available at the café were reduced.

The two men weren't tourists, for damned sure. Purpose coiled through them, and Adam was certain they weren't harmless business-men. He couldn't believe Susie had suggested it, but then, maybe he was seeing things that weren't there. Adam shook his head. He had a job to do. Hastily he prepared the two beverages and took them over to the men.

Deep in conversation, the older man said something the younger was not pleased by. As soon as Adam approached the table, they stopped midsentence. The only thing he'd had a chance to hear was the blond telling his companion, "No," in an emphatic manner. Well, that wasn't going to satisfy any of the town gossips. Adam couldn't work up any remorse, though, since he'd spent so much time as the subject of gossip.

Adam pasted on another bright smile as he placed drinks on the table. He made sure to make eye contact with both men as he did so, although those sexy blue eyes didn't meet his for more than a second before avoiding him. Well, that told the story right there. Not inter-ested. Too bad Adam could—*oh shit*—smell him. Clean, musky male under the scent of soap. Irish Spring, maybe.

The wattage of his smile dimming, Adam spoke again. "If you two gentlemen will be in town for any length of time, we have great lunch specials every day. And we're open until eleven each night."

Blond-and-Handsome looked at him, finally, an unpleasant expression marring his handsome face, blue eyes challenging Adam to...something. "Why? What do you mean by 'in town'?"

Uh, gee, what could he possibly mean by that?

"Carmichael! Enough." Apparently his companion thought he was out of line too.

Carmichael. Interesting name. First or last, Adam wasn't sure, but now he had a name to go with the face. Also interesting was the way Carmichael subsided under the exasperated scolding. His gaze dropped away, and he studiously ignored Adam once more. One more indicator Adam wouldn't be keeping this one company while he was in town. Too bad. The best ones were always straight or taken. Time to beat a strategic retreat.

"Well, if you need anything else, let me know. My name is Adam." He couldn't resist giving Carmichael one last bright smile, but the effort was wasted with the man refusing to look in his direction. Adam shrugged and returned to his post behind the counter, hoping he could ignore his attraction until the men left.

"WHAT THE FUCK was that about, Cardoso?" Carmichael was pissed but retained enough decorum to keep his voice low. He might be the junior partner, and younger, but that didn't give Oliver the right to talk to him like a bratty kid.

"You can't antagonize the natives, you know. We're going to need their help."

"Not his." He was certain. The kid had to be too young and irresponsible to know anything useful. Carmichael really, really didn't want him to know anything useful.

"You don't know that. In fact, he might be just what we need."

Need. *Yes, need.* Carmichael curled his fingers into fists. "What? No! How can you say that?"

"It's like I told you—we stick out. That's what the kid meant.

Look around." Oliver flicked his gaze over the rest of the people seated in the café. Unwillingly Carmichael copied him, even though he'd assessed every single person in there as a potential threat as soon as he walked in.

"Every person here knows damn well we don't belong," Oliver continued.

Yeah, Carmichael knew it too. Feeling all those eyes on him had made him uncomfortable, which was saying something, considering he was having inappropriate, lustful thoughts about the barely legal kid who'd not only served them coffee, but whom he'd almost flattened in the road not ten minutes ago. Guilt, lust, and embarrassment combusted into a volatile mix of emotions he hadn't experienced since he'd left home to join the army ten years ago. Felt like he was back in basic training, wondering if he had what it took.

Carmichael stole a peek at the kid—Adam—out of the corner of his eye and was treated to the sight of him laughing at something his coworker said. At the twitch in his groin, Carmichael brought his attention back to Oliver. No way was this kid going to break him.

"Fine. Sorry. How did you want to start?" Most times he got the answers he needed by roughing people up. This time, and in this place, that tactic wasn't going to work. But he didn't know if he had the finesse to get answers any other way.

"I told you this wouldn't be easy. No one's going to want to give us what we need. I think we could use Adam's help, if he's willing."

Carmichael's jaw locked. Oliver couldn't be serious. Why Adam, of all people? There had to be someone—anyone—else. He looked suspiciously at his partner, wondering if Oliver had come up with this ridiculous suggestion to torment him. Maybe he hadn't hidden his attraction as well as he'd thought. No, that couldn't be it. There was no good reason for Oliver to want Adam's help if he thought his presence would prove a distraction.

"Why him?" Carmichael knew there was only so much resistance he could put up before he had to come out and tell Oliver why he didn't want Adam's assistance. God help him, if Oliver didn't know he was gay, Carmichael wasn't going to tell him.

"Because he's the only one who, despite knowing we don't belong, hasn't given us any weird looks."

"Well, he should! We—I almost ran him over!" The effort required to keep his voice low became greater. "He should be more suspicious and hostile towards us than anyone. And if he's not, he's an idiot." Hmmm. That might be true. Adam had done nothing but smile at them. Carmichael couldn't believe anyone with their full faculties could shrug off an incident like that so easily. Someone a few cards short of a deck wouldn't be of any help to them.

"Stop," Oliver warned him. "Listen up. We need to get to the bottom of these disappearances, and soon. A friendly contact is the best start. There's nothing to say we won't find someone else, someone more appropriate for what we want. But right now a kid working in a coffee shop might like to make a few more bucks, you know?"

Carmichael bit his lip. Oliver was right. Everything since they'd arrived in Rothburg had thrown him off balance. He was so far off his turf, he was surprised he hadn't drowned. They did need help, but spending time with Adam was going to test his control like nothing ever had, not even the communal showers in basic, filled with wet, fit, naked men.

An image of Adam, dark hair slicked back, water streaming down his lean torso, slipped unbidden into his mind, and Carmichael let out a rather undignified squeak as he crossed his legs to hide the sudden bulge in his jeans. At least Oliver ignored the sound. This fucking nonsense had to stop.

"Fine, do whatever you want." Carmichael gave in, not at all gracefully.

"HEY, KID! ADAM!"

Adam turned toward the unfamiliar voice. Carmichael's companion waved him over. Well, they'd made short work of their coffees. A smile slipped back onto his face. *Kid*, huh? Adam knew he looked young for his age, but *kid* might be a little much.

"Need a refill?" Adam approached the table.

"No, not yet. Have you got a few minutes to pull up a chair?"

Well, yeah. But why? Carmichael didn't want him to, if the tense muscles and averted face were any indication. But then, sitting with the two strangers in town had to be more interesting than his job, so...

"Sure, why not?" Adam exchanged a quick glance with Susie, who nodded to let him know she'd be fine on her own, and pulled up a chair to sit between the two.

"Adam, we have a proposition for you," the older man said as soon as Adam settled into his chair. Adam's eyes widened in shock. Neither of them looked like they were cruising, and propositioning a random café employee didn't seem as though it would have a high degree of success. But he had never tried that particular tactic, so how would he know?

"Jeez, Oliver, what the hell!" Carmichael exploded. Oliver looked at Adam first, then at Carmichael.

"You're both aware that there is a perfectly innocent meaning to the term, right?"

Adam grinned, amused at Carmichael's extreme agitation. He suspected Carmichael was never anything but calm and icy, but twice in one day Carmichael had been thrown off his game, and it was clear he didn't like it.

Oliver smiled back, and Adam became aware that *both* of these men were attractive. Maybe an indecent proposition wouldn't be amiss after all.

"Excuse me. That was rather abrupt. I'm Oliver Cardoso, and this is Carmichael."

"Just Carmichael?" Adam teased.

"Just Carmichael." Carmichael stared intently at his coffee cup.

Okay, then, no sense of humor. Fine. "Nice to meet you both. I'm

Adam Farelli." He held out his hand, and Oliver shook it. Was it worth trying to shake with Carmichael? Yep, Carmichael was going to shake his hand whether he liked it or not.

Adam thrust his hand between Carmichael's downturned gaze and coffee cup. It hung there, obvious and uncomfortable, like a dick joke in a room full of nuns. Adam's smile stretched farther, feeling more like a grimace. How long was he going to push this before he gave up? Then Carmichael gave in and clasped his hand for a fraction of a second.

"You were saying, Oliver?" Adam gave up on making eye contact with those spectacular eyes.

"Yes, we were hoping to hire you to guide us around town."

"A guide? For Rothburg? It's pretty small, you know." Not that Adam wanted to give up the opportunity to get some extra cash, but taking money for that seemed criminal.

"But you live here, yes?"

"Born and raised." Adam didn't think it necessary to mention his time spent away at college. Why bother? It had no bearing on his life now, nor on the question asked.

"That's exactly what I was hoping you'd say. We're researching folklore and ghost stories in small towns, so we want a little more than a geography lesson. More like anecdotes, history of Rothburg, maybe a little bit on who's who in town. Things like that. I'm sure we can work around your schedule here at work." Sincerity shone from Oliver's brown eyes, his hands folded together on the table.

Folklorists, my ass.

TWO

Adam had come across a few professors of folklore in his time. Archaeology had enough overlap that he'd met several. Oliver might be able to pass as a professor. Might. Not accompanied by Brawny-and-Bristly, though. No way was Carmichael a professor or researcher. Not that they'd ever said they were professors. What alternative was there? Writers? Carmichael's demeanor didn't scream *writer* either.

Lying to him was suspicious, but they didn't seem dangerous or crazy, and helping them out would go a long way to battling the interminable boredom of living in Rothburg again. He could use the money, as long as Oliver was truthful about working around his shifts at the café.

"Just drive around town and tell you stories?" There were one or two that might fit the bill.

"Walk too. And not just in town, but maybe the surrounding area."

Adam bit his lip, wondering how mercenary it would sound to ask about the pay. Then he decided it didn't matter. He'd take whatever money they were willing to throw his way. What else was he going to do with his free time anyway? It would give him something to think about besides his depressing situation at home.

"Okay, I'll do it. When did you want to start?"

"Don't you have any other questions, kid?" This was the first contribution Carmichael had made since giving his name. The frown Adam got wasn't encouraging, but for a change, Carmichael was paying attention to him.

"Again with the 'kid'?" Adam could understand Oliver calling him that, but despite the world-weary look on Carmichael's face, he couldn't be more than five or six years older than Adam's own twenty-six. Carmichael's frown got deeper.

"Why are you agreeing so quickly?" Was that suspicion in Carmichael's voice? If he wasn't supposed to accept the job, why were they bothering to ask?

Adam looked over at Oliver. The two were not in accord over this job offer, and Adam didn't know what to make of that. Oliver merely shrugged and didn't say a word.

"You two might be the most interesting thing to happen to this town in a long time. I'm agreeing because I'm hoping you'll liven things up." True, as far as it went, but there was more to it than that. Not that Carmichael needed to know the specifics. But then, would the specifics cause him to gape in astonishment? If he couldn't have Carmichael, Adam could amuse himself by trying for that expression. It might be a new goal for him. "So do we have a deal?"

"I think we have a deal," Oliver said and reached out to shake his hand again. "When do you finish your shift? We could pick you up then."

Adam considered that. "Sure. I can call my parents from here, make sure they don't need anything. As long as they're fine, you can pick me up at four."

"You have to ask your parents' permission?" Carmichael sounded appalled. "How old are you?"

"What the hell difference does that make?"

"Carmichael!" Oliver did not sound pleased. That made three of them. Carmichael's eyes widened before he looked away again.

Was relieving his boredom worth this antagonism? Adam chewed on his lower lip while he considered the question and Carmichael's pecs. Adam wondered if he could master that same tone in Oliver's voice to control Carmichael. Mmmm. Controlling Carmichael. If only.

Yeah. His blue balls wouldn't thank him for the frustration, but it was still the most interesting thing to happen to him since he'd moved back to Rothburg. He had to try and make nice with Carmichael.

"I'm twenty-six." Adam intended to answer Carmichael's other question too, but Carmichael's expression made him pause. Contempt? Could that be possible? He didn't have any time to analyze it, though, before Carmichael pushed back from the table and stalked out of the café.

"Do you think you can put up with that?" Oliver asked.

Adam didn't bother to look at him, still tracking Carmichael's angry departure past the window and out of sight.

"Put up with what? Someone who hates me?" Like that would be a first, especially in this town.

Oliver snorted, and Adam looked at him.

"He doesn't hate you. He's just a little...rough around the edges."

Adam got the impression Oliver had intended to say more but thought better of it. Interesting. The more time he spent in their company, the less he thought they were telling him the truth. That didn't change the fact that Adam had little else to do with his time except go back home and take care of parents who didn't remember who he was anymore.

He'd tried so hard to keep them out of institutions, left his whole life behind as soon as it became clear that they were unable to function on their own. Being able to stay in their home had helped for a while, reduced their stress. But their deterioration was so rapid, and they required round-the-clock nursing, which Adam didn't have the skills for. Now he was just waiting for spaces to open up in a facility nearby.

It had been such a shock when Doc Ridley had called him up, out of the blue. He'd known his mother had early-stage Alzheimer's, known his father had been taking care of her. What he hadn't realized was that his father had been in total denial about his own condition. Adam had been so caught up in his PhD work that he hadn't noticed, not until the call.

Despite the doctor's efforts, his parents were losing the battle. Their surroundings were no longer enough to connect them with the here and now, and Doc Ridley had convinced Adam it was time to give in. The insurance, along with selling the house, would cover their expenses, and Adam could go back and complete his degree.

He'd had a hard time letting go, but between the cost of care, upkeep for the house, stress, and a lack of viable job prospects in Rothburg for an archaeology doctoral student, he had to admit that Doc Ridley had a point. With the nurses at home, he was at loose ends for the time being, and even dealing with a surly Carmichael was an improvement over the depressing task of packing up the detritus of a lifetime in preparation for his parents' impending institutionalization.

"Hey, you okay?" Oliver asked.

"Oh, sorry. Yeah, I'm fine," Adam replied, realizing he'd sort of checked out of the conversation for a few moments.

"So are you still in?"

"Yeah, I guess I am." Adam pulled a business card out of his apron. It wasn't his, but it had the café's number on it. "Give me a call a few minutes before four. I'll let you know if I can help out today."

Adam had the next day off too, but he'd wait to see how tonight went before volunteering that information.

"Good deal. Twenty bucks an hour work for you?"

"Sure thing." Wow. He didn't even have to ask and it was more per hour than he made at the café.

Oliver drained his cup and stood. "Thanks again, Adam. I think you'll be a great help." After pocketing the card, Oliver gripped Adam's shoulder with a friendly squeeze, then left.

Adam sat at the table for a few seconds, pondering, before he grabbed the dishes and took them back to the dishwasher.

"Well, so? What was that all about?" Susie's eyes were bright with curiosity; she was as bad as any of the town gossips.

"They're interested in the folklore of the region and want me to show them around."

"Folklore? Why are they interested in that?"

"Dunno. I guess they're writers. They didn't look like professors or students."

"Huh. Why you? Because of your degree?"

Susie had a point. If the two knew anything about Adam at all, he wasn't a bad choice for such a task. God knew if you got him started on his field, he could talk your ear off, or so he'd been told, more than once. But not many people were interested in excavations of villages that housed the workers who built the huge Egyptian funerary monuments—they involved neither pyramids nor gold.

Adam had lived in Rothburg most of his life. His parents' interest in the Native American traditions of the region no doubt influenced his choice of profession, if not his area of specialization. But Adam didn't think the two men had sought him out for his experience.

"Actually," he said to Susie, "I think they were trying to make up for nearly running me over earlier."

"What? Are you okay?" Susie patted him down the sides, as if she could determine injuries by touch alone.

"I'm okay. It freaked me out a bit. Them too, I think. They're going to pay me for my time. Twenty bucks an hour."

"Small price to pay for almost killing you. But you should have fun with it." Susie knew how strapped he was for cash.

"Probably as interesting as any teacher's-assistant position I've ever had, and they said they'd work around my shifts."

"Look, be careful, okay? You don't know anything about those guys."

Not true. Adam knew he'd like to take one of them to bed and not let him leave.

"Don't worry. I'm sure they're harmless."

"Hey, at least they're hot." Susie waggled her brows in an exaggerated leer.

Adam nodded. He wasn't sure if that was a bonus right now, especially if his dick continued to be as unruly around Carmichael as it had been so far.

CARMICHAEL SAW Oliver leave the café and crossed the street to meet him. What was the matter with him? He might be nothing more than an ex-military grunt, but he'd never been so unprofessional. Oliver was going to bitch, with good reason. There was no acceptable explanation Carmichael could offer without admitting his attraction to Adam.

He was going to get himself fired if he wasn't careful. Working investigations for the agency was an ideal job for someone like him, who'd gone into the army right out of school and been honorably discharged for a shrapnel injury. When he'd been recruited, he'd been desperate, not knowing what he was going to do with his life. Despite the weirdness, he had grown to love the excitement of this job and wanted to keep it.

"Let's go," Oliver snapped as soon as he was within range.

"But—"

"Here." Oliver thrust a napkin at him. "I got his address. Run a background check if it'll make you happy." Uh, no. He had a feeling Oliver would be even angrier if he did so. Nevertheless, he put the napkin in his coat pocket.

"Look, Cardoso, I'm—"

"Save it, Carmichael. I don't know what bug crawled up your ass, but you'd better get it out sometime in the next five hours. Now, we've got some equipment to set up."

Oliver strode ahead of him, heading for the car. Carmichael knew he'd been an ass. How could he want someone he didn't respect or like? His attraction to Adam was a weakness. Like a cornered animal, he was lashing out. For the sake of his job, he was going to squash his lust, shut up, and keep his head down.

THREE HOURS LATER, Carmichael had mentally prepared himself to spend an evening with Adam. He and Oliver had spent most of the time setting up equipment in Oliver's room. Thankfully his partner wasn't a man to sulk or hold grudges, so Carmichael was able to avoid an uncomfortable afternoon. For Oliver, the day was like any other workday.

Afterward, with little else to do, Carmichael returned to his room for a nap. Ducks were far manlier than cats, for damned sure. The Mallard Room didn't make him itch. Well, not as much, anyway. He hoped Oliver felt the ducks staring at him while he slept as much as Carmichael felt the cats. It would serve him right for making them stay in this place.

Fifteen minutes after four, Carmichael's bedside alarm went off. A few minutes later, while he was splashing water on his face, someone pounded on his door.

He flung the door open. "What?"

"Adam can't make it tonight," Oliver bit out, foul mood back in place.

"Why?" Carmichael tamped down a quick spurt of emotion. He couldn't tell if it was relief or regret and didn't want to analyze it. Adam hadn't canceled because of him. Surely not.

"Said his relief at the café called in sick and he had to stay until close. Said he was free all day tomorrow. But let me tell you, if he cancels tomorrow..." Oliver's forehead wrinkled into a frown, and Carmichael knew he'd be in deep shit if that happened. Because without a doubt, it would be all his fault. They could find someone else to do what they needed, but it would take a lot longer for one of the other townspeople to trust them.

Carmichael still didn't know why Adam had been so willing and open, but he hadn't sensed any sort of guile in the kid. Kid. Only two years younger, but it felt like a decade or more. Still, calling Adam "kid" might help keep Carmichael's cock and temper under control.

"If he cancels, I'll make it right." But Carmichael hoped he wouldn't have to.

Oliver nodded, accepting his promise. "I'm going to monitor the equipment. Doubt we'll see any activity tonight. That would be too convenient."

"I think I'll walk around a bit, get the lay of the land." Walking was often better for scouting than driving, and it would be dark soon, mitigating how much he didn't belong in this picture-perfect town.

THROUGH THE WINDOW, Bill watched Adam stroke his cock, feeling an answering hardness in his own groin. What he wouldn't give to be in there, smoothing his hands over that perfect body, instead of up in a tree, peering in. He'd wanted Adam from the first minute he saw him, but never thought there was a chance. Adam was back in Rothburg and would soon be ready for the taking.

They could be together in ways Bill hadn't ever imagined in those first early days when the sight of Adam as an eighteen-year-old high school senior sent blood thumping to his prick, hot and heavy. At first he hadn't understood his reaction. He hadn't understood Adam was meant to be his.

Bill had thought long and hard about how he'd claim Adam. He might need to be punished, just a little, for how long he'd made Bill wait for him. All those long hours with his right hand, a poor substitute for Adam's ass.

After stripping Adam naked, like he was now, Bill would bind Adam's wrists to the headboard. With ass upraised, straining to be filled, oh, he'd slide his cock into that hot, tight hole. Be like coming home, and Adam would know it. Adam would push back into the thrusts, whimpering, begging for a touch to his cock, promising anything in return for being allowed to come. He'd have to wait, though, wait until his ass was filled with hot spunk, wait until he was sobbing for release. That's when Bill would grant him permission. Only then would Adam get the pressure he craved.

Adam's hand stroked a little faster, his other hand snaking down to cup his balls. Bill licked his lips. With the window cracked open, and his newly enhanced senses, the scent of Adam's musky precum and the faint sounds of flesh on flesh reached Bill in his perch. The temptation was too great, and he pulled his pulsing erection from his pants. He gripped it tight, like he imagined Adam's sphincter would grasp, trying to keep the hot, hard cock lodged deep inside.

Oh yeah. Soon Adam would be his. Adam had smiled at him today. Shown Bill he was ready to be claimed. Before long, everything would be in place, and his long wait would be rewarded. He could show Adam how much he cared. It was fate. His new abilities, combined with Adam's return, were fate rewarding him for his patience.

Transfixed, he watched Adam's body buck and shift in preparation for orgasm. What was Adam thinking about? Maybe Adam was imagining Bill fucking him. Bill's hand sped up; he wanted to come at the same time. A geyser of cum shot from the end of Adam's long, hard dick, splattering across the almost hairless chest. With a subvocal grunt, Bill joined Adam in ecstasy, his cock firing an answering volley.

When it was over, he waited in the tree, watched his semen drip down the branch alongside the pine sap. Minutes after cleaning up, Adam fell asleep, and Bill climbed down.

It had been days since he'd had time to relax like this. He hoped he wouldn't have to wait so long before watching over Adam again.

CARMICHAEL PACED OUTSIDE by the SUV, the morning already warming up enough to make him reconsider his long-sleeved black tee. Days like this, he wished he smoked. Might give him something to do with his hands besides wringing someone's neck. Oliver was taking his sweet time with breakfast, and Adam was... Carmichael checked his watch. Okay, well, he wasn't late yet. Damn. Carmichael hated this. Stomach twisted in knots, he'd been unable to eat anything, although he'd choked down a cup of too-hot, sludgelike coffee. Right now he didn't know if he was hoping Adam would or wouldn't show up as promised.

If Adam showed, he'd have to spend all day with a kid—a man— he was incredibly attracted to yet wasn't sure he even liked. When he'd woken with his morning woody, it was the memory of those bottle green eyes along with a few quick strokes of his hand that had pushed him over the edge into orgasm. And that pissed him off.

Carmichael's shoulders knotted in frustration when he heard his name called. Turning around, he felt his heart begin pounding like parade drums. Dammit. Adam was every bit as gorgeous as he remembered, maybe more so. Today he was dressed in jeans that looked painted on and a loose red sweater that skimmed the top edge of the belt holding up the low-slung pants. If Adam lifted his arms a bit, the firm flesh of his abs would be visible.

At that wayward thought, Carmichael tightened his jaw, pulled his gaze away from Adam's midsection, and frowned.

"You're late," he growled.

Adam raised a dark eyebrow in response.

"So am I," Oliver said behind him, a warning clear in the tone of his voice.

Carmichael felt a flush of embarrassment ride up into his cheeks. God. He'd obeyed orders from commanding officers without question, including orders he hated or that were patently absurd. Almost ten years in the army, and he'd obeyed well enough, he'd never gotten a reprimand. Working as Oliver's junior partner for the past year had been even easier. Why was this case fucking with his head so badly?

Being pleasant and making small talk weren't skills he possessed, but he was going out of his way to be disagreeable, and that wasn't like him. Usually.

Head down in an effort to hide his reddened cheeks, Carmichael unlocked the SUV and got in the driver's seat. Adam opened the passenger-side door to the backseat.

Carmichael heard Oliver ask, "Are you sure you don't want to sit up front?" Shit, Carmichael hadn't considered that possibility.

"Nope, the back is fine. I don't mind," Adam replied. "Carmichael," he called into the car, making Carmichael flinch.

"Yes?"

"Okay if I put my skateboard in the back?"

Carmichael didn't bother to reply, just popped the back hatch. Skateboard. What self-respecting twenty-six-year-old man rode a skateboard? The thought went a long way toward dampening the arousal that had, well, never quite subsided, despite his jacking off this morning. *Skateboard.* Lived with parents. Worked in a café. Yep, worked like ice water down the pants.

He heaved a sigh of relief but made the mistake of looking in the rearview mirror when Adam climbed into the car. Those eyes caught his, and Carmichael was back where he'd started. At least his overcoat was in the car. Might be too warm out today for it, but it would save him a shitload of humiliation.

Oliver slid into the passenger seat and slammed the door shut with a little more force than Carmichael thought necessary. But he didn't dare say anything, not with the mood Oliver was in.

Carmichael started the engine. "Where to?"

"Adam, can you direct us to the library?" Oliver asked, flicking a minuscule piece of lint from the knee of his navy suit.

"Certainly."

Carmichael followed Adam's directions without saying a word to either man. He wasn't sure why Oliver wanted to go to the library, but he didn't feel like asking either. Better to keep his mouth shut. Less chance of getting into more trouble.

Within a few minutes, they'd pulled into the library's parking lot.

"Drop me off by the door," Oliver said with a slight wave.

What? "Where are you going?"

"Research. Towns like this often don't have back issues of their newspapers online."

"But...but..." Carmichael knew he was sputtering, but the knowledge did nothing to stop it. "Aren't you going to need help?"

Oliver opened the car door and got out. Sticking his head back inside, he looked at Adam. "Are you going to ride up front?"

"Oliver," Carmichael almost shouted. "Did you hear me?"

"I heard you." Oliver flicked an icy gaze over Carmichael, leaving frostbite in its wake. Obviously, Oliver had not forgiven him for his attitude. "But we'll get more done if one of us does this and the other gathers anecdotes with Adam. I know how much you hate library research."

A glare accompanied Oliver's last sentence, and Carmichael knew he had to shut up and deal. He'd spent too long in the military to start defying the man who was, essentially, his commanding officer. Carmichael gave a sharp nod, and the skin around Oliver's eyes crinkled, a prelude to a smile. He backed out of the car, leaving the door open for Adam, who bounded out of the backseat and into the front before Oliver had even ascended the steps to the library entrance. The car door thudded close, confining the two men in the car.

Pulling his seat belt across his lap, Adam turned to Carmichael, a huge smile on his face. Carmichael didn't smile but allowed his lips to give an answering twitch. It wasn't fair. Temptation had never been so compelling. And gorgeous.

"So are you going to give me more information about what we're doing?" Adam asked.

Oh holy hell. What the fuck had Oliver told him? Or not told him? Shit. He couldn't remember. Adam distracted him, and distractions affected his work. He couldn't afford that; work was all he had.

"What did Oliver say? So I won't repeat anything."

Adam gave him a look that Carmichael wasn't able to interpret.

"Twenty bucks an hour. Clock starts now," Adam said with a bright grin.

The expression was so genuine, Carmichael's facial muscles were surprised into unbending enough to return the smile. Although if Adam needed the money that bad, he should consider getting a job *not* in a café. Thinking about Adam's irresponsible life choices would make this day less endurable, so Carmichael shut off that line of thought.

"That's it?"

"And you wanted a guide around town. I'm a little unclear about what's going to take all day, though. Not much in the way of folklore around here."

Carmichael pulled out of the parking lot and guided the car back to the center of town.

"Let's start by hitting major landmarks and important buildings in town. I'll learn my way around, and while we're doing so, we can also cover any stories you might have about...I don't know...ghosts, weird lights in the sky, mysterious disappearances. Any sort of strange stories would be good."

For the first time in his short career with the agency, he was in charge of lying to informants about his investigation. And he hated it. He'd rather tell the truth, but he had a damn good idea of how well that would play out. Adam would think he was batshit crazy. Not that he cared what Adam thought of him, but it might make it awkward—more awkward—to work together. Why couldn't this be like the other jobs? How could Oliver think Carmichael was cut out for this type of subterfuge? Straightforward brawn, he was good at.

"Ghost stories? Weird happenings? Okay, yeah, there's a few of those. Why don't we walk around? Most of the places are in the historic district."

Historic district. Yeah, could be. Few of the cases he and Oliver had investigated had to do with anything too modern. Why that should be, Carmichael didn't know and never cared to ask.

"Sure, sounds good. Tell me where to go."

Carmichael heard a muffled snort through the hand Adam clamped over his face. Yeah, yeah, he'd sort of walked into that one, but he was glad Adam hadn't taken him up on the obvious dig. Carmichael had been an ass ever since they'd met. However, he didn't say anything else, just followed Adam's directions and pulled into a parking spot. Adam bounced, actually bounced, out of the car and stood on the sidewalk, waiting for him.

Taking a deep breath, Carmichael extricated himself from the car in a more sedate manner. He ignored his impulse to spend the day five paces behind Adam to admire his rounded ass. But that would be more overt than he'd ever been, and ever would be, in or out of the military.

Work. He was *working*. Squashing his desires down, Carmichael drew up beside Adam and gestured. "Let's get started."

"Over here..." Adam started walking.

Fumbling in his pocket for his digital voice recorder, Carmichael asked, "Mind if I record this?" At least he could be up front about this. Recording Adam without permission would have felt wrong, slimy. As irresponsible and immature as Adam was, he wasn't a shitheel like most of the people Carmichael encountered in the course of his job.

Besides, a folklore researcher? Would probably want to record everything. What the hell kind of occupation was that, anyway? Not for the first time, Carmichael wished Oliver had picked a cover Carmichael knew *anything* about.

FOUR HOURS LATER, Carmichael was ready to punch someone, Oliver at the top of his list. Adam had dragged him past every historic building and had some boring-ass story about each and every one. Not only was Rothburg tame beyond belief, but it had the most vanilla history Carmichael had ever heard.

If he never heard another story about ghostly cats and wailing women... Not one story was sinister enough, or recent enough, to have prompted the agency to send them out here. If ghosts existed, they were of no more concern to the agency than satanists were. Harmless, relatively speaking, compared to the scary shit the Umbrae were capable of. Residual energies had nothing on possession by evil entities from another world, turning people into some of myth's worst nightmares.

Carmichael's first brush with the Umbrae had been in Afghanistan. Oliver had told him after he'd joined the agency it had likely been an *afrit*, not a vicious hallucination, as Carmichael had assumed. Oliver had also surmised that the grenade Carmichael had lobbed at the monster had unintentionally closed the portal, preventing any more possessions. There had been a lot of similarities with the demon he'd killed in his first case with the agency, the same day he'd met Oliver. The day he'd realized he perfectly sane and there were more things in this world than he'd ever expected.

When Adam had mentioned disappearing pets an hour ago, Carmichael had gotten excited. Even if they were dealing with some-thing as mundane as a serial killer, disappearing pets might have been the start of it all. Until Adam told him it had happened a hundred years ago.

Researchers at the agency hypothesized that portals could reopen in the same place over and over throughout the ages, and there was some suspicion that any portal activity weakened the barrier between worlds, even after the portals were closed. But with no follow-up, no continuance of pattern, no dead bodies, well, Carmichael couldn't believe it had any bearing on this case. Now he was starving, and his knee ached. Adam was a good storyteller, and his voice was like a caress, but enough was enough.

"Isn't there anything more recent? More..." Did he dare specify what he was after?

"More what?" Adam stopped midstory and looked expectantly at him.

Fuck it. Oliver had left him in charge of this, and he wasn't going to second-guess himself anymore.

"More sinister. Unexplained deaths or disappearances."

Adam tilted his head to the side. Sunlight lit up a patch of skin where his neck joined his shoulder that called to Carmichael's tongue. Dammit. Carmichael draped his trench coat protectively in front of his groin.

"Can we break for lunch?" Adam asked.

Food. Sweet, sweet food. "God, yes. I haven't eaten since breakfast yesterday." Which was his own stupid fault, and partly Adam's, but explained a good deal of his fatigue and irritation.

"Yesterday? No wonder you're so grouchy." Adam grinned.

Carmichael growled in response. Getting cozy with strangers wasn't something he did well. So what? Most people weren't worth getting to know.

Walking into the diner, Carmichael scoped out the table farthest away from any potential eavesdroppers. The insatiable curiosity of the townspeople had been assuaged this morning, he hoped. Gossip had flown through the town like it was on a divine mission. After about an hour, and a brief introduction to five or six people, it had become obvious that all subsequent interactions were with people who already knew Carmichael's name and supposed purpose for being in town. Which meant more probing questions as to the nature of his work. Adam had deflected them with skill, leaving Carmichael surprised and grateful.

Adam amazed Carmichael yet again by leading him to the exact table he'd had in mind. Had Adam been able to sense how uncomfortable he was with all the attention and nosy questions?

"Hey, honey, what can I get you?" The buxom waitress was at their table before Carmichael's ass hit the seat.

Wow. Eager service. "Water and a burger," Carmichael said. No point in looking at a menu. Places like this always had burgers, and it was hard to fuck one up.

"No problem, honey." She continued checking him out, chest to package, and Carmichael realized why she was being so attentive. What he couldn't figure out was why Adam wasn't receiving equal or more attention.

"Ruthie, I'll get the same, please," Adam said pleasantly.

If Carmichael hadn't been watching, he might have missed the look of disdain that flickered over Ruthie's face when she deigned to glance at Adam.

"Sure." Her tone lost its previous enthusiasm, and she left. Curious. A bad breakup or something? Granted, most of the townspeople they'd met today had acted strangely around Adam, but Carmichael chalked that up to his own presence. None of them had been as overt about it as Ruthie, though.

Adam was very attractive. Maybe he'd slept around a lot, broken lots of girls' hearts. He could be the town's bad boy, but his disposition was alarmingly sunny, which didn't equate to Carmichael's notion of a bad boy. Maybe—

"Carmichael!"

He became aware that this wasn't the first time Adam had said his name. Warmth crept into his cheeks. Again. Fuck, what was it about this kid?

"Sorry, I, uh...was thinking of something else."

"Really? I hadn't noticed," Adam said with a good-natured grin.

"Well?" Carmichael tried to ignore the way his face heated further at the teasing. He hadn't known until he'd rolled into Rothburg that he was still capable of blushing. He'd always associated it with naïveté, and he hadn't been innocent in a long time.

"Well, what?" Adam asked.

"I assumed you wanted to say something. Isn't that why you said my name?"

Oh. Nice to see Carmichael wasn't alone in the embarrassment department.

"Er. Yes. Sorry." Adam's gaze shifted down to the table, and his long, slender fingers stroked over his cutlery, as though he were considering how to broach a difficult subject. A ring of braided, silver-colored metal on Adam's thumb caught Carmichael's eye as the well-shaped hands fidgeted.

Those amazing green eyes looked up at him, filled with apologies.

"Carmichael, I'm sorry. I can't do this."

"Can't do what?"

"Today, those stories, well, most of them aren't true."

Ghost stories. No one sane would believe they were true, outside of the agency. A year ago, Carmichael would have agreed. But he'd learned otherwise. A faint shiver traveled down his frame as he remembered the first case he'd investigated with Oliver. Probably the most important moment in his life, when his belief in what was real, possible, shattered.

Whatever. Didn't have anything to do with today. Or this investigation.

He might as well find out why Adam seemed so remorseful. He stared at Adam, silent, waiting for the explanation he knew would come. Most people didn't deal well with silence.

"Look, you don't have to pay me. I shouldn't have done it." Adam's gaze dropped back to the table.

"Done what?" Carmichael was confused.

"I made everything up. Well, no, not everything, but most of it."

It took longer than it should have, but the meaning behind Adam's words trickled into Carmichael's brain.

"You made it up. Made. It. Up. Four hours of my time, wasted." Yeah, Adam might be gorgeous, but that wasn't going to be enough. Carmichael stared, eyes narrowing, wondering if Oliver would let him get away with pummeling the little shit, just a bit.

"I'm sorry. I couldn't resist." Adam looked beseechingly at him. "But you and Oliver—you were both lying to me, so I—"

Carmichael coughed, surprised. "How? I mean, why?"

"Oh, honey, are you all right?" Ruthie raced over and patted him on the back, although it felt more like a caress than any attempt to aid him.

"I'm fine, miss." Carmichael didn't miss the flash of irritation in

Adam's eyes at the interruption. Good, they were on the same page. Ruthie needed to get lost so he could get some answers. She was *way* too attentive.

"Are you sure? Can I get you anything?" Ruthie was still rubbing his back, making Carmichael uncomfortable.

"No, thanks. I'm fine now." His tone was firm.

"Well, okay, you holler if you need anything."

From her? Yeah, like that would ever happen. Carmichael nodded and looked back at Adam as Ruthie moved away.

"What did you mean? What were we lying about?" Carmichael didn't want to give any more away than he had to, but something told him this mission wasn't going to go as smoothly as Oliver anticipated.

"You're not folklore researchers. That's obvious. I'd guess you're not professors or writers either. So since you lied to me about who you were, I lied about all those stories. I'm...sorry." Adam blushed, eyes downcast, voice more somber than Carmichael had ever heard.

He...lied. Carmichael wasn't quite sure what to think. Fingers drummed the tabletop as he considered the ramifications. Sure, Carmichael wasn't the best actor around, but damn, Adam was sharp. That'd show Oliver for coming up with such a dumb cover story. In fact, he couldn't wait to tell Oliver all about it, rub his nose in it. Screwing up might not be Carmichael's fault. The ridiculous stories Adam had told him flickered through his brain. Oh God. He snorted, a smothered laugh escaping.

It was enough. Adam looked up, incredulous. Carmichael pressed his lips together, trying to keep the mirth in, but he couldn't. Another laugh bled out before Adam started laughing too.

Oh, he was pretty. Carmichael's cock took a more definite interest, but the insane humor of the situation helped his control. The glares Ruthie shot at the both of them helped too.

Minutes later, she slammed their lunches down. Adam picked up a fry and popped it into his mouth, eyes still tearing. Carmichael didn't smile at him, but he felt like he'd overcome a hurdle. He could spend a while in Adam's company. It wasn't like they were going to get married. Or date. Or fuck. Not that he would mind. Yeah, right. Not mind. He'd fucking love to spend a whole lot of time naked with Adam, but he didn't know if the kid was straight or not. And Carmichael never made the first move. Ever. It wasn't prudent for someone lurking in the closet's door frame.

Oliver might kill Carmichael later, but Adam had given Carmichael the excuse he needed to do what he considered right.

He leaned back against the wall, reviewing the relative positioning of the people in the diner. Ruthie was still paying more attention to him than Carmichael was comfortable with. A police officer, younger than Oliver but older than Carmichael, had come in and sat down at the counter. Carmichael hadn't missed the searching glance he'd been treated to, but Carmichael had given him a faint nod, and the officer had accepted the courtesy. Local law enforcement could be problematic in his line of work, given the secrecy surrounding the agency's activities.

"Look, kid, eat up. I don't want to talk about this here, but I'll explain everything after lunch. My room, okay?" Still a lie. He couldn't explain *everything*. Not only would Oliver kill him, but there was no way Adam would believe him. *Hi, I work for a secret government agency. We investigate dangerous paranormal activity caused by a thinning of the barriers between worlds, and we shut it down. Yes, that would be the Metaphysical Investigative Agency. No, I'm not making it up.*

What a quick way to get committed. Thinking about trying to convince someone he wasn't a lunatic made his brain swim. Hell, Oliver hadn't even told him that much before he'd gone out on his first case. There was a limit to what most rational humans would accept, unless they had tangible, unequivocal proof. Proof he could not provide to Adam to support his case.

Adam nodded, swallowing. "So does this mean you still want to work with me?"

Want? A dangerous word. But Carmichael had already decided

he could explain some things to Adam, and once he did, there would be no point in recruiting someone else for this task.

"Sure, no problem," Carmichael said. Adam grinned at him again. God, he seemed so young but so damned appealing.

"I'll be back in a minute," Adam said as he stood. Carmichael nodded and absolutely did not watch Adam's sexy ass as he made his way to the restroom. Did not.

Adam hadn't quite reached the door when the police officer slipped away from the counter and slid into Adam's vacated seat.

"Afternoon," Carmichael greeted the cop. Shit, Oliver was much better at these encounters.

"Afternoon. I notice you're new around here."

"Yes."

More than curiosity or small-town friendliness prompted the man's actions. Otherwise why wait until Adam left the table?

"I'm the chief of police for Rothburg. Know Adam from the city, do you?"

What? Carmichael hadn't expected Adam's name to enter the conversation, even though his absence had triggered the visit. Carmichael had expected the show of power in the introduction. Most cops wanted you to know where you stood, right up front, in case you were a potential criminal. He peered at the nameplate on the brown-haired man's uniform.

"No, not at all, Chief Sarkovsky." Carmichael made an effort to keep his tone respectful. The chief could make his job very difficult if he chose.

"You looked chummy."

This was bad. Not for the first time, Carmichael wished Oliver were there. He must have walked into some long-standing issue the town had with Adam, and he didn't know what the fuck was going on. Was the cop trying to protect Adam, or was Carmichael somehow guilty by association?

From the piercing look the chief directed his way, Carmichael knew he'd have to cough up some explanation. He hoped it wasn't going to upset anyone.

"My colleague and I hired Adam to perform a few odd jobs for us while we're in town."

The chief nodded and stroked his clean-shaven chin. For whatever reason, Carmichael didn't think the man believed him.

"You know, lots of folks round here don't approve of our Adam."

Okay, this was totally fucked-up. Had to be a prank. "Why are you telling me this?"

"Just a friendly warning," Chief Sarkovsky said as he rose to his feet. "If you plan on spending time with Adam, you might want to be prepared." The chief returned to his stool at the counter and picked up his cup of coffee, as though he hadn't dropped the most surreal and obscure warning that Carmichael had ever received.

He couldn't even tell if the chief was one of the "folks" who disapproved of Adam. Might have been nice if he'd mentioned why. But then, these small towns had long memories. Whatever beef the townspeople had with Adam, Carmichael couldn't imagine it would matter; he and Oliver weren't going to be in town long.

Looking toward the restrooms, he saw Adam returning, a smile on his face, and Carmichael shoved the bizarre behavior of the police chief to the back of his mind.

"Eat up before it gets cold."

THREE

In a surprisingly short time, they'd finished lunch, and Adam followed Carmichael to his room at the bed-and-breakfast. Lunch, not overfilled with conversation, had been less stressful than any of Adam's encounters with Carmichael yet. Something had happened to allow him to relax, a bit, in Adam's company. He'd laughed, which Adam thought was a huge step forward. And he'd picked up Adam's tab at the diner, although that might have been part of the job offer that Adam had missed.

Maybe Carmichael's attitude was the result of nothing more than the concern of the überstraight man that a gay guy would pounce and make unwelcome advances at any opportunity. Perhaps spending the morning together had convinced Carmichael that Adam could demonstrate some self-control. Sure, Adam would give his left nut for a chance at that spectacular body, but few straight men would appreciate an obvious come-on, and Adam had no desire to get beat up. Would mess up their new working relationship, that was for sure.

Good thing Carmichael didn't know he'd starred in Adam's jack-off session last night. Beating off to visions of Carmichael naked and fucking him had given Adam the most intense orgasm he'd ever had on his own. Information like that might put Carmichael in a sour mood. Or back in a sour mood, anyway. Damn, though, his mind had conjured up images so vivid, he'd had a difficult time looking Carmichael in the eyes first thing this morning. He'd been afraid Carmichael would read the lust in his eyes like a flashing LED billboard.

Now, though, Carmichael had unbent enough to invite Adam up to his room. Sure, it was only one in the afternoon, and they weren't going for a little afternoon fuckfest, but Adam was pleased by the demonstration of trust. The library closed at four today, so it couldn't be too long before Oliver called for a pickup. Adam would rather get the explanations out of the way before dealing with Oliver. His staid, officious appearance made Adam feel like he was back at school, waiting for the principal to give him detention.

Intentionally screwing up a job was not something he did. Wasn't like him. So what if Oliver and Carmichael had lied to him? It shouldn't have mattered. They were paying him. They weren't asking him to do anything illegal, immoral, or unethical. He should have done the job to the best of his ability. The guilt had been eating him up, so he'd confessed. He should be glad his mother had never been the type to indulge in guilt trips, because he would have been a sucker for them.

"Hey, you okay?" Carmichael glanced at him as they got out of the car in the parking lot, voice soft.

"Yeah, fine." Thinking about his mother made him sad, but he was surprised Carmichael had noticed anything.

"Come on." Carmichael waved him in the door. Adam was glad the B and B had a separate entrance for registered guests. He wouldn't have relished the gossip that would spring up if he had to walk past Gladys in the middle of the day, with a good-looking man from the city.

"Which room did you get?"

"The Manx."

Oh, man. Hilarious. Adam swallowed a laugh at Carmichael's

curled lip and derisive tone. That alone might be proof Gladys had a sense of humor, putting a man like Carmichael in that room.

After Carmichael ushered him into the room, Adam glanced around. Unbelievable. He'd never been in this room before, but the overwhelming *catness* more than lived up to the comments he'd heard. Gladys should be strung up for this offense against aesthetics. Damned funny, though.

The presence of a sitting room might have accounted for Carmichael's comfort in asking him back here. Adam could see a precisely made bed through a partially closed door, and he shivered a little, imagining Carmichael spread out on those sheets, rumpling them. Naked. No...not naked. *Don't think about naked.* Adam's pants constricted, and frantic, he focused on the worst decorating disaster—the drapes.

"Have a seat," Carmichael said as he dropped into a chair on the other side of the table. "I don't have drinks or anything." He didn't sound apologetic, but then, it amazed Adam he'd thought about offering refreshments at all.

"No problem. We can always stop by the café, if need be." Adam settled into the chair, wondering if the end result of this little powwow would be his never seeing Carmichael again, never mind having the opportunity for a cup of coffee with him. It shouldn't matter either way, but money or no, Adam desperately wanted to spend more time with Carmichael. As stupid as that was.

Carmichael frowned, and Adam got the distinct sense Carmichael was considering how to edit what he was going to tell him.

"So...you were going to explain?" Adam prompted. If that didn't work, he would try to find out if Carmichael was his first or last name, and what else went with Carmichael, because it piqued his curiosity.

"Yes, yes, I know. Sorry, I've never told anyone about this before. I work for an agency called MIA—"

"MIA? What does that stand for? I mean, other than the usual 'missing in action.'"

Oh, that was an interesting expression. Adam didn't know how he knew, but Carmichael was going to lie to him. Again.

"Murrumbidgee Investigative Agency. And as I was saying—"

"Murrumbidgee?" Adam said. How idiotic did Carmichael think he was? But then, maybe this line of bullshit would work with most people. "You're a long way from home, then. Why is it you care about Rothburg, again?"

"What do you mean, 'a long way from home'?"

"Murrumbidgee is in Australia, mate," Adam said, putting on a heavy Aussie accent. There was that pretty blush again. Ha. Teach him to underestimate the *kid*.

Carmichael rubbed his face in his hands before he stared right into Adam's eyes. Gorgeous blue eyes held his, and Adam knew that this would finally be the truth.

"Look, you aren't going to believe me."

"Try me."

"Fine." Carmichael nearly knocked over his chair as he stood and walked over to the window, then twitched aside the curtains to look out.

"I work for a secret government agency."

"Really?" Adam couldn't quite keep the sarcasm out of his voice. He'd been so sure Carmichael wasn't going to lie again. There wasn't any point to this, and Adam stopped feeling guilty about his own lies. "Never mind. Don't bother trying to come up with anything else."

Head snapping back, Carmichael glared at him. "Stop interrupting. You wanted the truth; I'm going to give it to you. I don't care if you believe it or not, but you can't tell anyone else, got it?"

Okay, then. "Sorry. Lips are sealed and all that. Go on," Adam said, waving a hand.

Carmichael responded by stomping back to the chair and dropping down into it. Better. The whole forlorn, introspective, peering-out-of-the-window nonsense didn't suit Carmichael, not one bit.

"The agency *is* called MIA. But its full name is—Never mind. I can't tell you. It doesn't matter. It's the government. They love acronyms. Anyway, we're closely connected to the CID, but not actually military. We investigate unusual occurrences with no clear signs of criminal activity." Carmichael's speech pattern changed for the last sentence, letting Adam know he chose each word with care.

Adam sat for a few seconds, but it soon became obvious that Carmichael thought his explanation was complete. "Can I ask questions?"

Carmichael nodded. "I can't answer all, or even most, of them. I've already told you more than I should. A lot of what I work with is classified."

Uh-huh. He didn't look insane, but Adam had never heard anything so ridiculous. He wasn't the world's best judge of character, but he thought Carmichael was telling the truth, at least as he knew it to be. Man, oh, man. How could someone so fucked-up turn him on so much?

"Why all the secrecy if there's no criminal activity?"

Squirming a little in his seat, Carmichael opened and closed his mouth a couple of times. Yeah, Adam wasn't surprised he didn't know how to answer the question. How could he?

"I said no *clear* signs of criminal activity."

"And that makes a difference how?"

"Look, you send a group like the FBI in somewhere, people get freaked out. And the FBI would be hard-pressed to justify expending budget dollars on investigations that might not lead to prosecution. We have a little more latitude, but because of that, we're also secret."

Did Carmichael think this made any sense? At all? Adam thought about getting up, storming out, telling Carmichael where he could stick this stupid job. Then he remembered. Remembered his life—his boring, pathetic, lonely life. Did it matter how ridiculous and crazy Carmichael's story sounded? It was still the most interesting thing to happen to him since he'd moved home. And he might be able to forget, for a time, the depressing situation with his parents.

Most people would counsel Adam to forget it. If Carmichael and

Oliver believed the nonsense Carmichael was spouting, they could be dangerous. Adam knew damn well Carmichael was dangerous, but he also sensed he wasn't in any real physical danger from him. A broken nose if Adam made a pass at him. A broken heart, maybe. Adam had already endured a broken heart when Joel dumped him because coming back to Rothburg wasn't convenient or fashionable. He wasn't going to be foolish enough to fall in love this soon, especially not with a straight man. Unrequited lust was all he'd allow himself.

"Well, okay, then, secret-agent man. Does this mean I'm forgiven?"

Carmichael directed a glare at him. "Yes, if you'll help out. For real this time."

"What are you looking for? For real this time," Adam mimicked. "And why do you need my help in the first place? I'm not an investigator." He was an archeologist, or would be if he ever got the chance to finish his degree.

"I'm sure Oliver could explain a lot better."

"Why?"

"I've only been working for the agency for a year."

"Really?" Adam wasn't sure he should allow himself to be sidetracked, but he wanted to know more about Carmichael.

"Yeah, I was military police for the army, but I got injured. Shortly after my discharge, I was recruited by the agency."

Military police? The army? Hoo-boy! Adam was happier than ever that he hadn't made a move on Carmichael. He'd have been deader than dead. But it was nice to know he hadn't mistaken the whole military vibe.

"You were injured?" And badly enough to be discharged? Impossible. Adam didn't think he'd seen a more fit man in his life. And he'd spent some time searching.

"My knee. Shrapnel. Healed up well, but too much exertion..." Carmichael rubbed a palm over the knee Adam presumed was the injured one. Oh shit. Shame heated him as he realized how much walking they'd done, for no other purpose than to extract a little revenge.

"I'm so sorry. I didn't know." Adam flexed his fingers, wanted to reach out, touch, and soothe.

"What?" Carmichael looked confused, still rubbing at the affected joint. Adam glanced down toward Carmichael's knee, and Carmichael snatched his hand back, fingers curled into a fist. "It's nothing. Nothing."

"But—"

"No. Forget it."

Well, okay, then. Jeez, Adam had thought that they'd had a bit of a truce, but grouchy Carmichael—no, make that grouchy *Agent* Carmichael—had made an abrupt return. Adam sucked in a calming breath. Getting pissy wouldn't get him paid. But seriously, Carmichael needed to relax some.

Adam pasted on a bright smile. It wasn't totally fake, because he'd had a quick flash of how he'd like to help Carmichael relax. "Fine. You were going to tell me what you're looking for?"

CARMICHAEL STARED AT ADAM, amazed again by how imperturbably happy he was. Whatever shit Carmichael dished out, Adam took it and smiled. Yet somehow Carmichael didn't get the feeling Adam was a pushover. Immature, irresponsible, and on occasion childish, but not a pushover. Just a genuinely happy person, something Carmichael didn't quite understand. Happiness was not an emotion he had much familiarity with.

"What we're looking for. Right." So far, the explanation had gone well. Maybe he wasn't as shit at this covert stuff as he'd thought. However rotten it made him feel to deceive Adam, he knew it was necessary. He tried to take comfort in the fact that he'd told Adam as much as he could, more than he'd ever told anyone about his job.

"Like I said before. Mysterious disappearances. Unexplained

deaths. Maybe deaths that seem too convenient. But I wasn't lying about the weirdness. Sometimes people use existing stories of the paranormal—ghosts or whatever—to cover evidence of other activities. Dangerous activities."

The biggest problem with this covert stuff? All the damned talking he had to do. He might have said more in the past hour to Adam than he'd said to Oliver in the past week. Oliver was, without a doubt, better at the talking shit. But then, Carmichael had an attentive and attractive audience. Made him damned chatty.

Adam nodded and stroked his index finger across his lips, drawing Carmichael's gaze like a magnet to a lodestone. With deliberate precision, Carmichael placed both of his hands on the table to prevent himself from adjusting his cock, which responded immediately to the sight. Such perfect lips. He could only imagine how they'd feel on his own lips, his nipples, his dick.

He closed his eyes against the images as the unruly organ in question leaped at the idea. Carmichael scooted his chair closer to the table and opened his eyes again. He reached into his pocket to retrieve the digital voice recorder, taking the opportunity to surreptitiously adjust himself as much as he could, and placed the device on the table.

"If you think of anything, can I still record it?"

Adam nodded, still looking lost in thought. "The first thing that comes to mind is Allenton Woods."

Now they were getting somewhere.

"What about them?" Carmichael asked.

"People say they're haunted. Been stories about them for decades. Everyone avoids them. Of the tourists who come to the campground, there's always a couple of thrill seekers who venture off the trail. Sometimes teenagers on a dare. Usually a broken bone or something keeps them from going too far."

Interesting. "That sounds like a lot of coincidence."

"Yeah, I know. It does. But that particular area is very treacherous, which is why there are warning signs all over the place. My guess is that it has the reputation it does because of that danger. Some have reported loss of memory or strange, inexplicable sights—exaggerations, probably. The townspeople never go there, and the rangers make a point of scaring the curious off."

"How do you know what the rangers do? Were you one of those curious teenagers?"

"Maybe." Adam's lips curled into a wicked grin. "Actually, that was part of my duties. During the summer, I had a job with the park."

"You're a ranger?"

Compressed lips told him Adam had heard his unflattering, incredulous tone.

"No." Adam looked down at the table. "Another part-time job. With all the campers, there's too much work for the rangers. I've had some experience outdoors; I'm young, healthy, and familiar with the area."

"Oh." For a moment, Carmichael had been thrilled at the thought of Adam working a decent job. "Why haven't you tried to become a ranger full-time?" If what Adam said was true, there was no reason why he shouldn't get hired on. That had to be a better choice than the unskilled labor he was currently engaged in.

Adam's gaze lifted back up, and his eyes glittered. "I don't want to be a ranger; that's why." There was an unexpected bite to his tone, and Carmichael realized he sounded like someone's father. It wasn't any of his business, and the last thing he wanted to do was set himself up as a mentor or anything.

"Whatever. It was just a question." Carmichael brought his hands up, holding them palms out in a defensive gesture. "Any deaths in this particular stretch of woods?"

"Not that I recall. I mean, hikers disappear all the time."

"All the time?"

"I don't mean on a weekly basis or anything. But it happens. People don't take the proper safety precautions, or they have bad luck. Most times the bodies are found, but not always. And if they venture off state property, well, they take their chances."

"What do you mean?"

"A section of Allenton Woods is part of the national park. The rest of it is private property. The rangers know where the divider is, and neither regular patrols nor emergency searches will cross it. They won't leave park property, not near Allenton Woods. Don't know why, and it was never explained."

Carmichael frowned slightly. He didn't know much about the jurisdiction of park rangers and how it related to trespassing laws when it came to searching for a missing person. Was it unusual for an arbitrary line to thwart them in any way?

Unless it was that treacherous. No point in risking a ranger's safety without clear proof a person had ignored posted warning signs. A little callous, maybe, but it was something Oliver could look into. Liability and lawsuits made an awful lot of decisions these days.

Either way, he was certain Oliver would want at least one of them to check out the site in person.

"Hey, can I use your bathroom?"

Carmichael nodded and took the opportunity to watch Adam's gorgeous ass walk away. God. He adjusted himself again, not having to worry about Adam seeing. They had to get out of there.

Thinking of anything beyond how much he wanted Adam was impossible. Visions of fucking Adam, or being fucked by him, flitted through his mind with alarming frequency. The proximity of the bed increased the chance of Carmichael doing something stupid and humiliating. He wasn't as grouchy as Adam undoubtedly thought, but it was the only way he could keep himself under control. Never in his life had he been so tempted to give in. But without knowing if Adam swung the same way, it was a chance he couldn't take. Wouldn't take.

The toilet flushed, followed by the tap running. Carmichael tore his gaze off the door, embarrassed. He'd been staring, waiting for Adam to reappear.

Checking his watch, he realized it could be a couple of hours before Oliver called. Without any conscious direction, his gaze flipped back to the bed. Yeah, they had to get out of there. A couple of hours, with no real tasks to accomplish? Way too dangerous for his peace of mind.

"Well, I think that's enough to start with for now, unless you can think of any other unusual activity," he said as Adam sat down again.

"Oh. Right. Sure." Adam sounded disappointed, but Carmichael couldn't figure out why that would be. "Well, I guess I'll be off, then. Call me if you need any more help."

Adam started to get out of the chair. Wait, what? Carmichael's hand shot out and clasped Adam's forearm. "Where're you going, kid?" God, his skin was so soft and warm. Carmichael took a deep breath, trying to convince his hand to release Adam's arm and not give in to the almost overwhelming urge to caress, stroke. Even so, it was Adam's pointed look at his hand that gave him enough impetus to let go.

Sinking back into the chair, Adam looked at Carmichael, questions in his eyes. Carmichael was *not* going to blush again. Not.

"I thought you said we were done?"

"Sorry. You can go if you want. But I thought we could get a cup of coffee, wait for Oliver, see where he wants to go from here."

"Oh, okay." A wide, happy smile followed Adam's words, once again tempting Carmichael to return it. He didn't. "Want to go now?"

"Sure, why not?" The sooner they got out of here the better.

THE BED-AND-BREAKFAST WAS within walking distance of the café, but Carmichael chose to drive anyway, since he might have to go pick up Oliver. Technically the library was also within walking distance from the café, and Oliver could meet them there when he was done. If it were him, though, Carmichael wouldn't want to walk too far in one of those company suits. If Oliver had brought any other clothes with him, Carmichael would be shocked. Which meant Carmichael would be checking out the damned haunted woods.

He held the door open for Adam, who gave him a shy smile before ducking his head down and entering the café.

"Adam, what are you doing here?" The girl who'd been working the counter yesterday greeted Adam with a grin. With an unpleasant churning in his midsection, Carmichael wondered if she was Adam's girlfriend.

Not that he cared.

Nevertheless he paid close attention to their interaction.

"Hey, Susie. Just here to get a coffee."

An older woman at the counter turned to look at Adam as he spoke, and gave him such a venomous look, Carmichael almost stepped between them in a protective gesture.

"Hello, Mrs. Saunders. How are you today?" Adam sounded as friendly as ever. Had he missed the look? Adam had already proved how smart he was, so he couldn't be oblivious. Did he not care? The woman didn't look dangerous, but if someone looked at Carmichael that way, there's no way he could have spoken pleasantly to them.

"Adam Farelli. Not working again, I see." Mrs. Saunders's voice reminded Carmichael of his high school principal's. Thoroughly disapproving.

Carmichael stepped up beside Adam and brought his shoulders back, widening his stance. He knew doing so made him look larger and more intimidating, but the harridan didn't glance at him. Lucky for her, her glare had smoothed out to something less antagonistic.

"No, Mrs. Saunders. Today is my day off."

"Humph. This is one of the busiest days in the café. Instead Susie and Carol are working. You're shirking."

"Oh, I'd love to be working, but I don't make the schedule," Adam said without a trace of impatience.

"Hey, Adam, latte?"

"Susie, isn't mine ready yet?" Mrs. Saunders interrupted.

"Carol's finishing it up now. Adam, I know you're not working, but can you give me a hand with something in the back?" Susie asked.

"Won't take but a minute—Carol and I aren't quite strong enough to move the shipment that came in this morning."

"Sure thing. And a latte would be great." Adam flipped up the counter and slid behind it with practiced ease. He glanced back at Carmichael. "Black coffee, right?"

Carmichael nodded.

"And get Carmichael a black coffee, please," Adam said as he disappeared into the back room.

"Such a disappointment to his parents," Mrs. Saunders said at Carmichael's side.

Hell. All day he'd sensed odd undercurrents in every interaction they'd had with various townspeople. Maybe related to the strange warning the chief of police had given him at the diner. Many of the townsfolk must feel the same way as Mrs. Saunders. To his chagrin, Carmichael was part of that group. He had no right to care what Adam did with his life, and it was hypocritical of him to despise Mrs. Saunders for vocalizing her disapproval, when he agreed with her. But despise her he did.

"What? Why would you say such a thing?" Carmichael asked with more force than necessary for an uninterested party.

Mrs. Saunders glanced at him and blinked. "I take it you're a friend of Adam's."

"Not really, no." He might not have known Adam very long, but it felt strange, disloyal, to say those words. Something about Adam, besides his sheer sex appeal, made Carmichael want to protect him from everything, including whatever narrow-mindedness caused Mrs. Saunders's shrewish comment.

She stared at him.

"Don't you have anything better to do than gossip with strangers?" Carmichael couldn't believe the words coming out of his mouth. A further diatribe was rising behind his lips when Susie interrupted.

"Here's your cappuccino, Mrs. Saunders."

Mrs. Saunders took it and left without answering Carmichael's question. Not that he needed an answer. Any parent would be disappointed with a twenty-six-year-old who didn't go to school, rode a skateboard, and worked in a café. Especially one who still lived with them. But it didn't change the fact that Adam was gorgeous, funny, sexy, and even-tempered. Carmichael wanted him in the worst way, like a hypocritical ass.

"Don't mind her." Susie placed Carmichael's coffee in front of him.

"What?"

"She's a bitter old woman. Adam's a good guy." She winked at him. Was she flirting with him? Why would she care what he thought of Adam? At least she couldn't read his mind. Because almost every thought he had of Adam was X-rated.

Carmichael shrugged and paid. He waited for Adam's latte and grabbed a seat. After a couple of minutes, Adam reappeared and spoke to Susie briefly before ducking beneath the counter to join him. He didn't know what Susie had said, but Adam directed one of those belly-warming smiles at Carmichael, the kind that made Carmichael want to draw Adam into his arms and kiss him. Not that he'd do it, especially not out in public, but the desire became more compelling every time he saw those full pink lips curl and stretch into that happy expression. The dimples only made it worse.

"Oh, I could have paid." Adam dug around in his pockets. "I've got some cash."

"Don't bother. Consider it part of your salary."

"Cool, thanks."

They sat quietly for a minute. Several times Adam leaned forward, just a trifle, like he wanted to say something. Carmichael's coldness and his grim visage tended to put people off. It was useful on the job, both this one and in the army, but most times he dealt with dangerous criminals or murderous creatures. He didn't know how to turn it off when he was dealing with anyone else.

Taking pity on Adam, Carmichael gave small talk a try. "What do you do when you're not working?" He hoped the answer wasn't getting drunk or high.

Adam didn't launch into a laundry list of activities. Of the few emotions that crossed his face, regret and sadness were the most striking. And the most unexpected. But Carmichael had never been great at interpreting emotions.

Finally Adam spoke. "Not too much. Sometimes I do odd jobs, like lawn mowing, but most people use a lawn service around here. I read a lot."

No, not what Carmichael had expected. "What about your friends?"

This time there was no mistaking the sadness.

"Most of my friends don't live here."

Frustration seized Carmichael. Couldn't Adam see that they'd grown up, moved on, left him behind? Wasn't that enough motivation? What was the matter with him?

Oliver chose that moment to walk into the café, saving Carmichael from saying something as disapproving as Mrs. Saunders had. Either that, or he'd try giving Adam a hug. Both options would be mistakes.

Carmichael waved a hand, and Oliver nodded. He headed to the counter to place his order.

Leaning in toward Adam, Carmichael spoke quietly. "Don't say anything yet about what I told you. I'll break it to Oliver later that you know we're not folklore researchers."

"Of course. I wouldn't want you to get in trouble." Adam looked sincere.

How...sweet. Thoughtful. For all Adam's apparent irresponsibility, Carmichael knew he could trust him to keep his word.

"Thought you were going to call for a pickup," Carmichael said to Oliver when he sat down with them.

Oliver shrugged. "The café wasn't far. Figured I'd have you meet me here. How did it go today?"

Carmichael gave Oliver a summary of the day, excluding the

uncomfortable, probing questions from the townspeople and Adam's excellent storytelling skills. He glossed over those details—the subject would be easier to deal with when they were alone. True to his word, Adam kept his mouth shut, which boded well for his discretion in general.

"Interesting," Oliver said.

"Did you find out anything at the library?" Carmichael asked before Adam could. Funny how he could sense that Adam was dying to know. But then, Adam couldn't ask anything specific without Oliver finding out Carmichael had ditched the whole folklore-researcher cover story.

"Yes, there were a few items that might be what we're after."

Carmichael knew Oliver's vagueness was intentional, and he could see Adam's curiosity eating him alive. Oliver could see it too, because speculation appeared in his eyes.

"Carmichael, you'll have to check out those haunted woods."

"Yeah, I know."

"Adam, are you available to guide him? I didn't misunderstand when Carmichael said you'd worked for the park service?"

Adam bounced in his chair. "No, sir, you didn't. I'd be happy to guide him. How's tomorrow? Would take a whole day, at least."

"A whole day? Together?" Carmichael knew he sounded horrified, since both Adam and Oliver turned to look at him. Oliver looked surprised. Adam was hurt, though, no mistaking it. Shit. Carmichael royally fucked up, no matter what he did. He'd expected to be stuck searching the woods; he hadn't expected another whole day alone in Adam's company. His control was already slipping, and people had surrounded them most of the day.

"Don't you have to work tomorrow?" Carmichael tried to keep his tone mild. How could he be off Friday and Saturday all day? Weren't those the busiest days in a café, with the greatest potential to supplement income with tips? Why wouldn't Adam work them?

"I'm still the new guy," Adam replied. "I don't get the best shifts yet, unless someone needs time off. But if we're going tomorrow, we'll need to make sure we have the right supplies this evening."

"Perfect." Oliver looked pleased, almost smug. "Adam, if you could prepare a list, Carmichael can make sure he gets everything."

Oh goody. If he were Adam, the list would have a bunch of obscure shit for Carmichael to chase all fucking night, but he didn't believe Adam was that vindictive.

A few minutes later, Adam had written out a list on the back of a napkin and presented it to Carmichael. Adam's fingers brushed his. He barely suppressed the shiver of lust that threatened to shake his body, but he couldn't prevent the hairs on his forearm from standing up due to the electricity of the connection. Damn. He had never felt anything like it before. He hoped Adam wasn't aware of the effect he had on Carmichael. It would make—oh God—the whole day tomorrow more uncomfortable and humiliating than it needed to be.

With a quick look through his eyelashes at Adam, he couldn't see any indication Adam sensed anything out of the ordinary.

"Carmichael." Oliver drained his coffee. "Need any help getting the stuff together? Maybe Adam could help—"

"No," Carmichael yelped. He saw the flash of hurt again on Adam's face, but right now it didn't matter. His sanity was at stake if he didn't have some downtime away from the sexy Adam Farelli.

"That's fine. I've got to get home," Adam said and pushed away from the table. "I'll meet you at the B and B at nine tomorrow morning."

Before Carmichael or Oliver could confirm the plan, Adam left the café, his half-drunk latte still steaming on the table.

"What the fuck was that?" Oliver was pissed off. Again. Carmichael was going to be lucky to get this investigation wrapped up while he still had a job. At least this time he could divert Oliver's attention. They had to discuss what Carmichael had told Adam and the way that their cover story had changed. This time, however, it was much closer to the truth. Of course, Oliver might still be angry.

FOUR

Adam trudged home. He'd forgotten his skateboard in the back of Carmichael's SUV, but he couldn't bring himself to go back into the café to ask for it. Home wasn't too far away to walk.

Tomorrow. Why had he signed up to spend the whole day hiking with Carmichael? Oh, right, because he was an idiot. A horny, starry-eyed idiot completely smitten by a hot, sexy, straight man. He'd let his dick make the decisions, knowing full well there wouldn't be any opportunity, or even desire on Carmichael's part, to indulge. Dumb of him. Dicks weren't smart, as had been proven time and again throughout the ages.

Sure, the money wouldn't hurt, but damn. Adam was already more wound up over Carmichael than he'd ever been over Joel, and Joel had broken his heart.

Grouchy, lying, protective, gentle Carmichael. Susie had told him how Carmichael stood up for him. At the diner, Carmichael had ignored Ruthie's blatant advances to converse with Adam. Every time Carmichael snapped at him, Adam saw he regretted it. Adam could fall so hard.

Every time Carmichael did something sweet, he evened the

scales by lashing out at Adam. Which should have cured Adam of his infatuation, but damn it, it didn't. Carmichael's sharp words weren't malicious or hateful, just...accidental. Of course, the lack of respect hurt. Not that he wasn't used to it—no one who lived in this town respected him. But he'd never expected to see the town's attitudes mirrored in a stranger from the city.

Adam looked up, realizing his feet had brought him home on autopilot. He wiped away a couple of errant and unexpected tears. No man he'd just met should have the ability to hurt him like that, but somehow Carmichael's disapproval cut more deeply than the whole town's.

Walking in the door, he called to the nurse making tea in the kitchen. "Hello, Jennifer. How are you today?"

"Hi, Adam. I'm well, thank you. And your folks are doing fine," Jennifer said, anticipating his next question. "They had a good day."

Oh shit. Had his parents been lucid and he'd missed it? Those days came so infrequently in the past couple of months; he'd stopped believing the next one would come. Seemed strange that a genetic disease had a stranglehold on both of his parents—who weren't that old, dammit. Now they were merely animated bodies, reminding Adam of the many mummies he'd seen during the course of his studies.

He moved closer to Jennifer, muscles in his neck and shoulders bunching. "Are they still..."

"Oh, honey, I'm sorry. I didn't mean that. They weren't lucid today, but neither were they agitated. They're both sleeping now. I know it's early, but I think they might sleep all night."

The sudden tension washed away in relief, but he wasn't sure what he was relieved about.

Should he offer Jennifer the night off? Not that she wasn't getting paid, but Adam did feel guilty about not shouldering more of the care of his parents. Of course, if anything went wrong, he wasn't capable of helping. He was mere months away from getting his doctorate, but a PhD in archeology had no practical application when it came to medical emergencies.

Would he ever go back to school? Would he ever manage to finish those few final months of work?

"Some tea, honey?" Jennifer asked.

"Yes, thanks," Adam replied, pleased by the consideration.

God, what a lonely life he led. Last year at this time, he'd been a happy grad student, the beloved of Joel, with friends to party with, living in a part of the city filled with like-minded people. Now he was grateful for the company of one of the nurses he'd hired to care for his parents.

Joel had dumped him the minute Adam made the decision to give up his studies and return to Rothburg. Not that Adam blamed him, much. Joel wouldn't have fit in here, and if the townspeople hated Adam now, they'd have hated him more with Joel in tow.

Adam had spent time grieving for his failed relationship while dealing with the stressful and depressing decline of his parents. Now that he was over Joel and could think of him with wistfulness instead of tears, another man walked into his life and threatened to rip his heart out again. Thankfully Adam hadn't spent a year in a relationship with Carmichael. He didn't think he'd survive a breakup with that man. Watching him leave as soon as his investigation was complete was going to be harder than anything Adam would have anticipated, but infatuation was a funny thing.

Well, the best cure for getting over one man was to get under another, or so the saying went. Maybe not the best *plan* in the world, but a bad plan was better than sulking.

Adam became aware Jennifer had been talking, bits of nothing, small talk that didn't require his full attention, which was good because he hadn't been giving it. He smiled at her.

"I was thinking of going out tonight. I might not be home until morning."

Jennifer gave him a sympathetic look and patted his hand. "You go out and have some fun. You deserve a break. I know how hard you work, how hard this is for you, even if others don't."

"Thanks, Jennifer. I appreciate it." And he did. He had three nurses on a rotating basis, and they were all so kind. None of them were from Rothburg, though.

After a short nap and a shower, he stood in front of his closet. All his clothes were crammed into his small childhood room. The rest of his stuff was in boxes in the study.

When Joel had dumped him, Adam had lost not only a lover, but a roommate and an apartment as well. Today the advantage was that his club clothes were readily accessible. Within a few minutes, he knew what he'd wear. Might as well go in with the big guns blazing, because he needed to make the most of this opportunity. The cab fare and cover were an extravagance, but he needed to get his mind off Carmichael and his life. He needed this, no matter the cost.

That meant the mint green dress shirt that Joel said made his eyes light up. Not too original, but it always made Adam warm inside to hear it. And despite having bought the shirt at H&M, it was attractive enough that Joel never ribbed him about how little it cost. Joel was a bit of a fashion snob and spent a lot of money on clothes. But then, Joel had a lot of money to spend, much more than Adam ever did, although the past year had been an experience in near poverty that he didn't want to repeat.

He pulled the shirt and a pair of snug black pants out of his closet and threw them on the bed. Adam loved those pants. They were so low that without a shirt on, they barely covered his pubic hair. The sight of him in them had turned Joel into a quivering mass of lust on more than one occasion. The combination of pants and shirt almost guaranteed he'd score.

Before dressing, Adam returned to the bathroom to style his hair. He didn't know if the tousled, fresh-out-of-bed look was still in, but he knew it looked good on him, and anything that made gorgeous men think of him in bed was precisely the image he wanted to project tonight. Messy though it appeared, the style demanded a fair amount of time. The trick was to make sure it didn't look as though he'd spent hours making each lock sit just so. It was an art in which Adam had excelled, and when he viewed the finished product, he knew he'd not lost it.

The other skills he intended to employ tonight were rusty, but he was sure he hadn't lost those either. Blowjobs, fucking—you didn't forget how to do those. Labors of love, they were.

Adam checked the time. He needed to leave soon. Another skill he'd perfected in the city was arriving at a club early enough to not have to wait in line, but late enough to not appear desperate. Tonight he leaned more toward desperate, and he sure as hell didn't want to spend any time waiting outside in line.

He contemplated the pants, wondering if he should bother with underwear. No need to be coy, and boxer-briefs, his underwear preference, might show underneath. If the waist were higher, he'd choose silk boxers. Silk against his cock felt great, but again, he didn't want anything to ruin how the pants looked. Simple decision—no underwear. Made it easy access, and Adam had every intention of being easy tonight. Not for any man who asked, but surely he could find one who could fuck Carmichael out of his thoughts. Adam's mind wandered a bit as he wondered what kind of underwear Carmichael wore. Commando. Oh, please, commando.

Feeling his dick plump up at the thought, he realized he had to get lucky tonight. Otherwise spending the whole day tomorrow looking at that fine, muscular, ex-army ass, wondering what, if anything, was between jeans and skin, would drive him mad.

He ruthlessly pulled on his shirt and pants, thumping his cock to make it lie flat so he could zip up. Damn Carmichael. This was all his fault. One last task, and Adam could get the hell out of Rothburg for a bit.

He returned to the bathroom and stared at the bottles of cologne lining the counter. More than necessary. And he'd never be able to afford to replace them. Not now. He spent more on fragrance than clothes. Cologne dollars stretched further than clothing dollars. In the dark, no one remembered what you wore, but scents lingered. Joel used to laugh at how much time Adam spent assessing scents, but picking the right cologne was a science. He had four or five favorites, but the question was which one to choose.

Adam's fingers slid over the cool glass bottles. As much as his libido was driving him, he wasn't sure he wanted a random fuck. He wanted to go back to the B and B and crawl into bed with Carmichael, not go out cruising for a stranger. It had been years, long before Joel, since the last time he'd done it. Clubbing, sure. Cruising? Not so much. But desperate times and all that.

A rhomboidal blue glass bottle captured his fingers. The last gift Joel had given him. Flipping off the cap, Adam lifted the bottle to his nose, nostrils flaring slightly to bring the scent to him. This was Joel's favorite on him. In the bottle, it smelled like pipe tobacco and smoke. On Adam's skin, it smelled like leather-bound books and mahogany, making him think of old-world libraries filled with wingback chairs, first-edition books, fireplaces, and of course, sexy, arrogant men.

Not right for tonight, though. He was already wearing Joel's favorite shirt and pants. Wearing his favorite cologne would be pathetic beyond words. Adam's hand reached for his own favorite, the curved black bottle containing the woodsy, almost citrusy fragrance of Tokyo by Kenzo.

Perfect. Light and sexy. He hadn't worn it since his breakup with Joel, but then, there hadn't been much call for cologne in Rothburg.

He spritzed it on and inhaled, knowing by the time he got to the club the initial scent would have faded and transformed into his own. Now he was armed to face the gauntlet of gay men looking for a piece of ass.

BILL SUPPRESSED A SNEEZE. He'd never smelled cologne on Adam before, and the odor was almost painful to his enhanced scent receptors. Once Adam was turned, he'd understand. Bill would never need anything but the smell of Adam. Adam wouldn't need anything but the smell of Bill either.

It was all Adam's fault that Bill was gay—flaunting that hard little body in front of him, taunting him. Because of Adam, Bill had finally admitted to himself that he was gay. When Adam had come out, Bill had rejoiced. He'd known, somehow, that it would all work out. Bill could come out, and they could be together.

Then Adam left for college. Left him. It had shocked Bill into the realization that Adam, as the son of the chief of police, had a freedom Bill might never have. Not in this town. Until now.

As much as Bill wanted to remain on his perch all night and observe Adam's naked form, the clothes Adam pulled on announced the show was over for tonight. At least until later. Unfortunately Bill didn't have the luxury of returning. Not this evening—he had other obligations. He knew deep in his gut the reason Adam had donned a total fuck-me look. He was looking to get laid. Bill would volunteer, but Adam didn't know how good they could be together. And Bill couldn't show him yet.

Too bad killing Adam's one-night stand wasn't part of the plan. He couldn't allow his lust to overcome his good sense. After claiming Adam, Bill would ensure poaching on his territory was a fatal mistake. Soon Adam would be his, and there'd be no need for others. He'd already pulled some strings to get Adam's parents institutionalized faster. Once the nurses were gone and Adam's parents were taken care of, there was nothing stopping Bill from turning Adam— none of the pack would have grounds for complaints. Of course, Bill was in a position to overcome any objections, but he had to put the pack's safety and well-being first. Adam was a luxury, not a necessity, and right now he didn't fit into the plan. Soon, though, he'd be Bill's.

CARMICHAEL HAULED his purchases out to the SUV. Half the stuff did seem like Adam was punishing him, but Oliver hadn't been surprised at anything on the list. He *knew* Oliver was trying to punish him, though, which was why he was buying stuff for what appeared to be a camping trip.

A tent. The damned list included a tent. What the fuck? Weren't they supposed to be in and out? This shit was going to weigh a ton along with the weapons he wasn't leaving behind. Carmichael didn't have any intention of dragging the search out overnight. No way was his control that good. Pouncing on a man who hadn't demonstrated any interest was not in his job description. Oliver would kill him, of that Carmichael had no doubt.

As much as he hated research in the library, he'd given serious thought to trying to convince Oliver to take Adam on his camping trip. At least Oliver hadn't been too upset about Carmichael's coming clean, partially, with Adam. Oliver had dug up some disturbing trends in the archives, which Carmichael had every intention of sharing with Adam. Carmichael didn't think Adam understood the gravity of the situation, and only Carmichael and Oliver knew how bad it was and how bad it could get.

Adam needed to be careful. Oliver was going to dig further into county records, but what he'd uncovered was enough. Enough to convince Carmichael there was some seriously scary shit going on in Rothburg that had somehow failed to hit MIA's radar until recently. If the Umbrae ferreted out who Carmichael and Oliver were, and that Adam was helping them, Adam could be in a lot of danger.

Carmichael couldn't let anything happen to Adam. No matter how much Adam angered him, he made Carmichael want to kiss him, fuck him, smile back at his lopsided, dimpled smile, have those green eyes look at him with lust. Feelings that Carmichael shouldn't have, but he did, damn it.

He opened the back hatch of the SUV, preparing to heave his purchases inside, and caught sight of Adam's skateboard. Ah, fuck. His head dropped down as he realized he'd upset Adam enough earlier that he'd walked home.

Contemplating the colorful board with the scuffed black wheels, he rubbed the back of his neck. Maybe he should return it tonight. He checked his GPS. Adam didn't live too far from the café, but far enough that Carmichael felt like shit for making him walk all that way. He didn't know why he kept overreacting to Adam. It made no sense, but all these emotions kept roiling up out of nowhere, and all Carmichael could do was lash out at Adam with it. And Adam had done nothing to deserve it.

It wasn't Carmichael's place to tell him how to live his life. He was an adult, entitled to make his own choices, and if they weren't the choices Carmichael would make, well, it wasn't even like he and Adam were friends. After this was over, Carmichael would go back to the city and leave Adam to his feckless, responsibility-free life. Until then, Carmichael needed to keep both temper and lust in check.

Sighing, he glanced at his watch. It was getting late, but returning the skateboard tonight would let him see where Adam lived. Why he wanted to see that, he didn't know, but his decision was made.

TURNING ONTO ADAM'S STREET, Carmichael saw a cab in the driveway of Adam's house. Adam, looking more self-assured and sophisticated than Carmichael had seen him, hurried out the door and slid into the backseat of the cab. It backed out of the drive and headed away from Carmichael.

What the fuck? Where was he going at this time of night? Didn't he know people were disappearing around Rothburg? Maybe he didn't know how many. Carmichael hadn't until Oliver had given him the scoop, but damn. And did Adam think he'd be ready to go on a daylong, or more, trek at oh-nine-hundred tomorrow if he was going out now?

Carmichael resolutely pushed the word *date* out of his mind and followed the cab. He had an obligation to make sure his assistant was safe, didn't he? If he interrupted anything, well, there were consequences to irresponsible actions, and it would do Adam well to learn that sooner rather than later.

FIVE

"What are you doing here?" Grouchy Agent Carmichael struck again.

Adam was torn between telling him to fuck off and asking what Carmichael thought Adam was doing in a gay bar ogling, available, interested men. In the end, though, Carmichael's nearness, flashing eyes, and firm grip on his biceps dried up all the saliva in Adam's mouth and, with it, Adam's ability to speak.

He dropped his gaze to the tight, oh so heavenly, *tight* navy blue T-shirt straining across Carmichael's gorgeous pecs. And hello! It wasn't cold in here, was it? The dancing, writhing bodies created a warm, sweaty atmosphere. Thinking about tracing his tongue across the stiff nubs pressing against the thin cotton caused saliva to flood back into Adam's mouth.

Now he couldn't speak, for fear of drooling.

"Well?" Carmichael demanded.

What? Adam broke off his eye-to-nipple contact. Oh, right. Carmichael had asked him a question. But now Adam had a question of his own.

"What are *you* doing here?"

Carmichael's lips opened, then closed again. A wet pink tongue slid out to lick those kissable lips. Might have been a nervous reaction on Carmichael's part, but oh. Oh my. Adam's cock expanded. His pants had fit much better when he put them on earlier. Not constricting as they were now. It was a wonder his fly didn't burst from the pressure.

The brief moment of confusion passed for Carmichael, and his lips tightened, along with the grip on Adam's upper arms. Adam wondered if Carmichael would grip his cock that firmly, and he bit his lower lip to hold in a moan.

"I asked you a question." Carmichael ignored Adam's query.

"Hey, hon. Haven't seen you here in a while." A slender blond twink knocked hips with Adam, bringing him back to Earth.

"Oh, hey, how's it going?" Adam couldn't remember the guy's name, but they'd almost hooked up once, and Adam had seen him there several times. Before Adam had moved back to his parents' place, he and Joel had been regulars.

"Not as good as you, if this is who's keeping you out of the clubs."

Was it Darren? Adam was sure it was Darren. Probably Darren. Darren gave Carmichael the once-over and got a similar glare to the ones Adam received on a regular basis.

"Oooh. Possessive. You lucky little bitch. See you around." Darren patted Adam's ass then sauntered away.

Possessive. If only. Adam had no idea why Carmichael was here —almost back in the city—glowering at him, but it had nothing to do with possessiveness. Carmichael was straight.

"And how were you planning to get home?" Carmichael picked up their conversation as though there'd been no interruption.

However sexy Carmichael was, his attitude was fucking annoying. "Get the guy I hook up with to drive me home, or take a taxi."

Uh-oh. That answer made someone angry. Stunning blue eyes narrowed, and nostrils flared.

"You idiot. Don't you know how dangerous that is? Never mind that people have been disappearing." Carmichael's voice was low, rough, rubbing against Adam like a cat's tongue.

"What difference is it to you?" Great. Now Adam was reverting to a thirteen-year-old. He had been going to bars like this for years. Okay, not since he'd moved backhome, but he hadn't forgotten how to take care of himself, and Carmichael's scorn and lack of respect stung.

"C'mon. I'm taking you home now."

Carmichael propelled Adam through the crowd and out the door. Breath hitching, heart racing, Adam let him. Adam might have fought, some, but he was kind of getting off on the whole alpha-male thing. Even knowing the only relief he'd get that night would be from his own hand, he couldn't bring himself to sever their contact. But then, the reason he'd come here in the first place was because Carmichael had gotten under his skin. There hadn't been anyone in the club who came close to being worth going home with. Not since he'd met Carmichael.

When he got home, he'd stroke off to the way he wished the night would end.

Where was Carmichael taking him?

"Where did you park?" Adam started having second thoughts. Staying and having real human contact had to be an improvement over pining for a straight man he could never have, no matter how hot that man was.

They walked farther. "Seriously, I could have walked home already."

Adam was rewarded by a snort. Carmichael's opalescent SUV practically glowed from the shadows at the farthest and most over-grown end of the parking lot. If nothing else, the enforced march created more room in his pants as his lust waned.

After being steered around to the darkened passenger side, Adam reached for the door handle. Before he could touch it, Carmichael spun him around and pushed him against the vehicle.

Biting his lip against a gasp at the unexpected contact, he wished he could see better. The SUV blocked the lights from the club, obscuring Carmichael's expression. God. Should he be afraid?

There was no doubt in Adam's mind that Carmichael could be one terrifying dude when he wanted to be, but somehow Adam had never worried about that scariness being directed at him. Maybe going into a gay bar out of some overdeveloped sense of protectiveness had triggered Carmichael's raging homophobia.

"What?" Adam had made his tone deliberately provoking, perhaps more than was healthy, considering the disparity in their sizes. But he didn't truly think Carmichael would hurt him.

Carmichael shook his head. Adam could sense the eye roll. Then Carmichael brought his lips down on Adam's, firmly, no hesitation, with a nimble, wet tongue seeking entrance to Adam's mouth.

Adam's mind rabbited a bit with a quick chant of *ohmygod, ohmygod, ohmygod* before he parted his lips and met that thrusting tongue with his own. Zero to sixty, his pants went from fitting to viselike constriction. He'd wanted this from the very second he'd laid eyes on Carmichael, and after getting to know him better, the want had just gotten deeper.

Lust lit up his brain and made him more sensitive to everything. He'd barely sucked in a desperately needed breath when cupped his ass and stroke his neck with work-roughened hands. Carmichael's erection pressed insistently against his hip. And the touch of his pebbled nipples shocked Adam's skin right through two layers of cotton. Adam brought trembling hands up, craving touch, but a little afraid, despite the aggressive, hungry mouth devouring his. Could this be happening? It would suck so hard, and not in the good way, if it turned out he'd fallen on the way to the car and hit his head.

Adam placed his hands on Carmichael's back, muscles rippling under his palms like nothing he'd ever touched. Heat rising from that supple skin threatened to scorch him, convincing Adam he wasn't dreaming. The sensations dragged a moan out of his throat, swallowed by Carmichael's amazing, talented mouth. Imagining Carmichael's lips sucking him off made Adam's cock flex. Another refrain of *ohmygod, ohmygod, ohmygod* sang through his brain as he concentrated on not coming in his pants.

Moisture dampened the head of his cock, and Adam hoped it wasn't leaking through, but as excited as he was right now, he wouldn't bet money on it. Nearly ready to wrap his legs around Carmichael's waist and hump until they both shot, he nearly screamed when Carmichael pulled out of the kiss. Adam could tell Carmichael was looking into his eyes, but the lighting wasn't any better than before.

He wasn't done, was he? Adam might actually die of sexual frustration if this tantalizing taste was all Carmichael would allow him. Panting and trying not to squirm, Adam reached out a fingertip to trace those wet, swollen lips. If nothing else, Carmichael was as out of breath as Adam.

God. He could do this all night. Carmichael pursed his lips, a mere ghost of a kiss on Adam's finger, before he dove back in, angling for Adam's neck. Gentler than his original ferocious kiss, but determined enough to loosen Adam's limbs. A moan, unfettered now, escaped into the night, and Adam felt more than heard Carmichael's answering growl against his throat.

When hands fumbled at Adam's belt buckle and fly, he wanted to help, wanted to unzip Carmichael, get him naked or at the very least touch the exciting hardness pressing against him, but he couldn't make his body obey. He'd never been so helpless in the face of desire before. All he could do was thank whoever looked out for horny gay boys that Carmichael maintained enough dexterity to open Adam's pants, releasing a cock that felt like it'd been trapped for an eternity.

Carmichael's strong right hand delved past the waistband of his pants and—oh heaven—wrapped around his cock. Using his other hand, Carmichael loosened Adam's pants further, shoving them down Adam's hips, exposing Adam to the night air.

Under normal circumstances, the evening was far too cold to be half-naked. But these were not normal circumstances. Between Carmichael acting as his personal furnace and desire sparking fires all over his body, Adam welcomed the chill. Maybe the cold could return a little of his control.

It had been so long since he'd had another's hand on his flesh, warm lips tugging and nipping at his neck. Longer since he'd touched anyone he wanted even a fraction of how much he wanted Carmichael.

Carmichael's grip tightened, and his thick thumb rubbed through the moisture seeping from Adam's slit. Uh-oh. A few more moves like that...

"Yes," Adam whispered, trying to be quiet.

When Carmichael's left hand skimmed from where it had been squeezing the globe of Adam's ass to slip under his shirt and pinch at Adam's nipples, he moaned again, louder, no longer concerned about silence.

Hips thrusting helplessly into Carmichael's strokes, Adam tried to halt the rising tide of his approaching orgasm. This might be the best handjob ever, but he didn't want it to end too soon.

As though Carmichael could sense how close Adam was to blowing, he upped the ante with more pressure everywhere. Nipples pinched harder. Earlobe and neck bitten more firmly. Cock—oh God —cock stroked faster, fingers constricted more, wrist twisting on each upstroke as Carmichael's hand reached the bulbous tip.

Adam made the mistake of looking down at that strong hand, Carmichael's hand, practically blurring over the length of his erection. It was too much.

"Gonna come," he whispered.

Carmichael let Adam's ear slip from between his teeth, moved back an inch, and followed Adam's gaze down.

"Yes, come," Carmichael whispered back. Adam obeyed, orgasm pulled up from his toes, as he shot all over his stomach and Carmichael's hand.

"Oh yeah..." Adam groaned. The earthy scent of male pleasure floated up to his nose. Carmichael kept massaging him throughout, extending Adam's orgasm for what felt like several minutes. When his dick stopped jerking and the aftershocks ceased racking his body, Carmichael uncurled his fingers.

Adam grabbed Carmichael's slick hand and began licking cum off, captivating Carmichael's gaze. Adam still couldn't see his expression, but he knew damn well he had Carmichael's undivided attention. That tempting tongue licking lips in anticipation of a feast gave him away.

Once Carmichael's hand was clean, Adam drew the index finger into his mouth, tongue swirling like he was sucking Carmichael's cock, which Adam had every intention of doing, the sooner the better.

Even in the darkness, Adam saw Carmichael's gaze lift from Adam's mouth to his eyes.

"So hot." Carmichael gasped, and the shocks of Carmichael's orgasm vibrated through the finger in Adam's mouth.

Had Adam made the big, strong, ex-military man come in his pants? God. That was the sexiest, hottest thing that had ever happened to Adam. Even counting the spectacular handjob. His dick twitched and started to fill again.

Carmichael pulled his finger from Adam's mouth with a soft sucking sound and kissed him gently. "C'mon, let's go."

"Go? Where?" Adam bit his tongue to keep himself from begging Carmichael to fuck him. Or let him fuck Carmichael. He wasn't picky, but now that he'd had a taste, Adam discovered he wanted to be greedy.

"I'll drop you at your place later. Now we're going back to my hotel room."

Adam restrained himself from squeaking in delight or bouncing with joy. Carmichael had seen him act childishly and might appreciate a little more decorum under these circumstances. He managed a nod.

Carmichael stepped back and pulled car keys out of his pocket, giving Adam enough room to haul up his pants.

Climbing into the SUV, Adam found his body humming in anticipation, far hornier than he'd expected, considering he'd shot hard enough to see stars.

CARMICHAEL DIDN'T KNOW what to say, so he chose to say nothing at all. Tonight was a night of firsts—a lot of them, so it would seem. He'd never set foot in a gay bar. He'd never made the first move. He'd never invited anyone to his rooms. And he knew someone was getting fucked tonight. Coming in his pants... That wasn't a first, but it had been a long, long time. Maybe tomorrow he'd be embarrassed by it, but replaying the scene in his mind got him hot enough, the upholstery should be smoking. Not even the damp mess in his pants was enough to cool his lust.

Periodically stealing glances at Adam out of the corner of his eye, he noticed Adam glancing at him as well. Something about Adam had convinced Carmichael to throw out his long-standing rules.

He couldn't wait. From the looks of the bulge in Adam's pants, he was looking forward to it as much as Carmichael.

A thought struck him. Oh shit. "Hey, Adam, we gotta make a quick stop." He hadn't expected to indulge in any sexual activity on this trip, and he didn't engage with other men very often at all. Lube, he had, for jacking off, but condoms... Well, he didn't carry them around. Helped avoid temptation, but for Adam, Carmichael was willing to dive right in.

"What for?" Adam asked, his voice almost as breathy as when he'd told Carmichael he had to come. Sexy bastard.

"Uh, I don't have any condoms." Carmichael looked over again and saw Adam giving him an odd look. Not surprising. Most gay men he'd known considered condoms as important as their wallets, maybe more so.

"Don't worry. I have some," Adam said with a faint grin, patting his hip.

Carmichael rumbled low in his throat. There it was. The true reason he had followed Adam in the first place. The reason he'd gone into the bar. The reason he'd grabbed Adam and yelled at him. The reason he'd broken his rules.

If Adam wanted sex tonight, it was going to be with him. No one else. Carmichael had never wanted anyone enough to bother losing his virginity—the risks had always seemed to outweigh the rewards. But Adam called to him, deep in his bones. Finding out Adam was gay and wanting was enough to short-circuit Carmichael's common sense.

The smile Adam sent his way was so sweet, yet filled with the promise of carnality. Carmichael forgot about his jealousy and almost ran off the road. How fucking far away was the damned bed-and-breakfast? If it weren't for the investigation planned for tomorrow, he would have been tempted to stop at the first motel he found on the highway.

No, wait. Somehow that thought made it sound sordid, and—God, he was a fool, but he wanted his first time to be special. Sure, the B and B was a rental and filled with legions of cats, but it was his temporary home, and he wouldn't have to rush. If he was going to do this, he was going to do it right, dammit. He was going to have all the firsts he could handle.

His gaze must have given away some of his thoughts, because Adam's expression heated further, something Carmichael would have believed impossible before he saw it. Adam's beautiful, slick tongue snaked out to lap over his lips, reminding Carmichael how talented that tongue had felt licking his fingers. Adam reached out, and those long fingers played up Carmichael's thigh, ghosting near his burgeoning erection but never quite touching it.

His breathing picked up. How was it possible to be so hard so soon after coming? But he wanted Adam to touch him, he wanted to touch Adam, and he wanted to know what it was like to be fully naked with another man.

Carmichael opened his lips, let out a breath, and closed them again in shock. He'd been about to ask Adam to touch him, stroke him, something. He'd never asked any man for anything. Then he realized this was yet another first he could have with Adam.

"Please," he whispered.

"Yes," Adam answered, warm pressure stroking up his shaft and down to his balls. Oh, fuck yeah. That was it. Spreading his legs as far as he could without interfering with his driving, he humped up a little against Adam's clever fingers. Good, so good. Best ever. Adam knew how to keep the fires stoked, never providing enough pressure to bring Carmichael to the edge, keeping him keenly anticipating their arrival at a room with a bed.

Finally, the exterior lights of the bed-and-breakfast came into sight. Carmichael slung the SUV into the parking space before scrabbling at his seat belt. Fortunately Adam was also frantic, and his hands were clumsy enough that Carmichael was able to leap out of the vehicle and meet Adam on the passenger side after he extricated himself. Powerless against the impulse, Carmichael pressed into Adam like he had at the club, devouring those soft, intoxicating lips.

Adam fed a whimper into his mouth, along with that nimble tongue, but a few seconds later, Adam pushed at his shoulders and broke from the kiss.

"Upstairs. I need you naked," Adam whispered between gasps.

Right. Heaving in a great, shuddering breath, Carmichael forced himself to let Adam go. No point in getting sidetracked this close to the prize. Not a bad way in which to be distracted, but everything he'd experienced with Adam so far indicated that being naked with him would be explosive, earth-shattering. Carmichael wanted that so bad, he was close to ripping Adam out of his clothes right here and now.

"Come on," Carmichael said. They managed to reach the landing before Adam returned Carmichael's actions by the SUV, pressing him into the wall with a *thump*, aggressive and hungry. Hot, so damned hot. Adam smelled like sex and man, with an underlying hint of citrus, the scent clouding Carmichael's mind and making his cock throb against Adam's firm belly. An answering pulse, beating in time with Adam's heart, made itself known against Carmichael's thigh. Instead of capturing his lips as Carmichael expected, Adam pressed his nose up under Carmichael's ear before he bit down.

"Fuck!" The sting arrowed from Carmichael's neck straight to his dick, his hips flexing restlessly.

"Shhh," Adam cautioned.

"Why?"

"If Gladys catches us, I'll never hear the end of it."

Carmichael was a couple of years shy of thirty, and here he was sneaking around with his soon-to-be lover like they were a pair of teenagers, because God knew he didn't want Oliver to find out either. Again he should be annoyed or embarrassed. Maybe tomorrow he would be. But as his lips twitched, the first word that came to mind was *hilarious*.

His near smirk didn't go unnoticed by Adam, who let a muffled laugh escape. Carmichael had to bite his lip to avoid laughing too. If they were going to keep this a secret, being found in the stairwell, laughing like loons with matching erections, was not a good plan. He snorted, his amusement increasing as Adam stuck his fist in his mouth to stifle his sounds.

"Hurry up." Carmichael grabbed Adam's free hand, dragging him the rest of the way up the stairs. He let go long enough to fumble with the key, the impending laughter fighting for precedence over lust as Adam wrapped his arms around him from behind, those magical fingers unerringly finding his groin.

"Stop it." He breathed out, fighting not to chuckle. Adam didn't stop and bit his deltoid. If the door hadn't chosen that moment to open, Carmichael might have decided getting to the bed was too much trouble. Fortunately for Gladys's sensibilities, the door cooperated. Carmichael hauled Adam into the room, slammed the door shut, and leaned back against it.

Then Carmichael giggled. Adam looked at him, lips parted. Carmichael felt as shocked as Adam looked—Carmichael couldn't remember the last time such a sound had come out of his mouth, if it ever had.

Adam grinned at him and bounced through the doorway to the bedroom. His grin turned feral as he crooked a finger at Carmichael, beckoning. Transfixed, Carmichael watched as Adam slowly unbuttoned the shirt that Carmichael had rumpled not even an hour before, exposing his lithe, seductive chest.

With measured steps, Carmichael stalked forward, a broad smile on his face, the hysterical laughter easing. If he could have, he would have mirrored Adam's actions, but he was only wearing a T-shirt. Instead he grasped the hem of his shirt and leisurely pulled it up his stomach toward his chest, pleased by the intense attention Adam paid to each inch of skin exposed.

Adam's fingers stilled as he watched, those green eyes eating him up. Carmichael didn't think he'd ever had desire like this directed at him, and it pleased him immensely. He finished stripping off his shirt, edging closer to Adam, enjoying Adam's gaze on him.

Mere inches from Adam, he reached out and finished the job Adam had started on that sexy dress shirt. Adam didn't try to help but stroked his fingers over Carmichael's skin. God. So good. Fingers plucked at his hardened nipples, causing Carmichael to lose the ability to make the last button on Adam's shirt work. He moaned. With a sharp tug, the shirt parted, button flying off somewhere behind Carmichael.

Looking down the firm planes of Adam's torso, Carmichael wanted to lick him all over.

"So sexy. Naked, now." Adam's tone of authority made Carmichael shiver. But naked had to wait for a moment.

"I have no objection. Get naked. I'll be back."

Shock chased heat out of Adam's expression as he looked up into Carmichael's face.

Carmichael quirked a brow and shrugged. "Gotta hit the bathroom."

The grin returned to Adam's face as he glanced down at

Carmichael's groin, undoubtedly remembering Carmichael coming in his pants in the parking lot at the club.

"Hurry back." Adam flipped his shirt off his shoulders, hands going to the button on his pants. Carmichael knew Adam wasn't wearing anything beneath those sexy-as-fuck pants, and his knees wobbled.

Yeah, like Carmichael was going to take his time, with that sexy bastard waiting for him. He wondered if he should be nervous. He wasn't, only eager. Not eager enough that he'd make an ass of himself. He didn't think. Probably he'd crossed that bridge already by coming in his pants, but it hadn't deterred Adam any. Coming once tonight ought to give him a little more control.

Since he couldn't decide what he wanted to do first, maybe he'd give Adam the choice. After all, it wasn't like he was unaware of the basics. He was well versed in the theory.

ADAM STRIPPED IN RECORD TIME. Making sure he had a condom handy, he stretched out on the bed, languidly stroking his dick, waiting for Carmichael to return. Would Carmichael come back nude? Adam sure as hell hoped so. He couldn't wait to see that muscular stud in nothing but skin. Getting to see, and getting fucked by, the package he'd been fantasizing about was the cherry on the top of this incredible night. At least, he assumed Carmichael would top. Adam liked both, but he'd be more than happy to bottom for Carmichael. Again and again and again...

When Carmichael sauntered out of the bathroom, naked, with a bottle of lube in his hand, Adam wondered if he was going to come from the sight. Fucking gorgeous. The shy little smile Carmichael sported, an expression Adam had never seen him wear, made Adam almost as hot as the thick, mouthwatering cock rising from Carmichael's groin. The tip of its fat head was already leaking precum.

"Get over here." His words were a command, but Adam heard the pleading whine underlying them.

"There's something I should tell you." Carmichael suddenly looked down, refusing to meet Adam's eyes. Worse, not moving another step toward the bed.

Oh shit. Did he have a boyfriend? A husband? Adam had never cheated on anyone, nor knowingly slept with anyone who was in a relationship. Could he live with himself if he did? He wanted Carmichael more than anything, ever. He'd never had to make a decision like this.

"I've never done this before."

Adam blinked. Then blinked again, trying to fit those words into his thoughts.

"What? Never done what before?" Picked up a near stranger and had sex in a hotel room? Impossible.

"Fucked." Carmichael moved his gaze from the floor to Adam's dick. Gratifying, since Carmichael's own dick jumped, but at that moment Adam would have preferred to see Carmichael's eyes. Because it sounded to Adam like Carmichael was confessing to being a virgin.

"I'm sorry. You've never...fucked...before?" Looking at the stunning smorgasbord of man in front of him, Adam found the concept ludicrous. Adam needed clarification. Now.

"Blowjobs, handjobs—that's it."

Carmichael raised his eyes. Adam read the truth in those blue depths and the sexy blush on those sharp cheekbones. His heart squeezing, heat swept up Adam's torso, leaving him light-headed and breathless. Oh God. The *cherry* was going to be the cherry on this fan-fucking-tastic day. Adam thought he should ask *why him*, but gift horse, mouth, all that. If it weren't for the sensation of his hand clamping down on his dick in shocked response, he might have thought he was fantasizing.

Adam sat up, wondering if they needed to talk about anything.

He'd never popped anyone's cherry. Nothing about Carmichael looked nervous, though.

"What do you want to do?" Adam asked.

"Everything," Carmichael said with a grin. He took a few steps closer, but still not close enough for Adam to touch that beautiful golden-hued skin.

Adam snorted. No kidding. If Adam had waited until the ripe old age of...

"How old are you, anyway?"

"Twenty-eight."

Twenty-eight. Yeah, if Adam had waited until *two years from now* to fuck, he'd want to try everything too.

"Right, well, what I meant was—"

"I know what you meant," Carmichael interrupted while Adam searched for the right words. "And I meant everything. If we have a chance. Tonight, though, I'm in your hands. Your choice."

Adam shivered, lust shaking him like a leaf in a windstorm. His choice. Holy fuck. Wet dream come true.

"Well then, get your ass over here so we can get started."

Carmichael tossed the lube onto the bedside table before he slid into bed next to Adam. Adam was so revved, he didn't need much more stimulation, but Carmichael would. If it was truly his choice, Adam had every intention of sliding inside that awesome ass before the night was over.

Adam rose up and leaned over Carmichael, taking his lips in a soft kiss. Fingers trembling, he traced the side of Carmichael's face while he deepened the kiss. Strong hands grasped his butt, pulling his erection into contact with Carmichael's burning brand of a cock. Did he have any idea what a gift he was giving Adam? Even if the reason was nothing more than being tired of being a virgin, Adam was touched, awed, that Carmichael had chosen him. After all, there were dozens of men in that club tonight who would have killed to fuck Carmichael, virgin or not.

A complete lack of hesitation on Carmichael's part coaxed Adam into more aggression. Their tongues tangled and fought with each other, hands stroking madly without any plan but pleasure. Between them, moisture slicked cocks and bellies, smoothing the hump and glide.

Panting, Adam tore his mouth away from Carmichael's, pulling his chest up. For a man who'd never fucked before, he kissed like heaven. Staring into those eyes, the bright blue a mere ring around pupils blown with desire, Adam realized he couldn't take this as slow as he'd first thought. Not if he was getting into that ass before either of them came. Carmichael stared back at him, fingers biting into Adam's biceps as he continued to grind his pelvis against Adam's.

Nope. Not coming this way. This might be a one-time-only offer, and Adam wasn't going to waste it.

Adam pressed a quick kiss on Carmichael's lips before he separated their bodies. Leaning over, he moved his mouth along the soft skin under Carmichael's jaw. He nipped and licked his way down over finely striated muscles to the hard little nubbins that had first caught his eye in the club. Without giving Carmichael any warning, he opened his mouth over one, sucking strongly.

Carmichael groaned, deep in his chest, the vibrations transmitted to Adam through his lips. Swiftly he moved to the other one, this time tugging it with his teeth. Back arching into the stimulus, hips fucking air, Carmichael cupped the back of Adam's head.

After a few seconds, Adam broke Carmichael's hold, trailing his tongue over Carmichael's six-pack. Fuck. A thing of beauty. Letting his tongue trace each "pack," Adam could barely keep his mind on the seduction. Carmichael's breathy whimpers and moans tried to coax him into taking what he wanted.

God. He couldn't stand it any longer. Settling between Carmichael's spread legs, Adam held out a hand.

"Lube?"

Carmichael stared at him, dazed. Then the word filtered through to his brain, because Carmichael flung a hand toward the nightstand and fumbled for the plastic bottle.

Adam clutched his prize in one hand and pushed Carmichael's right knee up, exposing that tempting, wrinkled pucker.

First, though, he needed a taste of Carmichael's fat cock. Yep, he'd bottom for Carmichael whenever he wanted, ruddy prick tempting Adam to change his game plan. Pressing his nose to the base, he inhaled, smelling Carmichael's strong male scent. Meanwhile he flipped open the cap on the bottle of lube and squeezed some onto his fingers.

With the very tip of his tongue, Adam tasted the length of Carmichael's cock, right up to the flared head. He circled the ridge, teasing, enjoying the salty flavor that was all Carmichael.

"More. Harder," Carmichael commanded.

Yes, more, harder. Adam had every intention of obeying. Soon.

He pulled his tongue off that tasty dick but stayed close enough that Carmichael should be able to feel his breath. His finger stroked over Carmichael's hole. He opened his mouth and enveloped half of Carmichael's length while sliding his index finger into that tight, hot ass.

As expected, Carmichael thrust his hips up, feeding Adam the entire length of his cock. *Yes.* Adam groaned around the fat dick stretching his lips and pressed his groin into the bed, needing a bit of pressure on his achingly hard erection. Fuck, so sexy.

Adam sucked and laved the scorching flesh in his mouth while sliding his finger in and out, simulating what was to come. He eased another finger in, getting a response similar to what he had from the first intrusion. Oh, Carmichael was going to love being fucked. Adam could tell.

Wiggling his fingers a bit, he found Carmichael's prostate, judging by the keening, wordless wail that erupted from Carmichael's throat. Adam didn't want Carmichael to come on his fingers, though. He wanted to feel that tight hole milking his prick, so he eased off the gland and slid yet another finger inside.

Pulling back, he continued to love on Carmichael's dick, but only the head, as he concentrated on stretching that snug hole.

"Dammit," Carmichael cursed. "Fuck me already."

Adam glanced up to find Carmichael watching him, face tense and scrunched in a desperate, horny, gotta-come expression. Oh yeah, this was going to be so much fun.

Adam slid his fingers free, let Carmichael's dick go with a *pop*, and grabbed the condom. Sheathed, he smeared more lube on, pushed Carmichael's other knee toward his shoulder, and lined up. As he pressed in, feeling the tight ring of muscle stretch and give way around his cock, Carmichael lifted his head, seeking Adam's lips.

Oh God, sweet, so sweet. Again their tongues dueled as Adam slid home. Carmichael winced and gave a short, pained gasp, but he never softened, which meant Adam had learned something from his own very painful and embarrassing deflowering.

"Wait a minute," Carmichael whispered, pulling out of the kiss before biting his lower lip in concentration.

"As long as you need," Adam whispered back, determined to hold still as long as Carmichael required.

Beneath him, Carmichael's hips began shifting, and he sought Adam's lips again. Adam took that as permission to move. He pulled out almost all the way and stroked in again. Carmichael's breath huffed out of his nose, mouth still occupied with Adam's.

Amazing. Adam had never felt anything as fabulous as Carmichael's tight sheath gripping him like it never wanted to let go. He began stroking in harder, with long, measured thrusts, while plunging his tongue into Carmichael's hot, wet mouth.

Finally, needing breath to moan, Carmichael broke their kiss to fling his head back against the pillows, hips meeting each of Adam's thrusts with equal strength.

"Oh God, oh God, oh God. Adam. So good." Carmichael grunted, a faint sheen of sweat breaking out all over his body.

And it was so good. Adam could see Carmichael was close. Adam was close.

Wait. Adam was ready to come, probably harder than he ever had in his life, and he still didn't know Carmichael's first name.

"What's your name?" Adam asked. He had to repeat himself so Carmichael could hear him over the increasingly loud groans.

"Carmichael," he replied in the middle of gasping out his pleasure. "Harder."

"No, your first name." Adam slowed his thrusts, backing away from the pinnacle beckoning to him.

"I...uh...please, fuck me," Carmichael pleaded, ignoring Adam's question. In response, Adam stilled his movements altogether. The muscular body beneath him writhed, and he gritted his teeth, determined to hold out. Adam grasped Carmichael's chin, forcing the other man to look into his eyes.

"I will be damned if I shout out your last fucking name when I come, understand?"

Carmichael nodded, whimpered, then stuttered out, "Lachlan."

"Lachlan." Adam breathed, letting the name resonate through his mind. Until Carmichael's—Lachlan's—ass gripped him tighter. In a flash, he was back on the precipice, poised and waiting for heaven. Adam slammed in and out of that heated tunnel, reaching a hand beneath to grip a rock-hard ass, tilting Carmichael up. The slight alteration in position was enough. Carmichael yelled Adam's name, and cum sprayed between them.

Between the hot, sharp smell, the insanely tight grip on his prick, and Carmichael's sounds of completion ringing in his ears, Adam rocketed over into orgasm, calling Lachlan's name.

Once Adam could breathe again, and his vision wasn't threatening to blacken around the edges, he slid slowly out of Carmichael.

Carmichael reached up a trembling hand and stroked the side of Adam's face. "Thank you," he whispered and pulled Adam's face down for a soft, sweet kiss.

"Anytime," Adam replied and meant it more than anything he'd said in his life.

Best. Fuck. Ever.

Carmichael clearly agreed, since he was already asleep, the harsh planes of his face softening.

After cleaning up and getting rid of the condom, Adam slid into bed beside Carmichael—*Lachlan*. Damned if he was going home now. He might be conscious, but no way were his legs in any condition to walk anywhere. He was totally melted, utterly sated, and—like an idiot—halfway in love.

SIX

Carmichael woke to a morning woody, the scent of Adam's cologne, and elation. Who would have guessed the kid had such mad bedroom skills? When he reached out a hand, hoping for an early-morning repeat, all he found was an empty bed. He lay there, listening carefully, but he couldn't hear a trace of Adam anywhere. Yet he knew Adam had stayed after fucking him into oblivion, because he still had the sense memory of holding Adam to the curve of his body.

Both elation and erection faded. Shit. He'd had his night of firsts, but he hadn't expected Adam to duck out before he was awake, the sexual equivalent of a dine-and-dash.

Hauling himself to the shower, he tried to tell himself it was for the best. No reason for his emotions to be involved—God, you'd think he was a marshmallow. As he soaped himself under the spray, he wondered at his sanity. What made him think having sex before a lengthy hike was a good idea? His ass ached—a good ache, to be sure, but he'd be feeling Adam's dick all day. He'd never be able to concentrate on his job; this would be way more distracting than anything else on this double-damned mission.

Dressed, he stood before the door, reluctant to put out his hand to turn the knob. Dammit, was he going to have to explain to Oliver why Adam wasn't here? And what explanation would he give? They'd had sex, sex with no strings, like he wanted. Why did he feel let down by Adam's absence? He hadn't been nervous last night, but he had doubts about his level of proficiency if Adam had needed to escape before Carmichael awoke.

Once downstairs, he poured himself a cup of coffee, wondering when Oliver was going to appear. He took a quick sip and forced himself to swallow. Thankfully there was no one in the room to observe his disgust. No disguising the fact that it wasn't café coffee. Eyeing the breakfast offerings, he wondered if he could bring himself to eat anything. He knew he should, but his churning stomach convinced him otherwise.

Soft footsteps alerted him to the presence of another person, and Carmichael whirled to look.

Adam.

Adam's black lashes shadowed eyes that couldn't quite hold Carmichael's gaze. But the pink cheeks and upturned lips combined with the coffee and paper bag from the café dispersed Carmichael's apprehension.

"Hi, Lachlan." Adam's eyes swept up, letting Carmichael see his intense green gaze.

Unaccountably shy and turned on at the same time, the tips of Carmichael's ears heated up. *Lachlan.* He'd hated the name for a long time, but hearing Adam call it out as he climaxed, as well as hearing it now in Adam's soft voice, well, maybe he didn't hate it quite so much anymore.

Adam smiled. "Coffee? Breakfast? I had to go home to change clothes, thought I'd stop by the café."

Change clothes. Of course. Adam couldn't have gone hiking in the outfit he'd worn to the club last night. If nothing else, it'd have required explanations to Oliver that Carmichael would rather not give. A smile stretched Carmichael's face, and Adam took a step toward him, desire infusing his expression. Carmichael moved forward but stopped when he heard someone coming down the stairs.

Instead of reaching out to Adam like he'd been going to do, Carmichael looked around and found a place to ditch the substandard B-and-B coffee.

"Morning, Adam," he heard Oliver say. "Thanks for thinking of us."

"No problem," Adam replied in his normal voice, not the lower, sensual timbre that he'd used with Carmichael seconds earlier.

Carmichael turned back. "Good morning, Oliver."

"You're in a good mood today."

"Uh, yeah, I guess." He hoped Oliver wasn't going to ask why. He caught sight of Adam's bottle green eyes over Oliver's shoulder.

Adam was trying not to laugh, and another smile pulled at Carmichael's lips. A wicked gleam brightened those hypnotic eyes while Adam licked his lips, and Pavlovian-like, Carmichael's cock began to swell.

"Here." Adam moved past Oliver, extending a cup to Carmichael. That seductive, breathy voice was back. Oliver was a trained investigator, but Carmichael sincerely hoped he hadn't noticed anything out of the ordinary, besides Carmichael's good humor.

Nothing like a couple of spectacular orgasms to banish a bad mood. Especially when it looked like there was every chance to get more.

"Thanks," Carmichael said, amazed to see Adam shiver. But then, his own voice was more smoky than normal.

Adam ran his thumb along Carmichael's fingers as the cup changed hands, braided ring providing a sharp counterpoint of sensation. God. Carmichael wanted to throw him down on the floor and lick him all over. They hadn't had as much time to explore last night as Carmichael would have liked. Nor did they get through all the firsts Carmichael had in mind.

"Ready to go?" Oliver asked as he dug in the paper bag.

Appetite having returned with a vengeance, along with his good mood, Carmichael was ravenous, and he grabbed the bag as soon as Oliver pulled out a muffin.

"Sure thing, boss."

Oliver narrowed his eyes. Shit. He'd have to tone down this whole *happy* thing.

"Great. I'll drop you at the park entrance. Then I've got more research to do. Carmichael, you've got the sat phone?"

Carmichael nodded. Good thing he'd explained some of their purpose to Adam, because how could he explain why folklore researchers needed a fucking sat phone?

"Good. Give me a call when you're done, and we'll arrange a pickup."

"Where are you going while we're out in the woods?" Adam asked.

"I'm going to the county seat to follow up on some of the leads I got at the library."

Adam followed Oliver out to the car, and Carmichael made up the rear, allowing him to assess and appreciate Adam's firm ass. Adam hoisting himself into the seat behind Oliver was a sight Carmichael could watch over and over again. He moved around to the passenger side, opened the door, and lifted his foot to the running board. The soreness in his ass made itself known, and Carmichael hissed. His gaze flew to Adam, who gave him a knowing look and winked. Fuck. Soreness or not, he'd do it again in a flash. Heat pulsed in his groin, and he hoped Oliver didn't notice his erection. This was what he'd been afraid of all along, but somehow he couldn't work up any distress over it.

He winked back at Adam, who made a teasing show of licking sugar off his fingers. Asshole. Carmichael glared.

"Are you getting in the damn car, Carmichael?" Oliver asked.

Oh. Right. Carmichael flicked another quick glare at Adam before he hopped in.

THEY EMERGED FROM THE CAR, and Carmichael handed Adam a fully loaded backpack. Well, almost fully loaded. Carmichael had tried to take most of the burden when he'd packed, and Adam didn't have any of the weapons. Didn't know Carmichael did either, he didn't think. He noted with a bit of discomfort that Adam's skateboard was still in the car.

After slamming the hatch down, Carmichael tapped the car a couple of times with his hand, and Oliver drove away.

"I've been meaning to ask..." Adam said.

Carmichael swallowed a groan. This could be bad.

"What's with the car? I mean, aren't you big, bad secret-agent types supposed to be driving around in black SUVs like they do in the movies?"

Carmichael rolled his eyes. Yes, dammit, they were supposed to be driving around in black SUVs. No matter what Oliver said, every time he got in the car, he felt like he was sitting in a target. The only things lacking were concentric black rings.

"That's exactly why we don't drive the black SUVs. It makes people suspicious." Or so he'd been told.

"So you chose pearlescent off-white to throw them off the scent?" The teasing sarcasm was clear in Adam's voice.

"Not my fucking choice." His words were harsh, but Carmichael couldn't help but be amused, and he knew Adam heard it, considering he got a sexy, dimpled smile in return.

"Well, this is it." Adam flung his arms around expansively.

Carmichael glanced around at the RVs, children playing, sunburned adults with beer. This didn't fit his idea of a danger zone. At all. If anyone disappeared around here, they were boning someone they shouldn't be, in the wrong RV or tent.

"Are you sure?"

Adam chuckled, the sound hitting Carmichael in his balls. Fuck. Was he suddenly going to find everything Adam did sexy as hell? Oh wait. That wasn't sudden. Most everything Adam did *was* sexy. The immature, irresponsible stuff pissed him off, but he was willing to ignore that for sex like they'd had last night.

"Yes, I'm sure. Obviously it's not right *here*, here. We've got a couple of hours' trek ahead of us. This is the camping version of the bunny slopes. C'mon." Adam shifted the pack on his shoulder. His pack was lighter, but out here in the woods, he didn't look as delicate as Carmichael had expected.

"Lead the way."

"You just want to look at my ass," Adam said.

"Shhh." Carmichael glanced around. It didn't appear that anyone had heard the comment.

Adam rolled his eyes.

Well, that was good to know. Adam wasn't in the closet. Good thing Carmichael wasn't going to be here for long. He had no desire to be outed by his...lover? Could Adam be considered his lover after one night? It wasn't like they were going to start a relationship or anything, but Carmichael had every intention of Adam warming his bed as often as possible. A sex partner for several days could surely be called a lover.

"Let's go. We need to check in at the ranger station first."

Carmichael nodded. Common sense dictated you told people where you were going; otherwise, if you got lost, no one would know when or where to look for you. However...

"Don't mention exactly where we're going."

"I know. I'm not an idiot." Adam didn't bother to look back at him. He hadn't meant to imply Adam was an idiot, but Carmichael believed it was better to be clear up front than to have misunderstandings later. Although he'd known Adam for a very short time, Carmichael trusted him. He did not trust anyone else in Rothburg, including park rangers.

As they moved away from the worst of the tin-can RVs, Carmichael saw a small wooden sign directing them to the ranger station. He followed Adam, wending their way along a well-maintained path. Around a curve, a log cabin came into view, secluded and quiet, considering its location mere minutes from chaos. The scent of beer and burning hot dogs lay thick in the air as a reminder.

Carmichael had never set foot in a campground or national park —at least not in this country—but the station didn't look as he'd expected. The door stood open, and Carmichael could see racks of shelves with Twinkies and bread and other assorted goods.

"This is a ranger station?" he asked.

"Yep. Well, the only permanent, year-round one."

Carmichael reached out a hand to pull Adam to a stop. "Explain, please." He hated going into a situation blind, and he didn't want any surprises.

"There are a few temporary stations scattered throughout the park, but no one lives in them; they're used by the rangers on an as-needed basis. I know this looks like a general store, and it is, partly." Adam paused to wave at the building. "But this place is manned year-round. The head park ranger lives here. The back of the building extends farther than you'd think."

"Where do the other rangers live?"

"In town, mostly, along with the cashiers for the gift shop. There's temporary living quarters not far from here, for short-term rangers transferred from other parks."

Carmichael nodded and let Adam's arm go. "Thanks."

Adam smiled sweetly, making Carmichael regret that he didn't feel comfortable expressing his desires. If he did, he'd have Adam back in his arms in a heartbeat, his tongue giving Adam's mouth a thorough cavity search. He'd taken a step forward before he realized what he was about to do, and gestured Adam to continue on to the station.

"Adam, honey, so nice to see you." The twenty-something buxom blonde behind the counter waved as Adam stepped through the door.

"Hey, Maddie, how are you?"

Well, after last night, Carmichael could be pretty sure that Maddie wasn't one of Adam's exes.

He moved through the store while Adam chatted with Maddie and did whatever he had to. Carmichael was leafing through a book on indigenous wildlife when he heard a man's baritone call out Adam's name. Looking up, he saw a tall, good-looking ranger in his late thirties approach Adam with a smile.

A strange possessiveness welled up inside. He set aside the book and reached the little reunion in time to see the ranger hug Adam. He could be an ex of Adam's, dammit. A growl rose up from his throat, which he quickly changed into a cough. What difference did it make if this asshole was an ex-lover of Adam's? Or even a current lover?

Carmichael bit the inside of his cheek as shock lanced through him at the thought of Adam having a current lover. He told himself it didn't matter. Adam was a temporary indulgence, nothing more.

"Who's your friend, Adam?" Carmichael couldn't see any jealousy over Adam in the man's eyes, but that didn't mean it wasn't there.

"Smokey, this is Carmichael. He's hired me to take him on a guided tour of some of the hiking trails. Carmichael, this is Ranger Goldman. He's the head park ranger here."

Ouch. With an introduction like that, no one would have any reason to be jealous. Not a hint of the intimacy he and Adam had experienced the previous night found its way into Adam's words. Like Carmichael thought he wanted. He hadn't realized it would bother him, though.

"Nice to meet you, Carmichael," Smokey—*Smokey*—said as he offered his hand for Carmichael to shake. Carmichael took his hand and pumped it once, not wanting to touch the man any longer than he must. The ranger was taller than Carmichael, and his hand was larger, but he was much leaner, less muscled. Which was Adam's preference?

Shit. If he could kick his own ass, he would, for even thinking that question. For the last time, it didn't fucking matter.

"Adam, are you coming back to work next season?" Ranger

Asshole placed one of those big hands on Adam's shoulder, and it was all Carmichael could do to keep from knocking it off.

"I don't know, Smokey. Maybe. It was a lot of fun."

"Yep, it sure was. Remember when—"

"We should head out now," Carmichael interrupted. Damned if he were going to listen to fucking reminiscing. Thankfully Adam nodded.

"Don't be a stranger, Adam. We've missed you around here," the ranger said. Yeah, Carmichael just bet he had. He hustled Adam out of the store before ol' Smokey could touch him again.

When the door closed behind them, Carmichael couldn't hold it in any longer.

"Smokey?" he asked, incredulous. "As in Smokey the Bear?"

Adam shrugged. "I know. Silly, isn't it? But he likes the name. And he's a good ranger."

Carmichael pressed his lips together. None of the words fighting to escape his mouth were going to be useful. "Where to now?" he asked instead.

MINUTES PASSED as they steadily worked their way along the trail Adam had chosen. Adam was glad they'd stopped at the ranger station before setting out, for a couple of reasons. First, the rangers were a little more accepting of him, especially Smokey, than other people in town. Adam didn't know why that was, but he was grateful for it. It was one of the reasons he had so enjoyed working at the park.

The other reason was more selfish, but the more people Adam saw Carmichael come into contact with, the more he realized Carmichael was surly by nature. Which didn't make Adam happy, but knowing he wasn't responsible for Carmichael's habitual grouchiness lifted a weight off his soul.

The sounds from the campground faded, leaving his ears filled with the soft sounds of nature. He enjoyed being outdoors, but he preferred his dusty excavations to this humidity. At least it was shaded. Even with the majority of the leaves shed in preparation for winter, the evergreens provided plenty of cover.

Adam was content to walk in silence, for a while anyway. Carmichael had given him a lot to think about, both last night and this morning. Between sexual exhaustion and nerves, he'd not had a chance to let his mind play over it. Here in the woods, with the sound of their boots on the leaf-strewn earth overshadowing all other noise, Adam still couldn't think. Everything that had happened was like sitting next to a campfire—it felt good on his skin, made him warm and happy inside, but if he looked too closely, he'd get burned.

The memory of Carmichael's laughter stuck with Adam almost as vividly as the actual sex. The sounds had been rusty, mixed with shock. Without a doubt, laughter wasn't a sound Carmichael made very often. He wasn't sure Carmichael knew how to be happy, and Adam looked forward to wringing more happy sounds from him.

Never in a million years would he have guessed Carmichael was a virgin. But then, he'd not pegged him as gay either, so what the hell did he know?

Every time he thought about holding Carmichael's tight, muscular ass as he thrust into that snug, warm hole, Adam couldn't help but plump up. If Carmichael noticed the increased frequency of crotch adjustment, he didn't give any indication. Despite Adam's desire to throw him down on the ground and have an instant replay of the previous night, this wasn't the time or place, condoms and lube in his pocket notwithstanding. However, the place he planned to stop for lunch was *quite* secluded.

Sure, Adam had questions, but he didn't want to voice them, afraid putting anything into words would make the dream dissipate. That was the last thing he wanted. No one had ever made him feel this shiny before, and he wanted to keep the feeling as long as possible.

"We need to talk." Carmichael's voice was overloud in the stillness.

Fuck. Really? Suddenly the muffin this morning didn't seem like such a good idea after all. Adam was getting dumped after what was little more than a one-night stand? That was new. And sucked. So sex *wasn't* just like riding a bike, because apparently Adam had not done a good job of initiating Carmichael. Carmichael hadn't looked regretful this morning and in spite of his shower, the man had that well-fucked look about him.

Carmichael looked over at him, and Adam huffed out a facsimile of a grunt in response, because he sure as hell couldn't get any words past the sudden ligature around his throat. Getting ditched wasn't going to change the fact that Carmichael was the sexiest man Adam had ever seen. So much for that secluded lunch spot.

"Oliver found a few things in the newspaper archives that disturbed both of us." A slight frown drew Carmichael's blond eyebrows together.

With a snap, the pressure on Adam's chest eased. He drew in a breath, shocked he cared so much, but grateful those horrible four words hadn't prefaced what they normally did. It was maybe too soon in their altered—Adam hesitated to call it a relationship—*interaction* with each other to tease Carmichael about what those words meant to most people. Perhaps Carmichael had never experienced the dread that accompanied them and was oblivious to their import.

"What did you find?"

"I'm surprised you didn't know about it. There have been a number of disappearances in the past year, but they were quickly suppressed, or the search was directed to other areas besides Rothburg."

Adam considered that for a moment. "Well, sure, I'd heard of some, but we were told they got resolved. Mistakes, people found later. No one I knew."

"Of the people found later, all were dead."

"All dead? That's not possible."

"All dead. All conveniently discovered several miles away. Most were considered to be victims of animal attacks."

"That would have to be a record number of fatal animal attacks. Are you sure?"

"Yes," Carmichael said. "It would be a record if the bodies weren't spread out over such a large geographical distance."

"And you're sure they disappeared from here?"

"Oliver's pretty sure. I know you don't know us well, but Oliver's usually right about these things. There's some indication the local vagrant population may have been affected, and to my knowledge those bodies have never been found."

Adam nodded, processing what Carmichael had said along with the information regarding the agency Carmichael said he worked for. They both had more expertise in these matters than Adam, so there wasn't any reason for him not to take them at their word.

Vagrants. A memory tweaked in Adam's brain. He'd had the responsibility of rousting them more than once from various places within the park. They'd complained about some of their number gone missing, but Adam hadn't given it a second thought. Vagrants were transient by definition, weren't they? God, could he have done something to prevent this earlier if only he'd paid attention?

Adam stopped in the middle of the trail, unable to go forward. "How many?"

Carmichael took a couple of steps before he turned back.

"How many what?"

"How many dead? How many missing?" Adam didn't want to know, but he had to.

"Oliver says at least twenty-seven dead that he can connect to Rothburg or this park, maybe as many as forty-six. That we know of. For disappearances, the numbers are harder to tally."

"Forty-six? In the last year?" Adam couldn't quite catch his breath. He squeezed his fingers into fists, trying to force the words out. "You think this is the work of a serial killer? Not wild animals?"

Carmichael nodded and looked puzzled.

"I... It might be my fault no one knew about it until now. I mean, they told me, but I didn't listen. I thought they were drunk." Tremors shook Adam's body.

"Hey, no, it's not your fault." Carmichael stepped toward him. Adam wasn't sure if he or Carmichael closed the gap, but next thing he knew, he was shaking, with Carmichael's arms wrapped around him. Or as best they could with Adam's backpack in the way.

Carmichael dropped a light kiss on the top of Adam's head, so light Adam was surprised he felt it.

"Calm down. Whatever it is, it's not your fault. Trust me," Carmichael murmured soothingly into Adam's hair. After a couple of minutes, the shaking eased.

"Tell me what that was about," Carmichael said without letting Adam go.

"Early in the season, I was given the job of rousting the vagrants." Carmichael tensed, and the grip around Adam tightened. "The park's not a bad place to live, even in winter. Once the season starts to ramp up, the homeless have to go. Doesn't give the right impression, and I imagine the park service is concerned about associated crime."

Adam felt Carmichael nod. He slipped out of Carmichael's arms, dropped his pack, and sat on a nearby log. Not that he wasn't deriving comfort from Carmichael's embrace, but it was weird talking about this while hugging in the middle of a nature trail. He was pleased all out of proportion when Carmichael dumped his own pack to come and sit beside him. There was no embrace, but Carmichael sat close enough that his thigh and shoulder pressed against Adam's. The warmth seeping through their clothes comforted Adam too.

"Go on," Carmichael said. His fingers twitched, making Adam wonder where Carmichael was planning to put his hand, but in the end he left it resting on his thigh, a fraction of an inch away from Adam's.

"I had to do it, move them, several times, because they'd shift their camps around from place to place. They complained about friends of theirs disappearing. Strange sounds in the woods, like screams.

"I didn't take it seriously at all. Then they were gone, and as far as I know, no one thought of it again. Including me."

And what did that say about him? A gay man ought to have a little less tolerance for labels and shouldn't be dismissive because of them. Yet he'd done to them what his hometown had done to him.

"I should have listened. I should have done something."

"There wasn't anything you could have done."

"Sure there is. I could have reported it, followed up, something. If nothing else, you and Oliver might have showed up sooner."

Fuck. The tremors started again. How many people had died because he'd ignored Western society's version of the untouchables?

"Hey," Carmichael said sharply and grasped Adam's chin, twisting his head, forcing him to look into those lapis lazuli eyes. "Listen to me. The person or persons responsible for this are dangerous. I know you started helping us on a lark, probably bored."

Uh, yeah, that was true.

"I understand," Carmichael continued. "But you need to understand something too. There's more planning here than we—Oliver and I—expected. You could get hurt if the people behind this figure out why we're in town and that you're helping us."

"What do you mean, more planning?"

Carmichael pressed his lips together into a fine line before he spoke. "Oliver could explain this better."

"I don't want *Agent Cardoso* to explain." He sounded like a sulky child, but Oliver was such an authority figure, he made Adam feel like he was back in school, unsure and recalcitrant. Carmichael made him feel uncertain at times too, but now that they'd had sex—great, mind-blowing sex—Adam's comfort level with Lachlan had increased.

"As far as I know, this is the first time we've seen such organization, along with what appears to be a deliberate suppression of potential alarms. Which may be why it took a year for me and Oliver to be sent here."

Adam tapped his lips with a finger. He didn't want to be the target of a serial killer, but Carmichael made it sound less like a serial killer and more like a murderous conspiracy. How could they be sure about all this? So far it sounded like a lot of supposition.

Opening his mouth to ask that question, he was halted by the rueful smile on Carmichael's face. Jeez. Adam's heart and libido were going to go into overdrive if orgasms made Carmichael smile at him all the time.

"I know what you're going to say. I can't tell you everything I know. I've already told you more than I should. I need you to be careful."

Sweet. He wasn't sure if Carmichael's admonition to be careful was a personal desire, but Adam chose to take it as such.

"So Oliver's, what, checking out some of the disappearances, seeing how big the stories got nationally? If there's any other connections to Rothburg?"

"Pretty much. The stories stopped cold a few weeks ago. Oliver's also going to find out if bodies stopped showing up then or not."

"The stories stopped," Adam repeated. "Isn't that funny?"

It had never occurred to him until now, but then, he didn't bother with the local paper. Anything of note filtered through the café as gossip anyway.

"You okay to keep going?" Carmichael asked.

"Yeah, I'm fine now. Thanks."

Carmichael stood, and Adam followed suit. They picked up their bags and hoisted them onto their backs.

"We don't want to be out here all night." Adam had every intention of spending tonight in Carmichael's bed. Again.

"Not out all night? Why the hell am I carrying sleeping bags?" Carmichael asked. His affronted tone made Adam want to laugh, but he refrained.

"We need to be prepared for anything out here, but I have no intention of missing my shift tomorrow."

Carmichael nodded and gestured for Adam to lead the way, although he stepped into place beside Adam as he walked.

"So what's funny?" Carmichael asked as they continued down the trail. Adam had to search his memory for their recent conversation because, for a couple of seconds, he wasn't sure what Carmichael was referring to.

"Right. The editor of the *Rothburg Review*, which I assume is the archive Oliver was looking through..." Adam waited for Carmichael to give him confirmation. "Well, he had one of those incidents I told you about. I think it was a month and half ago. Got lost out here for three days. When they found him, he had no recollection of where he'd been or what happened to him. They chalked it up to exposure, but it's still odd."

Carmichael looked thoughtful. "Yeah, that is weird, although Oliver should have come across it in the newspaper."

"Nope, wasn't in there. The editor wouldn't allow the story to be printed. Guess he was embarrassed."

"Hmmm. I'll let Oliver know when we get back."

"What, you're not going to call him on the sat phone?" Adam teased.

Carmichael tossed him a glare. "Emergencies only."

Oho. Adam guessed he'd used up all of Carmichael's loquacity minutes for the day, perhaps the whole week's worth. Too bad, because Adam had other things he'd like to discuss.

They stopped speaking as the trail became rougher and soon became no trail at all. The place Adam intended to stop for lunch was well off any trail, although not as far-off as their eventual destination.

SEVEN

Breaking through the brush, Carmichael followed Adam into an idyllic clearing. Small but private.

"Let's stop here for lunch." Adam pulled off his backpack.

Carmichael's tongue twitched in a mouth filled with saliva. Adam had sweat as much as Carmichael; his T-shirt hung damply against the firm, lithe muscles in his back. Carmichael's mouth craved the opportunity to taste those gorgeous contours.

"Sure, sounds good."

Swiping sweat off his own brow, Carmichael looked for the best place to sit down and get comfortable for a bit. It wasn't basic training or anything, but he wouldn't say no to a break and some food.

He dropped his pack to the ground. Humping this shit through near jungle for an hour would have put him in a super-pissy mood if Adam weren't such good company. Also he got to follow that bitable ass. Which, come to think, was something he'd not had the chance to do the night before. On the agenda tonight, for sure, whether or not they were stuck in this hellacious wilderness. He didn't have a condom or lube—dumb—but there were other safe ways they could have fun.

Adam knelt underneath some shade and pulled supplies out of his pack. Carmichael unrolled one of the sleeping bags for them to sit on.

Leaning back against a tree, Carmichael made quick work of the simple meal while watching Adam eat. Beads of sweat dotted his forehead and upper lip. The black hair that had looked so artfully messy last night now just looked messy, with bits of bramble and twig sticking out.

Carmichael assumed his own hair sported vegetation as well, but he'd never paid much attention to his appearance. Not like Adam did.

Reaching across, Carmichael plucked the biggest twig from Adam's hair, who flushed fire engine red when he saw it, hands immediately going up to pat down and remove any offending bits, sunlight glinting off his ring.

Adam glared at him, making Carmichael laugh a little. The glare got worse before Adam grabbed a bottle of water and lifted it to his lips. Watching those pink lips wrapped around the bottle, throat working to swallow, combined with the scent of clean sweat, inflated Carmichael's cock. He'd been sporting half wood the whole damned morning, but within seconds of looking at Adam now, it became fully functioning, fully grown wood, throbbing in his cargo pants.

Adam finished his sandwich and licked his fingers. Carmichael pounced, toppling Adam—who grunted in surprise—over backward. Straddling Adam's hips, Carmichael lowered his pelvis to rub against Adam's—oh thank God—erection. As Carmichael dipped his head, lips meeting lips, Adam twined his hands around Carmichael's neck, anchoring him in place.

One gentle nibble at those lips was all Carmichael could take before he plunged his tongue inside, eating Adam up. He tasted like mustard and the addictive taste of pure Adam that Carmichael had discovered last night.

Adam moaned into his mouth, pressing his hips up.

Carmichael tore his lips away from Adam's succulent mouth and, loving the extra-salty tang, tasted his way down Adam's neck to his collarbone, where it peeked out of the neck of his white T-shirt.

He slid his hands up Adam's belly underneath the shirt, coaxing it off. Adam helped by grabbing Carmichael's T-shirt and tugging it off.

Fucking decadent it was, with the sun warming Carmichael's back through the filter of the leaves.

Seeing Adam like this, desire clear on his face, nothing hidden in the light of day, made Carmichael desperate to see all of him. Attacking one of Adam's pink nipples with his lips at the same time as his hands attacked the fly of Adam's jeans, Carmichael wrestled him out of his clothes and boots in record time. Adam's sexy moans echoed through the clearing, but Carmichael didn't care if anyone heard, if anyone saw. Those moans were for him, and if anyone else came upon them, they'd be insanely jealous of Carmichael's good fortune.

Carmichael rocked back, pulling his lips away, and stroked the pale, sweat-slicked skin. A barely there trail of dark hair on Adam's lower belly led the way to his goal—Adam's ruddy, pulsing cock, already leaking clear fluid.

Sweeping his fingers across the head, Carmichael captured as much of the moisture as he could. Adam's gaze fastened on him, intent, hot, as Carmichael brought his fingertips to his mouth and sucked.

Adam let out a breathy whimper, accompanied by a jerky thrust of his hips, and Carmichael's cock leaped in aching response.

Carmichael pulled his fingers out of his mouth and slid them down Adam's balls, which were pulled tight against his body. Unable to keep his mouth off any longer, he dived down to suck on one of those tender balls, causing Adam to gasp and fling his legs wider, giving Carmichael more room to maneuver. He lavished attention on the other side of Adam's furry sac, loving the smell of him, so strong here.

Curling his hand around Adam's heated shaft, he didn't provide any friction. In between rough licks, Carmichael stuck his fingers back in his mouth, then slid one finger down into Adam's crease, right into his pucker, one of many body parts that had been consuming Carmichael's thoughts since he woke that morning.

Adam almost shrieked, and thrust himself down toward Carmichael's hand, the hole fluttering open with ease. Carmichael had to close his eyes and count to ten. Twenty. Fuck. He could only imagine what that would feel like gripping his prick. Would it feel better than getting fucked? Because that had been an unexpectedly toe-curling pleasure.

Dammit. Why the hell hadn't he thought to bring condoms?

"I thought..." Adam panted between strokes.

Carmichael eased another finger in, stealing the rest of Adam's words, except for his name moaned over and over. Carmichael thought he could get used to hearing Adam use his despised first name, as long as he kept saying it in that lust-filled, raspy voice that told Carmichael he was doing something very, very right.

Adam propped himself up on his elbows so he could observe Carmichael's labors.

"I thought..." Adam began again. Carmichael started stroking Adam's long cock in time with his finger fucking. "You...were...a... virgin." Heaving breaths punctuated each word.

Carmichael smiled. It felt like a wicked smile. Judging by Adam's expression, he'd given exactly the smile he'd meant to. God, Adam's eyes were even more mesmerizing with blown-out, dilated pupils.

He licked the tip of that rosy head bobbing in front of him, tongue slipping around the ridge.

Pulling away, Carmichael said, "I do have the Internet, you know!"

A look of mild confusion passed over Adam's face. "What?"

"You asked about my virginity." Hmmm. Saying that word aloud, at least in reference to himself, would normally make Carmichael squirm. As he'd discovered last night, being this close to blowing his load superseded any and all embarrassment.

"I have the Internet," Carmichael repeated. "And I know how to use it." He punctuated his words with deep, gliding strokes into Adam's ass. Too bad this was all they could do right now.

Understanding flooded Adam's face before his head dropped back between his shoulder blades as his hips pushed up into Carmichael's fist.

"Lachlan." Adam's voice held the same faint note of command Carmichael had heard last night. "Fuck me. Now."

Carmichael froze, pushing away his impending explosion by sheer force of will. Thankfully his cock was still trapped behind his fly, because otherwise he'd have been inside Adam as fast as he could manage, regardless of any safe-sex precautions.

Helpless, aching to fulfill Adam's orders, he looked into Adam's eyes. "I didn't bring any condoms or lube." Fuck, was he stupid. Those orgasms last night must have melted his brains along with his muscles.

Adam returned Carmichael's earlier wicked smile, with interest, making Carmichael's prick jump, seeping ever more precum into his boxer-briefs.

"I did." Adam purred.

Oh thank fuck. It warmed Carmichael inside to know Adam had planned to get into his pants during the hike. He disengaged his hands from their pleasurable pursuits and scrambled toward Adam's pack, fingers scrabbling to release his pants.

"Where?" he snapped, all patience for play at an end.

"Front pocket. Hurry," Adam snapped back, body shifting restlessly on the sleeping bag. His hand hovered over his dick, and Carmichael knew exactly what Adam's dilemma was. Torn between needing touch and wanting to extend the pleasure until they were fucking.

Carmichael shucked off boots and pants, grabbed his prize, and scooted back over to the hot, writhing male waiting impatiently for him. He ripped open the package and slid the condom down his dick, wincing at how sensitive and eager he was. God. What if he hurt

Adam in his desperation? Carmichael understood he wasn't going to be perfect at this, not the first time out, but he didn't want to... well...fuck up.

Closing his eyes against the delicious temptation in front of him, he took a couple of deep breaths and listened to his heart pounding like parade drums in his ears. Once again he'd expected to be nervous, not like a stag in full rut. Feeling the imminent orgasm retreat, he slicked up his fingers and slid them back into Adam.

"Stop playing around. Fuck me already." Adam hissed.

Well, he'd have to trust Adam on this, and he wasn't inclined to argue at this point. His dick was hard enough to carve obsidian.

Lining up to the small, puckered hole, Carmichael had another moment's hesitation. His dick looked much larger in comparison. Adam's cock was thinner than his, and Carmichael was still feeling him, hours later. It was a good ache, but an ache nonetheless. Would the burn be greater for Adam?

"Do it. Now. I can't wait," Adam ordered.

Adam flipped over, arching his back, legs spread, crease beckoning. Carmichael slid his palms reverently over the smooth, rounded ass cheeks. Beautiful. Fucking beautiful.

Adam moaned, and Carmichael realized he'd said the words aloud. What could he say? Best ass he'd ever seen. More bitable than he'd imagined. Leaning forward, he nipped at Adam's left cheek, leaving a strawberry red mark on that perfect skin. Adam yelped and glanced back at him, bucking his hips in invitation.

To hell with waiting. Adam seemed to want it as bad as he did. Carmichael pressed in, the tight ring of muscle giving way, allowing him to sink all the way inside, his balls touching Adam's.

Oh holy fuck.

Sweat rolled down Carmichael's temples as he adjusted to the sensation of the tightest sheath he'd ever imagined rippling around his cock. His fingers dug into Adam's hips. Slowly he pulled almost all the way out, then thrust firmly back in. Adam yowled and thrust back against him, back arching so strongly, he looked like a contortionist.

Hips finding a natural rhythm, Carmichael leaned over Adam's back and mapped the bumps of his spine with his tongue. After a few minutes, Carmichael's orgasm boiled in his balls. Trying to stop it now would be like trying to stop a freight train with a trip wire. Be nice if he could hold off until Adam came, but it wasn't meant to be; he no longer had conscious control of his hips, lost in the heated thrust and glide.

Thrusting faster, Adam started sliding along the soft fabric, grunting and keening. Carmichael had shifted, hoping to adjust his position enough to reach around to stroke Adam's cock, when Adam screamed Carmichael's name, a red flush crawling up his spine, cords standing out on his neck.

Carmichael was surprised enough that it took a second for him to notice Adam's ass clutching his dick in a near-painful grip, before it yanked his load right out of him.

"Adam!" he yelled and fell forward against Adam's back, hips jerking sporadically as he rode it out. His lips sought out Adam's neck, and he latched on, sucking at the salty flesh.

Despite the trembling reaction in his arms, Carmichael pushed himself up enough so that most of his weight wasn't resting on Adam. When the grip on his softening prick eased, he heard Adam whisper, "Slowly on the way out."

Carmichael nodded, stupidly, since Adam couldn't see him, and withdrew. He slumped onto his back, chest heaving. Adam rolled over and snuggled up into the crook of his arm, pressing soft kisses onto his chest.

"That was spec-fucking-tacular," Carmichael said as soon as he could form a coherent thought.

"Uh-huh." Adam sounded breathless. "Never better."

Carmichael raised an eyebrow. "Lying to make me feel good?"

"Nope, not at all. You're a natural. But if you're interested in more practice..." Adam's sentence trailed off as he bit Carmichael right near the join of shoulder to pec. The sweet sting made his dick consider taking a renewed interest in the proceedings, but as much as he might like to practice more, right now they were still working.

A sudden thought surprised a laugh out of Carmichael.

"What?" Adam asked.

"This is the first time I've literally fucked around on the job," he replied.

Adam stared at him for half a second before he started laughing also. "Me too!"

Carmichael reached down to deal with the condom, and Adam sprang up toward his pack.

"Hang on," he said.

Hang on? "To this?" Carmichael asked, holding the limp latex. What the fuck?

"You don't think I'm going to let you litter out here, do you?" Adam produced a small, clean sandwich bag. Carmichael might never look at Ziploc bags the same way again.

Condom disposed of to Adam's satisfaction—in Adam's pack, he could carry it back to civilization—Carmichael eyed the mess on the sleeping bag. Unbelievable. These damned things were dry-clean only, weren't they?

"Guess if we're out here all night, we'll be sharing your sleeping bag."

Adam looked at the same spot on the sleeping bag before he blushed and giggled at the same time.

"I don't have a problem with that." Adam came in for a full-body press. Damn, his skin felt amazing against Carmichael's naked form. But they had to get dressed. He gave Adam's ass a friendly squeeze before he grabbed his clothes and pulled them on.

With a slight grimace, Carmichael rolled up the sleeping bag, jizz and all, and reattached it to his pack.

"How much further?" Carmichael asked.

"Depends. The edge of the park is about another hour away. I don't recommend straying too far out of park property, but how far and how long we do is up to you."

"How come you know this area so well? I mean, I can see a full park ranger, maybe, knowing the areas off the trails, but I don't imagine everyone in town would have this familiarity."

Adam made a face that Carmichael couldn't interpret, his features smoothing out before Carmichael could call him on it.

"My parents loved to hike around here. They brought me here several times when I was younger. My mother used to be a professor of Native American studies, and she often scoured the area looking for remains of Native American settlements and such."

Huh. Somehow that wasn't the answer he'd been expecting.

"What does your dad do?" The question was one Carmichael had never asked anyone before, partly because he had never cared and partly because he had never wanted the question to be returned. He didn't know who his real dad was. His mother had him at sixteen and had spent most of his formative years in and out of jail. His grandfather, the man he was named after and who had raised him, sort of, was an unemployed, abusive alcoholic. Questions about Carmichael's family life were never welcome from anyone.

"Oh, well, my dad's retired too. Used to be the chief of police."

Oh. Wow. Somehow neither of those professions meshed with Carmichael's previous assumption of indulgent, wealthy parents. Adam wouldn't meet Carmichael's eyes, and Carmichael wondered if that was because he was well aware he was sponging off his folks far longer than a grown man should. But saying so would ruin the afterglow.

"Huh. Did I mention I met the current chief?"

"No, when?" Adam looked at him, more animated than before.

"At the diner, while you were in the restroom."

"Really? What did he want?"

"Don't know." The interaction still puzzled him.

"He's never liked me much, even when he was my dad's deputy. Maybe he figures I'm a bad influence on newcomers."

"Oh, you are." Carmichael was happy and wanted to tease.

Adam looked stunned. "What do you mean?"

"Well, I was in town for how long?" Carmichael let out a short bark of laughter. "You managed to seduce me and take my virginity."

Adam sputtered for a moment before he began laughing. He wrapped his arms around Carmichael's neck and kissed him, light and sweet. "That's me, seducer of innocents."

Carmichael rumbled deep in his throat and nuzzled at the accessible cheek, the slight stubble rasping his lips. He nipped at Adam's ear, enjoyed the resultant squirm, then pulled out of the embrace.

"C'mon. Work to do."

AN HOUR LATER, the overhead canopy blocked most of the sunlight, and the undergrowth was thick near the ground but much easier to slog through than the previous pseudojungle. Were there poisonous snakes in this part of the country? Carmichael didn't know, but he kept a close eye on where he placed his feet.

Adam stopped moving. "Here it is."

Carmichael turned around in a circle. He'd expected a fence to demarcate the national park from private property. He looked more intently and saw it. A small, battered, red metal sign nailed to a tree, somewhat above average eye level. It proclaimed private property, lack of liability, and potential danger.

"That's it? That's the notice?"

Adam nodded. "Yep. There's one tacked to a tree every hundred yards or so."

"Fucking ridiculous."

"Yes and no. When visitors enter the park, they're told not to venture off the trails. Not one official park trail crosses any part of this border. But with the reputation of this place, well, there are a few unofficial trails; that's for sure."

Hell. If they'd gotten here by using one of those unofficial trails,

Carmichael suddenly had a lot more respect for those curiosity seekers. They had to have a shitload of curiosity riding them to go through all that work.

"Who owns this property?"

"Don't know, actually. Crazy Mary Winters lived in a cabin in the middle of Allenton Woods while I was growing up. I don't know if she went into a home or died, but I heard her cabin was abandoned, and I never heard about any heirs."

Oliver was going to have to keep researching that. "Crazy Mary Winters?"

"Er...that's what we called her. Everyone avoided her, and she rarely came into town."

"No one visits there?"

"Not that I know of. The reputation of the woods keeps people away. No reason for anyone to go out there, I don't think. We don't even get a lot of hunters around here."

Carmichael wondered if she had been the first victim of the Umbrae. Oliver had a theory that the portals would open up in the same places over and over again throughout time, that the fabric of the universe was somehow weaker in those places, and the stories throughout the ages of werewolves, vampires, and demons were the result of those portals opening.

"All right. Let's keep heading in this direction. You said it was dangerous out this way. I assume you aren't talking about ghosts. What are we on the lookout for?"

"The area is rocky, and there are lots of hidden crevasses. Deep ones."

"That's it?"

"What more do you need? Slip and fall out here, you've got a broken leg. And with rangers reluctant to pass over the boundary, who's going to find you before exposure or animals get you?"

Carmichael nodded. Made sense, although he'd expected something a little more sinister. But then, he grew up in the projects.

Later, the army only stationed him in deserts. What did he know about fucking forests and shit?

About five minutes into the trek through the private property, Carmichael felt it. This was the first time ever he'd been able to sense a significant change in the atmosphere. The idyllic nature walk became something else, something dangerous.

"Wait up," Carmichael whispered, reaching out to grab Adam's arm.

"What?"

"Wait a minute." Carmichael strained his ears. In addition to a strange sense of decay in the air, like an unpleasant taste in the back of his throat and a film on his skin, there were no sounds. No birds, no chittering, just the dark stillness.

Shit on a shingle. Was this what Oliver kept hoping would happen to him? Or was this why Oliver was always so adamant that there was an open portal in the vicinity when they'd arrived at a site?

Adam was obviously confused by Carmichael's actions, but he remained still and silent, waiting. A faint howling reached Carmichael's ears.

"What's that?" Adam asked, his already light skin bleaching further.

"Don't know. Sounds like a wolf."

"There are no wolves around here," Adam said.

"You sure about that?"

The howling got louder but still sounded quite far away.

Adam shrugged. "The rangers said wolves left the area decades ago. I've never heard of a wolf sighting."

The wind shifted, and the sense of decay was now accompanied by a rather strong scent of the same. Adam wrinkled his nose.

"Where's that coming from?" Carmichael asked.

"Why? You don't want to find whatever dead thing it is, do you?"

Nope. He definitely didn't *want* to, but Carmichael knew he should. He could try following his nose, but fuck, he wasn't Daniel Boone or whatever nature boy. That was Adam's job, strangely enough, even though he'd looked so urbane and sophisticated at the club last night.

"If it's close, I think we'd better take a look."

Adam rolled his eyes but turned and headed toward the sickening rotten-meat smell. As they traveled, Carmichael realized the area *was* quite treacherous. The sharp, rocky outcroppings became larger and more tightly packed the closer they got to the smell.

After about ten minutes, during which Carmichael nearly sprained one ankle or the other every thirty seconds, he was about ready to call a halt and turn back. It wasn't worth one of them actually injuring themselves out here on the ass end of nowhere.

Adam stopped and pointed toward a rocky edge, holding his nose. "I think it's down there."

Carmichael flattened himself on the rocks to safely peer over. The carcass rested about ten feet below, well decomposed. Carmichael thought it might be human, but at this point it was hard to tell. Given that all other potential victims had been disposed of far from Rothburg, this could be nothing more than a bear cub. Regardless, he pulled out his smartphone and zoomed in on the body, snapping pictures. He also took a few pictures with a small, old school camera as back up. Oliver might be able to determine more from these pictures.

Scanning the area, Carmichael noticed a clear footprint in one of the few earthy sections. He zoomed in and took a photo of it.

Showing the photo to Adam, he said, "Still think there's no wolves?"

"Huh. Guess not. I mean, it could be a dog print, but..."

Problem was, even though the camera worked now, there was no guarantee the pictures would still be available for Oliver by the time they returned. Damned portals. There was no predicting how they'd affect the equipment, especially if the portal was nearby. Carmichael inspected the sides of the crevasse. It'd be a bitch, but he was sure he could get down to the body, maybe confirm it was human, see if there was any identification.

"I'll be right back." Carmichael shucked his pack.

"What? What are you doing? You can't go down there. It's too dangerous."

"I'm fine." Carmichael could have jumped the ten feet down, maybe, but he didn't want to land on the corpse.

"Carmichael, come back here." Adam's voice was low but conveyed his upset.

Carmichael dropped the last couple of feet to the ledge. Fuck. The stink was worse down here. Inspecting the body as best he could without disturbing it, he wished the skull were present. Probably rolled even farther down. Skulls were the most distinctive identifiers.

He looked a little closer. No reason for a bear cub to have a shirt collar. Without a doubt, this was a human corpse. After snapping a few more pictures, he grabbed a stick. Poking around, he tried to locate a wallet, but without proper tools, he was leery of disturbing the scene too much. Besides, every poke sent a fresh wave of stink into his nostrils.

"Carmichael, what the hell are you doing? Get back up here."

Nothing more he could do down here. "I'm coming."

Carmichael hauled himself back to where Adam was. It was much easier going down than up.

"What did you find out?"

"Nothing. Probably a bear cub." He shouldn't have lied to Adam, but he didn't want to upset him. He didn't want to ruin the day they'd had. How fucked-up was that?

Eerily the mournful howl they'd heard before wafted through the forest. "Yeah, that doesn't sound like a dog." Adam looked around as though he expected to be attacked any minute.

"Let's get back." Adam's apparent concern was valid. They could get attacked, and it was Carmichael's job to prevent that. "As it is, we might not get back before nightfall."

Adam agreed and led the way back to civilization. Sweaty and exhausted, they met Oliver at the entrance to the park as the sun faded to red on the horizon.

———

THEY TOOK QUICK, consecutive showers alone, despite Adam's attempts to entice Carmichael to conserve water. His argument that showering would take a lot longer together was more than likely correct. Adam had every intention of finding out for sure tomorrow, since his shift at the café didn't start until eleven a.m., and Carmichael was going to have to shove him out the door if he didn't want Adam to stay the night.

Adam dressed after his shower and curled up in one of the horrible, cat-upholstered chairs to wait for Carmichael to finish cleaning up.

What an awesome day. Well, the stinky-weirdness interlude wasn't awesome at all, but the sex was everything he'd hoped for. He'd always wanted to have sex outside like that. Not that he hadn't had a quick and dirty fuck beside a building before. Joel and he had done that a couple of times. But fully naked sex outside, in the sun, was something he'd never done before, and it was something he'd never forget.

Sex aside, Carmichael had been a great companion for the hike. He hadn't been prickly or grouchy at all, and he'd been protective of Adam. Again. It was sweet, although Adam was certain Carmichael would not approve of anyone's applying that adjective to him. He'd also been entertaining and pleasant.

What Adam wanted to talk about—but didn't—was Carmichael's lack of sexual experience. Not that Adam thought he was lying about being a virgin. There hadn't been a lot of hesitation, but there'd been enough, along with a few unguarded expressions, to confirm Carmichael's claim.

Once Carmichael got more experience under his belt, so to speak, Adam wasn't sure he'd survive the experience. Of course, that would be long after Carmichael left Rothburg. The thought of Carmichael leaving made Adam sad, so he shoved the thought away.

It did explain why he was so quick on the draw that night in the club parking lot. If Carmichael had just been getting handjobs and blowjobs, probably he'd been with a lot of strangers and quick hookups. Licking cum off your fingers? Not usually on the agenda during those.

Adam could understand why Carmichael hadn't fucked or been fucked while he was in the military. He wasn't exactly proper, but he seemed to be a believer in rules, even if forced to bend or break them. Although the majority of his service would have occurred after Don't Ask, Don't Tell had ended, Adam suspected coming out in the military wouldn't have been easy.

A year, though. Carmichael had said a year had passed since he'd been out of the army. Somehow he...what? Never found the time? He was so gorgeous and buff, he could have walked into a gay bar anywhere and had his choice, with or without anyone knowing about his cherry. He'd had no issue translating theory to practice; if he hadn't said anything, Adam might not have guessed.

Which was the source of Adam's confusion. Why him? Adam knew he was relatively good-looking. Knew they had chemistry between them. But that couldn't be a first for Carmichael. No fucking way. So what had made him, at the ripe old age of twenty-eight, decide to lose his virginity with a virtual stranger he hadn't appeared to like until he'd stuck his tongue down Adam's throat?

Again. Why Adam?

Only problem—Adam wasn't sure he was going to like the answer, so he hadn't been able to bring himself to ask. The question wouldn't have occurred to him if he weren't starting to care—too much—for Carmichael.

Carmichael emerged from the bathroom fully dressed. More of his "we'll spend too long fucking, so let's avoid temptation" nonsense, no doubt. Shame. With a bare chest and a towel wrapped around his waist, Adam would have done his damnedest to tempt Carmichael into a little—no, a lot of—immediate gratification. He was already tempted, but easy access would have been key to convincing Carmichael.

Ah well. Maybe this debriefing wouldn't take too long. They needed to eat too. He was starving.

"Ready?" Carmichael asked.

"Whenever you are," Adam replied, unsure if Carmichael heard and understood the double meaning Adam had intended.

Carmichael looked away for a second, then handed Adam his key. "I'll have to talk to Oliver after we talk to you. Will you stay?"

Adam hadn't considered the secretive "need to know" bullshit. If he'd thought that far ahead, he would have planned to sit outside Carmichael's door. This was better. He took the key and tucked it in his pocket, trying desperately not to squeal with glee.

"What about dinner?" Oliver had already eaten by the time they'd called for a pickup, and both of them had felt too grimy to stop anywhere on the way back to the bed-and-breakfast.

"We'll order pizza when I'm done."

Carmichael gave him a hungry look, and Adam almost had to sit down again. That look wasn't for pizza. That look said the pizza was destined to be eaten cold. Yummy.

EIGHT

Adam had never been in the Mallard Room before. The ducks were less obnoxiously cute than Carmichael's cats, but they were overwhelming in their overt duckyness. The piles of electronic equipment and cords didn't match the image of stodgy hunter in hip waders the room's decor evoked. Adam couldn't imagine a hunter of any description staying in the B and B instead of the motel on the highway about twenty minutes out of town.

"What's all this for?" Adam waved a hand at the equipment. Agents Cardoso and Carmichael might belong to some super-secret government organization, but their investigation was so nebulous. A whole platoon of FBI agents wouldn't need this much surveillance equipment. He didn't think. Of course, he didn't know what MIA truly stood for. He'd tried a quick internet search but hadn't turned up anything useful.

"Surveillance equipment," Oliver said.

Adam rolled his eyes. Not helpful. He'd already guessed as much. Oliver's stoic expression led Adam to believe he wasn't going to get any more information, though. Maybe he could make Carmichael talk later, the same way he'd gotten Carmichael's first name. Oh fun.

Adam looked over at Carmichael's crotch, then up to his face. Eyeing Carmichael's pinkening cheeks, Adam was certain if he looked back down, he'd see that tasty dick hard and pressed against Carmichael's fly. Adam didn't want to join the boner brigade, not yet anyway, so he made a point of keeping his gaze above the waist.

"Sit down." Oliver turned his attention back to the computer screen. "I'd like to hear all about your trip. Give me a minute to finish up here."

Oliver typed a few more commands into the strangest computer Adam had ever seen. Looked like something from a movie. Thinking about all this equipment made him wonder if the agency Carmichael worked for dealt with computer crimes.

Huh. Computer crimes. Made sense. Maybe. It didn't mesh with the whole serial-killer scenario he'd been working on out in the woods, but with all this computer equipment, maybe there was something on the Web connecting the disappearances. Maybe they'd tracked the killer as far as Rothburg but weren't able to pinpoint his exact location or something.

Adam knew enough about computers to get by, as well as what he saw on TV, but he was an archaeologist, for Christ's sake. His head was stuck far in the past. He was smart enough to know the unerring precision with which television detectives were able to determine the identity and location of computer users might be a convenience for the show rather than demonstrating reality.

Then again, he was much better at making deductions from the detritus of civilizations. He'd never make a true investigator.

"So, tell me what happened today," Oliver invited.

Adam heard a choked gasp from Carmichael and he chuckled. Carmichael had better be grateful tonight that Adam was going to pass up on this incredible chance to tease.

"Are you okay?" Adam asked with an excess of solicitude, desperate to hold in the laughter.

"Fine," Carmichael coughed out.

Like Adam would tell Oliver *everything*. He wasn't sure he

wanted to share with anyone what had happened with Carmichael. He wanted to hug it to himself like a special treasure.

Oliver raised a brow but pulled his chair away from the equipment so that he could pay attention to Adam. Carmichael took a seat on the far side of the table, as though afraid Adam might do something naughty. As much as he'd like to, Oliver was Carmichael's boss. Adam had too much respect for people's work and careers to do something inappropriate. Like fuck Carmichael on the clock. *Oops.*

Adam bit his lip. Well, at least nothing had happened in front of Oliver. *Technically* it was a loophole. Besides, he'd never done anything like that before, although he was more than willing to try it again. With Carmichael. Lachlan.

Considering how close to the vest Carmichael kept his sexuality, Adam didn't know if Oliver knew which way Carmichael swung. Adam would be more likely to whip out his dick and masturbate in front of the police station than out someone on purpose. Which meant a quarter after never. Thinking about being naked around the current chief of police was a guaranteed dick shriveler.

He already had a sharp, bitter taste of how painful the derision could be when he'd come out before heading off to college. His parents had been supportive; most of the townspeople had not. He'd not been able to get out of town fast enough, and he wouldn't subject Carmichael to the possibility of that when he didn't know how Oliver would react.

"Whenever you're ready," Oliver said.

"I don't know what help I can be. I didn't see anything unusual except for the decomposing animal. And I didn't even see that, just smelled it. We also heard some strange sounds, like howling wolves. I'd always been told there weren't any wolves in the area, but with the sounds and the paw print Carmichael found, well, I have to consider that might be wrong."

Oliver rested his forearms on his knees, brown eyes intent on Adam's face. He was a good-looking man, although he was older than Adam went for.

Too bad his air of authority made Adam want to confess to every minor indiscretion, like the time when he was eight and stole a candy bar. Until these agents from MIA had stepped into his life, there hadn't been any indiscretions for a long time, well before his relationship with Joel. His reckless and irresponsible actions over the past few days were unlike him.

"Lach—I mean, Carmichael has the photos." Shit. Adam had to be careful. Until he knew why Carmichael didn't like to tell people his first name, it was a word best left in the bedroom. "There's not much there. I didn't look, because *ew*, but I'm guessing the dead animal we found was a wolf kill." Lachlan's theory did seem reasonable, given the paw print they'd found.

The only corpses Adam had dealt with were long, long dead and hadn't smelled so hideously foul. Adam's stomach rebelled slightly at the memory. Thank God he hadn't heaved up his lunch in front of Carmichael. That would have been humiliating beyond belief.

"You okay?" Oliver asked.

Adam nodded. He hadn't realized his distaste had been so obvious.

"I can see why rumors sprang up about that area being haunted." Adam wanted to think about something—anything—else. "It was pretty creepy. But if there're hungry wolves in the area, I'd want to steer clear too."

"So that's it? Nothing else out of the ordinary?"

Adam shrugged. *Besides your partner's fine, fat cock?* Between that, Carmichael's hot, wet mouth, and his talented fingers, Adam wasn't sure much else could have made an impression. His brain could only handle so much sensory input at a time.

"Fine, then." Oliver sat back in his chair. "I think we can call it a night."

Weird. Maybe Adam's theory about computer crimes was wrong. No one was using computers out where they'd been traipsing around today. Drugs? Maybe.

Whatever. Adam nodded and stood, ready to return to

Carmichael's room. The room key was practically branding him through his pocket.

"Hold on." Carmichael held a hand out. "You need to tell Cardoso about the editor."

"The editor? Oh, right." Adam dropped back down.

"What editor?" Oliver's intent gaze came back to Adam.

"From the *Rothburg Review*. The paper itself reported a few disappearances but there is also an associated blog which was always a little... out there. Not exactly tin foil hat time but it could have ended up that way."

"Yes?" Oliver prompted.

"It's all gossip. I mean, I'm not friends with Arthur and I never read the blog or the paper, but I'd heard about a month and a half ago he'd been hiking up there and he himself disappeared. Was found wandering a county road three days later, disheveled and suffering heat stroke."

"Three days, you say," Oliver repeated.

"Uh-huh." Adam nodded. "He's the closest person I know to have experienced all that hokey alien-abduction stuff."

Oliver's eyebrows climbed up his forehead.

"Alien-abduction stuff?" Oliver sounded more surprised than Adam would have expected, even for a total skeptic like himself. "What do you mean?"

"Just that he couldn't remember anything about those three days. Not where he was or why he was there."

"Three days. Amnesia. Interesting." Oliver grabbed a tablet and tapped at the screen, then made a couple of notations on a legal pad.

"Yeah, it sounded like total bullshit at the time, and I didn't think anything of it until Carmichael mentioned that the stories in the paper stopped about that same time. I remembered thinking the whole thing had been made up. No one wrote about his experience in the paper. And it's not like a lot of fascinating stuff happens in Rothburg. Not even purse snatchings, usually. And the blog posts that came after apparently lost any conspiracy theory undertones."

"Shit." Oliver stopped typing and exchanged a cryptic look with Carmichael.

More secret-agent shit, no doubt. Adam didn't know why the story bothered Oliver, but judging from his new twitchiness, it did.

"We might be looking at this all wrong," Oliver said.

Carmichael frowned. "Yeah, I was starting to wonder about that myself."

Oh, if only Adam knew what they were talking about. Sooner or later he'd make Carmichael tell him. Or at least he'd have fun trying.

"Forget the haunted-woods, ghost-story crap," Oliver said. "I think someone's using that as a cover. Adam, think carefully. In the past year, can you remember anyone who's been 'out of town' for three days?"

"And hasn't remembered where they were?"

"No, no. I think that was an isolated case," Oliver said. "I'm wondering about people, possibly influential people, who had a legitimate reason for leaving town and were gone for three days."

Was he serious? Adam looked over at Carmichael for confirmation. He also looked eager for an answer. Were they both on crack? Adam was barely accepted by the townspeople—most of them blamed him for his parents' ailment. He sure as hell didn't pay attention to their fucking social calendars.

And over the past year? Hell no. That was a long time to pay attention to people who hated him or ignored him.

"Why would I know such a thing? Why would I care?"

"It was a bit of a long shot. What about people who regularly hike or camp overnight in the park? Maybe a three-day trip about a year ago?" Oliver wouldn't let it go.

Maybe Adam would have to revisit his decision regarding the sanity of these two. "You'd have to check with one of the rangers. I wasn't working in the park a year ago."

A year ago he'd moved back home after losing the man he had thought he'd have forever, to prepare for losing his parents. Sure as he was gay, he wouldn't have given a flying fuck who was going on a camping trip.

"Hey, calm down." Carmichael patted his knee gently. Oliver looked from Carmichael to Adam before giving Carmichael a questioning look.

"Can't you see you're upsetting him?" Carmichael said. Protecting him again.

It made Adam feel all warm inside. And like he wanted to lick Carmichael all over, but that had been a constant desire since meeting him.

"Sorry." Oliver turned back to Adam. "Look, I know these are strange questions. You'd have no reason to remember. But please, think about it. Because the more questions we have to ask, the more people we have to involve, the more likely someone will figure out why we're here. I'd like to delay that as long as possible."

"I'll think about it," Adam promised. He knew it didn't matter. He didn't know anything and wasn't going to remember any more.

CARMICHAEL WATCHED ADAM LEAVE, focused entirely on that ass and what he wanted to do with it. He couldn't believe he'd asked Adam to stay, handed over his key to a guy he'd known less than a week. As long as he didn't fall to his knees and beg for those spec-fucking-tacular, Adam-induced orgasms, he'd probably be okay. Unless Adam cut him off. Carmichael was becoming addicted to the pleasure he experienced with Adam. If Adam ever said no, Carmichael might beg or plead or do something embarrassing and unmanly.

Leaving Rothburg after this investigation was going to take a shit-load of willpower. But he didn't think Adam would be interested in occasional covert hook-ups. Adam seemed more the relationship type. If Carmichael had any intention of stepping out of the closet, he wasn't sure he could do it for a man who hadn't really grown up, no matter how intense the orgasms. Driving out here regularly because Adam didn't have a car would piss Carmichael off anyway.

He did like Adam and enjoyed his company in and out of bed, but building a life required similar goals, similar life views. Opposites might attract, as he and Adam proved, but it was lust, not something lasting. For something solid, Carmichael would be willing to come out. Probably. But he had spent most of his life alone and was accustomed to it.

Oliver waited in silence until the door thunked shut behind Adam. "That was interesting."

Carmichael turned his attention to his partner.

"Yes, it was." Had Carmichael concealed his avid interest in Adam?

"You're in a good mood. "Glad to be ditching the groundwork and actually do something?"

Carmichael smothered a cough. "Yeah, sort of." Glad to do *someone*—definitely do someone. Oliver was going to draw some accurate and unfortunate conclusions if Carmichael couldn't get this happiness thing under control. Happy felt so good, though. He wasn't sure he wanted to hide it.

Oliver fiddled with the equipment again. "Well, what do you think?"

This was part of his mentoring as an MIA operative. He had no doubt Oliver had everything figured out, but the question was how closely Carmichael's deductions matched Oliver's. Carmichael thought he'd put it together. Most of it.

"Werewolves, right?"

"Yes, I think so. They're acting a little out of character, though."

"I noticed that. This time it seems as though they're planning. More than normal, anyway."

Oliver nodded. "The werewolf manifestation is always cunning, but you're right. I can't tell if this is a new tactic or if it's related to the first person turned, since the pack will take their lead from the alpha.

I'm hoping Adam can remember something helpful. Either way, I think you're going to have to go back."

Fuck no. Carmichael couldn't go back to the city. He wasn't ready to give Adam up. Not yet.

"Back?" Arguments rose on his tongue. Oliver needed him here.

"Yeah. Don't tell me those woods and one dead body freaked you out. You've seen worse."

Oh. Back to the haunted woods. Sure, Carmichael could do that. No problem.

"No, that's fine. I was thinking of something else." Thankfully Oliver let it go.

"How come Adam doesn't know it was a body?"

"He didn't get close enough to it to see for himself. I told him it was a bear cub. I didn't want to upset him."

Did he just admit that to Oliver? Could he be more obvious? He might as well post a selfie of him and Adam in bed, sheet artistically arranged over their groins, #ImFuckingAdam.

"Good. After this is over, we'll retrieve it, see if we can make an identification, but for now, no harm in leaving it there. The closer our scent is to the kill, the more dangerous it will be for us."

Right. Those damned heightened werewolf senses.

"You mentioned going back to the woods?"

"I found some old surveys. I haven't tracked down the owner of the land yet, but there's a building on site. We need to check it out. Might be a den."

"We? Or me?"

"Depends. Finding out who owns the land might help us figure out who was turned first."

"I'll go on my own." Carmichael dreaded another hike in the goddamned woods without the sexy interlude he'd had earlier.

Oliver frowned.

Carmichael frowned back. "You can't mean for Adam to go with me? We both agree it's werewolves, yeah? It's not like we can explain that. How can you suggest exposing Adam to that kind of danger without letting him decide if he wants to?"

Carmichael stood up, tipping his chair over. Heat warmed his cheeks as he realized his emotions were showing, but he couldn't help it. The thought of putting Adam in danger made him anxious, which also pissed him off.

Werewolves were one of the most dangerous manifestations of the Umbrae. They killed first, without bothering to assess the consequences.

"Hey, hold on." Oliver held his hands out in a defensive gesture.

"Sorry, sorry." Carmichael knew Oliver wasn't literally trying to throw Adam to the wolves, but he hated this idea

"Normally I'd go with you, watch your back. And normally I'd agree that we'd have a better chance at playing dumb, assuming anyone tried to ask questions. But the Umbrae are covering their tracks more thoroughly than usual. The presence of a native townsperson might be a form of protection. In fact, you might be able to drive right up. There's a dirt road, I think. Adam could stay in the car, see if he recognizes anyone."

"And what's wrong with surveillance photos? He could identify people from those without any danger. Besides, what if he sees someone transform? How am I going to explain?"

Oliver shrugged. "You know you're lucky your phone worked at all so close to the portal. You might not be as lucky next time. Up close and personal is best. We need to know who's behind this, and fast. We can't wait too long—Adam's scent is all over the border between private and public land."

Oh fuck. Would it be better, in spite of the danger, to have Adam by his side, where he could keep an eye on him, or not? That was the million-dollar question. One that he had to answer the next day. He knew Adam wouldn't agree to taking a day off from the café with no notice, so if Carmichael intended to bring Adam with him back to the wilderness, he'd have to wait until at least the following day.

TWENTY-TWO-FUCKING-HUNDRED. Took Oliver long enough to review the data. Carmichael left Oliver's room, anticipation ratcheting up as he wondered what he and Adam would do tonight. Today would be a hard act to follow, but Carmichael was up —in more ways than one—to the challenge. He almost regretted not doing this sooner, but he couldn't remember any other man who'd tempted him to come out of the closet.

He should be thankful he'd not encountered Adam earlier in life. Inviting Adam to stay in his room had been surprisingly easy. One of the easiest things he'd ever done. Carmichael had spent the last twenty-eight years thinking he had control of his own cock, but this mission had disabused him of that notion. His prick was all Adam's to control, whether he knew it or not.

Carmichael adjusted his pants and raised his hand to knock, then noticed the door was not completely closed.

Shit. Blood pulsed in his temples, and his lungs clenched. More afraid than he'd ever been in his life, afraid for someone else, he reached for his gun, only to find his shirt—no holster, no gun. Fuck. His gun was in his pack, inside the room. He had to get his mind back in the game before someone—Adam—got hurt or killed.

After considering for a moment getting help from Oliver, he discarded the notion. If he had to fight a goddamned werewolf, Oliver would hear it and come running.

Slowly he opened the door and edged into his room. The only eyes he saw were the spooky cat eyes staring back at him. He closed the door behind him with a soft *click*. Sniffing the air, he didn't notice anything out of the ordinary, just the lingering scent of soap from their earlier showers. No blood or other worrisome scents.

No physical evidence of a struggle, and Carmichael hadn't been so engrossed in his conversation with Oliver that he would have missed the sound of fighting. Had Adam been ambushed? Was he here, unconscious? Or had they taken him away?

Moving a little farther into the room, he saw his bedroom door ajar, dim light seeping out.

Huh. Carmichael would have left the entire place dark and, if he'd had the time, disconnected the light switches. Dark was better for surprise attacks. He crept closer to the door and peered through the opening, tensed and ready to repel an attacker.

Oh, fuck him blind. Soft yellow light was perfect for the tableau in front of his eyes.

Adam stretched out on the bed, naked, eyes closed, dark hair splayed out on his pillow. Most eye-catching was the long cock, hard as Adam lazily stroked it. Condoms and lube sat on the bedside table. Adam gave no indication that he knew Carmichael was there. Fucking gorgeous. Blood responded to Carmichael's instant hunger, surging into his dick, swelling it painfully in his pants.

Damn. The scenario of a sexy, naked man in his bed hadn't crossed his mind once he'd noted the open door. He grinned. So many possibilities. Get naked and pounce? Pounce now, strip later? Stay right here and watch? Oh, the agony of indecision. He pressed the heel of his hand against his throbbing prick.

As he watched, Adam's strokes picked up speed, got a bit firmer. A drop of moisture appeared at the tip of the engorged head, making Carmichael's mouth flood with saliva.

Mesmerized, he followed the drop's path as it slid down the head to the ridge, ready to fall. Adam swept his fingertips along the flared head, catching the slick fluid and bringing it to his lips.

Oh my fucking God. Carmichael's faint moan was drowned out by Adam's rapid inhalations. No fucking way was Adam finishing without him.

Carmichael slammed open the door and dived for the bed. Adam's eyelids lifted, and in the dim light, Carmichael saw no surprise in those lust-filled eyes.

"About time you got here." Adam's breathy, husky voice would forever be associated with sex.

Carmichael didn't bother to respond. He knelt on the bed and spread Adam's legs apart, shoving his knees to his shoulders. Flinging Adam's hand away from its plaything—that was Carmichael's now—he opened his mouth and swallowed Adam's cock, almost to the base.

"Oh shit," Adam whispered as his hips jerked upward, shoving the last inch of his penis down Carmichael's throat. The shock overcame any gag reflex; Carmichael could deep throat when he wanted, and had done so several times. Today he wanted. Wanted badly.

Adam began sawing in and out of Carmichael's mouth, immersed in the sensations Carmichael provided, whimpering and moaning his name.

So fucking sexy. He had never seen anything like Adam, never been turned on like this. Never been so completely under someone's thrall that their pleasure mattered more than his own. Yet here he was. He wanted Adam to come, content to wait for his own orgasm. Nothing mattered but Adam's pleasure right now.

"Lachlan, dammit," Adam panted out.

Carmichael looked up but didn't stop sucking and swirling his tongue around the salty treat filling his mouth.

ADAM THRASHED ON THE BED, anchored by his dick lodged deep in Carmichael's mouth. He had done this before, Adam could tell. Best blowjob he'd ever had. Everything Lachlan did was the best.

Looking down the length of his naked body, he wasn't sure he'd ever seen anything as hot as Carmichael's eyes gazing back at him. Until his gaze moved past those plumped, wet lips wrapped around his dick. Carmichael giving him fantastic head, fully clothed in contrast to Adam's complete nudity, had him close to blowing his load way too soon.

Decadent? Kinky? Adam couldn't think of the right word. Wasn't sure he could think at all with Carmichael vacuuming his brains out through his dick.

"Oh God." Adam whined. He fucking whined. Couldn't help

himself. So good. He lifted up on his elbows to get a better look and moaned as he noticed Carmichael humping the bed. Was there anything better than a man who got off on giving head? Hell no.

Tide rising in his balls, Adam ignored the temptation to empty himself down Lachlan's throat in favor of a new idea that had taken hold of his brain. Shivers rippled through his body as he thought about it.

"Stop, stop." Adam panted, pushing Carmichael's head away.

Carmichael complied, those blue eyes looking at him questioningly. "Everything okay?"

Goddamn. Adam grabbed the base of his dick and squeezed, the breath from Carmichael's words almost setting him off as he thought about how much more than okay everything was.

"Fuck me now. I want to come with you inside me," Adam said.

Carmichael smiled, happy and lustful at the same time. He grasped the hem of his T-shirt and began to pull it up.

"No. No. Just unzip. Please, now." Adam couldn't tell if he was begging or demanding, but he didn't care as long as Carmichael did what he asked.

Carmichael's eyes dilated farther, and he let go of his shirt to direct trembling hands to his fly. One zip, one slight adjustment, and Carmichael's incredible, fat cock was poised and ready, moisture leaking from the tip.

"Oh shit." Adam whimpered. Definitely a whimper.

Carmichael looked horny, depraved, desperate for him, and that was a bigger turn-on than anything. Adam flipped a condom at Carmichael and grabbed the lube. Carmichael's movements stilled as he watched Adam slick himself. His face flushed dark red, Carmichael's tongue flicked out to wet his lips.

As much as Adam got off on teasing Carmichael, putting on a show, he wasn't going to be able to wait. He didn't even want much prep. Adam wanted to feel the burn as that thick penis slid inside. He wanted to feel it the next day and the day after. Make him horny all day, sensing that empty ache in his ass.

Whipping his fingers out of his hole, Adam pulled his knees back to his chest, offering up his wanting ass.

"Now," Adam said.

"Are you—" Carmichael asked, clearly entranced by Adam's slutty display.

"Now," Adam repeated, louder. His dick quivered, a steady stream of precum dribbling onto to his belly. It wasn't going to take long.

Carmichael crawled forward, the dark clothing a fascinating contrast to Adam's pale skin. As he moved in, his jeans brushed against Adam's thighs. He bit his lip, waiting.

"Lachlan, please." Adam couldn't stop himself from pleading.

"Don't worry, baby. I'm here."

Baby? *Oh God.* Adam's orgasm boiled closer to eruption.

Carmichael slid home in one long thrust. Adam arched and gritted his teeth to keep in the moans. Oh, it was perfect. Exactly what he'd wanted. He grabbed Carmichael's neck, pulled him down, and pressed their lips together.

Moving his hips in short, staccato bursts, Carmichael plunged his tongue into Adam's mouth in the same rhythm. If Adam's mouth were free, he'd be yelling, crying, screaming out his pleasure to the entire bed-and-breakfast. So fucking awesome.

Carmichael's large hand slid into the small of Adam's back and pressed him up, tilting his ass. Carmichael's next thrust caught his sweet spot. Once, twice... Adam's whole body stiffened, his ass clamping down on Carmichael's invading prick as his cock erupted, splattering cum all over his neck, chest, and chin.

Carmichael fed him a groan in return, and Carmichael's penis pulsed as he came in Adam's well-fucked, sensitized channel.

Pulling his lips away, Carmichael dropped his forehead to Adam's, their breath mingling as they panted. Relaxing further, Carmichael fit his head into the crook of Adam's neck, placing gentle kisses underneath Adam's ear.

"So good, baby," Carmichael whispered.

Adam shivered. He could so get used to Carmichael calling him *baby*.

Carmichael slid his softening prick out of Adam.

"Okay, naked now." A wide, goofy smile stretched Adam's face.

Carmichael rolled his eyes, but he grinned back. "Good idea. I seem to have cum all over my shirt."

Adam giggled as Carmichael went to the bathroom to get rid of the condom.

ADAM SNUGGLED into Carmichael's chest, enjoying the warm arm around him, holding him close. They were both slick with sweat and cum from their recent exertions and needed a shower, but Adam was content to wait or fall asleep like this. He'd never known this kind of contentment with anyone, not even Joel. He wondered if there was any way to continue seeing Carmichael after this case was done, because he couldn't imagine giving this up. He had never dated anyone in the closet, which he assumed Carmichael was, given his skittishness and lack of experience.

"So where do you live? I mean, do you have an apartment or anything?" Adam wasn't sure if Carmichael would tell him anything personal or not.

"Yeah, I have an apartment about twenty minutes east of the college."

"That's not too far." Might be near the same area Adam would look for an apartment when he went back to school. And not too far from here. Seeing each other would be possible.

"Not far from where?" Carmichael asked.

"Here. That's, what, a little over an hour's drive?"

"Closer to two."

"Still, it's doable."

"Doable for what?" Carmichael tensed up beside him.

Loath to give up the comfort of Carmichael's warmth, Adam thought it might be better if he sat up. God, this was hard.

"Well, I thought, maybe... We're having a good time, right?"

Carmichael's eyes narrowed as he waited for Adam to continue.

"No reason for this to end after you go home, right? We could still talk, hang out..." Adam gestured to their naked bodies. "You know..."

Carmichael sat up, drawing the sheet up over his waist. "Look, kid, yeah, we're having a good time—"

"Kid? Again with the kid? I'm two years younger than you." Was Carmichael making excuses?

Turning his face away, Carmichael swung out of bed and pulled on his pants. "It's been fun, but there'd be no point in continuing after I leave."

It's been fun? Like a phantom fist had plowed into his midsection, all the air left Adam's body. Somehow he'd never imagined this response. Not after the best sex of his life.

They'd only known each other a few days. It shouldn't hurt like this. But it did. He'd never felt so comfortable, so right, with anyone else. Carmichael had to feel the same, didn't he? Why else would he have chosen to given up his virginity to Adam? Why would he have been so sweet and protective?

Adam pulled on his jeans, his nudity making him feel vulnerable in the face of Carmichael's clothed state. A complete about-face from their earlier, sexy...fuck. Just sex. That's all.

"Why? What would be so terrible?"

"Look, you need to grow up a bit. You may be almost my age, but you're so young. I'm sorry, but you need to go to school or figure out what you want to do with your life. You need a plan. You're a little old to be working odd jobs, aren't you?"

Adam blinked, unable to formulate words. What the fuck? Somehow he'd expected the biggest objection would be Carmichael's wanting to stay in the closet. Not that Carmichael apparently *disapproved* of him. Like the rest of this stinking town.

"What the fuck does that mean? That I'm irresponsible? That I haven't done all the things you have, so therefore I don't have the right to choose how I live my life?"

Carmichael shrugged, still refusing to meet his eyes. "I've heard from more than one person that you've disappointed your parents. Can't you see they're right? You're a smart guy. You could do so much better."

Asshole. Not that Adam had explained about his parents, but still... "Leave my parents the hell out of this. They have nothing to do with us."

"There is no us."

"Oh, you've made that clear, you self-righteous prick." That caught Carmichael's attention. He actually looked at Adam. "You know nothing about my life, and you come in here and judge the choices I've made. Choices you know shit about. I shouldn't have to explain anything or justify myself."

"No, you don't. I'm explaining why it would never work."

"Those flimsy assumptions are why you think you couldn't see yourself with me? I'm good enough to fuck but not spend time with? Not hang out with? I guess you'd be embarrassed to tell your friends what I did for a living. Because that's what should matter in a relationship. Superficial details."

"A relationship?"

The disgusted tone was not flattering. Why couldn't Adam be enough for anyone?

He wasn't making any headway and he wasn't sure he wanted to anymore. After all, he'd almost begged Carmichael to date him. Pathetic. Like getting dumped by Joel all over again, but for it hurt a hundred times more.

His eyes started burning. If he was going to leave this room with a smidgen of dignity, he needed to get out before the tears started. Damned if he'd let Carmichael see how much he'd flayed Adam's heart.

He grabbed his shirt from the back of the chair and headed

toward the door. "Fuck you," he spat out before he flung the door open and left.

ON THE WALK HOME, Adam managed to avoid any actual tears, but they'd threatened to spill the whole way. Standing in his driveway, realizing Carmichael had no intention of coming after him, of apologizing, he couldn't stop them any longer. Wetness tracked down his cheeks. Scrubbing the tears off his face didn't help—there seemed to be an endless supply.

At least he was home. He'd sneak past Jennifer or whichever nurse was on duty; he didn't want to have to explain his upset to anyone. Now if he could avoid both Carmichael and Oliver for the remainder of their investigation, he might be able to pretend this had never happened. Might be able to pretend he hadn't opened up his heart again—stupidly—after Joel had stomped all over it.

NINE

Carmichael woke with gritty eyes. He wished he could blame hunger for the yawning emptiness in his gut, but he wasn't willing to lie to himself. Not about that. He missed Adam. He'd only known Adam for a few days, but he didn't want to leave things this way. He wanted Adam in his bed as long as he could have him.

And the hurt in Adam's eyes, like he'd kicked his dog. He never wanted to put that look in anyone's eyes again.

Those pained green eyes had haunted him all night, enough so Carmichael was amazed he'd slept at all. He wasn't going to be at his best today, and he hoped Oliver wouldn't notice.

He needed to apologize. Adam didn't have to live his life to suit Carmichael; he'd been right about that. But Carmichael had panicked at the suggestion of a long-term affair. He'd never had a relationship before and wasn't sure he was ready for one now. Not with someone so irresponsible, anyway. He still needed to apologize for the things he'd said, but he also needed to be clear there wasn't anything beyond sex for the two of them.

What did he know about relationships? Even if he decided to keep coming back here for sex, the gossips in this town would know sooner or later. Right now, he couldn't deal with everyone knowing he was gay. Didn't know if he ever could.

He stretched out, and a couple of joints popped. He turned his head to look at the bedside clock. Damn. Oh-nine-hundred already? He never slept that late.

Oliver expected him to check in soon. No way could he slip over to Adam's place to get it over with. He'd have to wait until Adam's shift started at the café. Noon, Adam had said yesterday.

Carmichael hopped out of bed and took a quick shower before pulling on his clothes. How could he long for company in his shower? Now he regretted refusing Adam's suggestion to shower together. If he hadn't, he'd have a sweet memory of a naked, wet Adam in this shower.

A vision of the shower in his own apartment flashed through his mind. Empty, cold. He wasn't sure how to transplant the mental picture of Adam's slick, slippery warmth into that frigid loneliness. Why hadn't he ever realized how dreary and lifeless his apartment was?

This was not the way to get his head back on straight. Werewolves were too dangerous to fuck around with. If he wasn't paying enough attention, they could kill him. Kill more innocent people.

Finished dressing, he took one last glance at his rumpled bed, wishing it had been messed up from frantic, mind-blowing sex. Instead the sheets were twisted because of his solo, guilt-ridden, restless night. Whatever. He could fix that. At noon.

Carmichael walked over to Oliver's suite and hammered on the door.

"You're late." Oliver opened the door but his attention was on the equipment on the table, not on Carmichael. Thankfully.

"Yeah, sorry, boss. What's up?"

"I'm getting some spikes on the readout. Not sure what they mean. We've never stayed this long near a portal creating werewolves before."

"Huh." Carmichael sat down and tried to interpret the data on the screen. He was no slouch when it came to computers, but he logic had little to do with understanding the Umbrae, as far as he could tell. Of course, he didn't have an enormous amount of experience with MIA yet.

"Usually werewolves are violent, impulsive, and all about instant gratification. They come to our attention quickly, and as dangerous as they are, there's usually not enough of them to cause a problem when we shut them down."

"*Shut them down.*" Made it sound innocuous, and yet the truth was so far removed from how it would go down, it might as well have been on Mars.

"So what do we do now?"

Oliver was still engrossed in the screens.

"Well, I've been comparing the data to past Umbrae breaches. Maybe you can check out the satellite imagery around that structure referenced on the maps, see if you can determine how many of them there are."

"Shit, Oliver, how many could there be? We've never encountered a nest of more than three."

"There's a first time for everything. I'm not comfortable with the differences we're seeing in their behavior. I'm worried we'll encounter something unexpected. We may need to bring in a couple of other teams."

No fucking way. Sure, werewolves were vicious fucks, and strong. The Umbrae gave the possessed many of the unnatural attributes in werewolf mythology, but silver bullets worked like a dream. It wasn't that difficult. And closing the portal sometimes save those who'd been turned.

"Don't discount the possibility, Carmichael. It might be a big nest, bigger than we've seen. Or what if it's a combination of werewolves and some other creature?"

That didn't ever bear thinking of. Carmichael pulled the screen with the satellite images closer, peering intently at it. Heat-signature data would be a fucking bonus, but the damned portals did a real number on electronics.

When his eyes started to throb, he pinched the bridge of his nose and looked up.

Shit. Past noon already?

Gaze glued to the monitor, Oliver muttered and made notations on the pad of paper beside him.

"Gotta take a break." Carmichael interrupted Oliver's droning. "I'm heading to the café, maybe talk a walk."

Take a walk. Sure. Maybe convince Adam to return with him to the bed-and-breakfast for a horizontal lunch break. If Adam accepted his apology. Which he might not. Apologizing was not a particular skill of Carmichael's.

"Need anything before I leave?" Judging from the muffins and pastries Oliver had appropriated from the breakfast bar this morning, he could survive a week without leaving this room. Assuming the damn ducks didn't make him lose his mind. Carmichael had gotten used to his cat decor, especially since it made him think of Adam's catlike green eyes.

"No," Oliver replied, the first intelligible word Carmichael had heard from him in hours. "Ask Adam when he can go back to the woods with you."

Sure, yeah. No problem. If Adam would even talk to him.

Carmichael slid out the door, determined to make things right— as right as he could—with Adam.

CARMICHAEL APPROACHED THE COUNTER. "Hi, Susie. Can I talk to Adam?"

She looked at him strangely. "Isn't he with you?"

Carmichael's brows drew together. What the hell had Adam told her? One more aspect of Adam's irresponsibility. Which Carmichael had already decided shouldn't matter to him, but shit. Surely Adam could have kept his mouth shut about the sex.

"I mean, I thought he was doing some work for you and that other guy. I assumed he was running late and hadn't had a chance to call me."

Carmichael stared at Susie, letting the words filter in, concern replacing his anger.

"He's not with me. Er...doing a job for me. Are you saying he hasn't shown up for his shift?" The worry grew exponentially, making Carmichael's gut turn over.

"No, he hasn't. I was getting worried. He's never missed a shift without calling, and he's only ever called in when he's been very sick. This isn't like him at all, but he was so excited about working for you, I thought maybe he was distracted." Susie looked like she wanted to nibble on her thumbnail, but glanced around and settled for squeezing her hands together. Her distress scared Carmichael like nothing ever had.

"He's half an hour late. Surely that's happened before."

"No, Adam's never been late for his shifts. Ever."

Ever? Adam might not be living up to his potential, but he had a good work ethic. Carmichael had noticed that before but had chosen to ignore it, like an ass.

"And it's been an hour and a half," Susie added.

"What?" Jesus fuck. An hour and a half? Adam was supposed to start at eleven today, not noon. Fuck.

"Did you try calling his parents?"

"His parents? They wouldn't know anything, and I wouldn't want them to worry." Susie progressed to wringing her hands.

Wouldn't want to worry them? Why not? Adam was their son, for God's sake. Okay. *Don't panic, don't panic.* It'd been ninety minutes. Maybe Adam overslept. Or had an accident on his skateboard—Wait, that thought caused panic too.

But the skateboard was still in the SUV, and Adam had walked home—again.

Shit. Remorse scalded him. He was a total asshole. But there'd be time for him to wallow in guilt later. Right now, he had to figure out where Adam was.

Without the skateboard, he could be hurt on the way to work, unrelated to the existence of werewolves in the area. Either way…

"I'm going to go look for him. Can you call my cell phone if you hear from him?" Carmichael slid one of his plain business cards across the counter to Susie.

"Sure, yeah. You have the number here, right? Call me and let me know what you find out?" Susie's eyes looked suspiciously shiny, and Carmichael nodded before getting the hell out of the café. The fiery ball in his stomach gnawed at him, even more now that Susie was on the brink of tears.

He leaped into the SUV and slowly drove toward Adam's house, peering along the sidewalks for any evidence of an accident or abduction.

Nothing. He saw nothing unusual. By the time he reached Adam's house, his stomach was fluttering. He'd never felt trepidation like this before, and he'd seen some scary shit overseas. Fuck, getting his leg damn near blown off hadn't freaked him out as much as the thought of Adam in the hands of those damned werewolves.

Once parked in the driveway, Carmichael jumped out of the vehicle. He stopped himself from pounding frantically on the door, because he didn't want to frighten anyone inside without reason. There was no obvious evidence of unlawful entry. Taking a deep breath, he tried to tell himself there was nothing to worry about. Because if he couldn't at least pretend to believe that, his agitation would upset Adam's parents.

With a reasonable facsimile of Oliver's official agency cardboard demeanor, Carmichael calmly knocked on the door.

A woman in nurse's scrubs opened the door. She didn't look anything like Adam, and not what Carmichael had expected Adam's mother to look like, but what did he know?

"Good afternoon, Mrs. Farelli. I'm Carmichael."

Lachlan. A soft voice that sounded like Adam's whispered his name in his mind. Hearing Adam cry out his name in ecstasy had obliterated Carmichael's hatred of his first name, but he wasn't up to using it himself yet.

The blonde woman snorted. "So you're the one," she said with derision.

"I'm...the one what?" Carmichael had an idea what she was going to say.

"You're the one who lit Adam up like I've never seen. Until yesterday, that is." Mrs. Farelli clucked disapprovingly.

Shame heated his face. Oh no. He had never met anyone's parents before, and the day after fighting with his lover—oh God, Adam *was* his lover—might be the worst possible scenario. Regret scorched its way up his throat. None of it mattered now. He no longer cared if everyone—even Adam's mom—knew Adam was his lover, if it meant Adam was safe, here, sulking.

"Look, Mrs. Farelli, that's why I'm here."

"Oh, son, I'm not Adam's mom. Call me Jennifer."

Not Adam's mom? Then who was she? Stepmother? Boarder?

"But..."

"Didn't he tell you about his parents?"

"Uh..." Carmichael tried to remember what Adam had said, if anything, about his parents, but nothing came to mind. Nothing beyond their heated words last night and Adam's continued need to check in with them. No matter how confused he was, though, there were more important issues at stake.

"Jennifer, ma'am, I'm looking for Adam. I need to apologize..." And make sure he was safe.

"Uh-huh. I should think so."

Carmichael's ears burned as his flush flared hotter.

"Is he here?" Carmichael was almost afraid to ask, but Jennifer, whoever she was, didn't seem concerned.

"I thought he was supposed to be working at the café this morning, but since he hasn't checked in with me, I assume he's in his room."

Carmichael blinked. He wasn't ready to let go of his anxiety, and as much as he wanted to run to Adam's room and check, there were too many oddities in his conversation with Jennifer so far.

"I thought Adam checked in with his parents. He never mentioned you."

"Oh, that boy. I swear, this town has him twisted up tighter than a pretzel." Jennifer shook her head. "I shouldn't butt in, but he's such a good boy."

Carmichael cringed at her use of the word *boy*. Jennifer was starting to make Carmichael feel like a cradle robber but Adam was a man, a very sexy man.

"That boy doesn't get the credit he deserves, partly because he doesn't talk about it."

Okay, enough cryptic statements. "Who are you? Are you a relative of Adam's?"

Carmichael itched to head up to see Adam, and he'd meant to ask where Adam's room was. Getting sidetracked by the chatty, disapproving Jennifer wasn't getting him any closer to his goal.

"Never mind. It doesn't matter. Where's Adam's room?"

Jennifer raised her brows at him and took a step back. "Yes, he mentioned that about you."

A brief spurt of pleasure warmed Carmichael's belly, knowing Adam had talked about him, but he wasn't sure what Adam had said, good or bad, to prompt that odd statement from Jennifer.

"His room?" Carmichael asked again, unwilling to waste any more time. Figuring out Jennifer's role could wait.

"Upstairs, first door on the left." Jennifer turned and headed back into the kitchen.

Carmichael took the stairs two at a time and wrapped his hand around the doorknob, halting himself before he flung the door open. Should he give Adam a chance to prepare himself? No. Under normal circumstances, he would, but he couldn't shake the feeling that Adam wasn't in his room.

Fuck it. If Adam was naked, well, maybe they'd have sex before Carmichael apologized, but he need to know—now—Adam was safe.

Carmichael turned the knob and opened the door forcefully, slamming it into the wall. Striding inside, he raked his gaze over a room that appeared frozen in time. High school, specifically.

No sign of Adam anywhere. Carmichael couldn't tell if Adam had slept in his bed or not. The bed was made, somewhat haphazardly, but no Adam.

He crossed the room and opened one of the doors he saw there. A tiny bathroom met his gaze, the shelf above the toilet covered with bottles, including four or five colognes. Carmichael didn't know why, but he grabbed the nearest one, a black one with fine streaks of orange and red on the label. Bringing it to his nose, he sniffed, and his legs nearly gave out. Adam had been wearing this cologne, smelling clean and sexy, the night he'd broken Carmichael's resolve, the night they'd first had sex.

Fingers trembling, Carmichael replaced the bottle. The silver ring he'd seen on Adam's thumb rested on the shelf as well. Carmichael picked it up. A strange impulse prompted him to slide it onto his hand. It fit on the middle finger of his left hand, and somehow he felt a little closer to Adam. He backed out of the room.

Determined to make a thorough search, he opened the other door. The closet was packed full. So many clothes hung from the rack, Carmichael was amazed they hadn't exploded into the bedroom.

Leaving the room, he began calling for Adam.

Jennifer rushed out of the kitchen, hands on her ample hips.

"You hush now! You're going to disturb my patients. I just got them down for their nap after lunch."

What? Carmichael's mouth opened, ready to yell back, but he didn't want to wake whoever it was up. This was all too fucking weird.

He had to find Adam. Living with his parents, acting like a kid, his complete lack of ambition—irrelevant. None of it mattered, because if someone hurt Adam, they would irreparably damage a piece of Carmichael he'd never known existed. And maybe it hadn't existed before Adam.

ADAM THOUGHT about opening his eyes, but he didn't want to. Someone wasn't actually flailing a tire iron against his head, but it sure as hell felt like it. Was he hungover? He didn't remember getting super drunk last night. Pain squeezed his heart. Alcohol might have been the answer after his vicious fight with Carmichael, but he couldn't even remember taking the first drink. Burrowing his face into the pillow, he sifted through his memories, uneasy, but nothing gave him the information he needed. God, he felt like shit.

As clarity returned, the pain in his head localized at the base of his skull. He must have hit his head somehow. Raising a hand, or trying to, shocked Adam into full wakefulness. What the fuck? Why couldn't he move his hands? Shit. Had he been in an accident?

When he lifted eyelids masquerading as hundred-pound weights, it took a second for Adam to focus and realize he was looking at the walls of a log cabin, not the sterile whiteness he'd expect from a hospital. And his wrists were tethered to the wrought-iron headboard of the bed he was lying facedown on.

Fuck! Adam pushed himself up as far as he could, vision blurring, and swung his head around as much as his limited range would allow. He'd never seen this place before in his life. Where was he? How long had he been here?

More importantly, why the fuck was he naked? Had Carmichael done this to him?

His stomach lurched, and he forced himself to relax as best he could. He eased himself back down to the bed, careful not to jostle his head too much.

Flashes of memory filtered back, and he remembered going home, alone. Shit. Carmichael had totally freaked out when Adam suggested their little fling might extend once Carmichael's job here was done. Then Adam found out what Carmichael truly thought of him. It wasn't as though he hadn't suspected. But hearing it aloud had hurt.

But Carmichael wouldn't do this to him, no matter how much he wanted to dissuade Adam from wanting a long-term relationship. Adam couldn't imagine Carmichael following him home and ambushing him. After those hateful words Carmichael had spoken, Adam assumed Carmichael would be happier never seeing him again. Returning to the city would accomplish that. And ignoring Adam while in Rothburg.

No, Carmichael had not done this.

Fear and a hint of anger grew, overriding the disorientation. Adam didn't know where he was, and some unknown person or persons had tied him to the bed, naked. No way was this a good scenario, unless he was filming porn. He would have remembered signing up for that.

Adam ignored the pounding in his head for more important issues. He tugged at the rope around his wrists but couldn't get enough leverage to stretch the ropes, much less break free, assuming he had the strength. Shit. He twined his fingers into the headboard and tried pulling back on his haunches, but the damned thing didn't even creak.

Should he call for help? No. Better if his unknown captors were unaware of his return to consciousness. Adam flipped over to get a better look at the room. He was able to endure the painful, twisted position only for a few moments before he returned to his former belly-down pose.

With the closed bedroom door behind his naked ass, vulnerability loosened his guts. Regardless, the position was marginally better than the cock-up, pretzel position he'd been in on his back. Sure, he'd be able to see whoever came in the door, but he had no leverage for kicking or fighting or anything. Because damned if he wasn't going to get himself out of this. He had to. Fuck, it was possible that no one knew or cared he was gone. No one was coming to rescue him.

"PATIENTS?" Carmichael stared at Jennifer, confused as all fuck. "What patients?"

"Adam's parents, of course." Jennifer's tone implied Carmichael was an idiot. She wasn't far wrong.

"What's wrong with Adam's parents?"

Jennifer shook her head in resignation. "I shouldn't be the one telling you this, but I think you need to know how badly you misjudged that boy."

Misjudged? Adam must have confided an awful lot of details about their fight last night. Carmichael needed an explanation, though, and he needed it now. He wasn't sure if this had anything to do with Adam's disappearance, but given how fucked-up his head had been since he'd arrived in Rothburg, more information had to be useful.

"So tell me." Carmichael was a breath away from punching his hand against a wall.

"His parents both have Alzheimer's. Adam pays me and two other nurses to take care of them, hoping familiar surroundings will stave off the inevitable. The insurance covers only a fraction, their savings are gone, and Adam had to move back home and sell his car to make payments. But they're both too far gone now. Within a month, they'll be institutionalized, and Adam will need to sell the house to afford their care."

Fuck. As if he needed proof he was an ass, here it was, served up by this nurse. Carmichael had no idea how to reply to that bomb. Saying, *Guess that explained the skateboard*, sounded flippant and insensitive even in his head. Adam might be one of the nicest, most selfless people Carmichael had ever met, and the urgency to make sure he was safe increased further.

Hold on. Alzheimer's? *Both* of them?

"How long?" Carmichael asked.

"Adam moved back here a year ago. I was the first nurse he hired on, but as they got progressively worse, he needed more help. Now one of us is here around the clock."

"And they're both getting worse at about the same rate?"

Jennifer pursed her lips. "Normally talking about it is a breach of privacy, but the whole town knows about it, so yes, I can confirm that. One of the strangest cases I've ever seen."

Jesus. He needed to tell Oliver about this. More than likely, Adam's parents were one of the first aborted attempts the Umbrae had made to possess someone in this area. They weren't able to fully possess everyone they came across, and failed attempts manifested as some sort of neurological disorder.

"I'm going to look around a little more, see if I can figure out where he's gone." For the moment, Carmichael chose to ignore the pain her revelation caused. From the look on her face, though, Carmichael didn't think he'd fooled her any.

Jennifer tsked. "Do it quietly. My patients need their sleep."

Carmichael moved through the rest of the house. There was little out of the ordinary except for the study.

Cardboard boxes, some with Adam's name on them, were piled haphazardly in a corner. Flipping open the top of the nearest box, Carmichael glimpsed a couple of brown frames.

Wondering if he could convince anyone he had a good reason for snooping, besides his rampant curiosity about the only man he'd slept with, Carmichael pulled out the frames.

Oh fuck.

Degrees. Adam's degrees. A bachelor's and a master's. A letter fluttered out from between the two frames. Carmichael snatched it from the floor and had to read it twice. Both times it said the same thing: due to a family emergency, Adam was granted extra time to complete his doctorate. In Egyptology. Could Carmichael have fucked this up any more? He deserved to be beaten for the assumptions he'd made about Adam. Assumptions a trained investigator shouldn't have made.

Acidic guilt burned his throat as he stumbled backward into the desk chair and sat down heavily, hands still gripping Adam's degrees and the letter from the university. The cutting words he'd slashed at Adam the previous night replayed in his mind. What a bastard he was. Why the fuck had Adam wanted to spend any time with him, much less continue to do so?

It was bad enough that contempt had no place in his relationship with Adam, whatever that ended up being, but to know he'd flung those hateful words at Adam when they'd had no basis in truth... Once Adam was safe, Carmichael could worry about how to apologize, beg Adam's forgiveness.

Under the desk, a bright blue flyer caught his eye.

ADAM SCRUNCHED his eyes shut as he tried to piece together what had happened after his fight with Carmichael.

He'd gone home in tears. He hadn't expected their affair to end that badly after so few days. Adam had locked down his heart after Joel, or so he'd thought. Carmichael was vulnerable, sweet, protective, sexy, a giving lover—Adam could have worked on the respect thing. Too bad he hadn't been as appealing to Carmichael as Carmichael was to him.

Jennifer had been on duty again when he'd come home, and although he'd tried to avoid her, she'd drawn him out. Got him to talk about it. Been supportive. Almost like having a mother again. Bittersweet, but welcome all the same.

Once more in control of himself, he'd gone to work packing and sorting his parents' things. He had been putting it off, and he sure as hell wouldn't be able to sleep after the emotional firestorm with Carmichael.

Adam's eyes flared open again. The flyer. There had been an old blue flyer in his parents' study for a three-day law-enforcement retreat. Took place approximately a year ago. Not too close to the wolf kill, but definitely near old Mary Winters's cabin, he thought. Three days. It couldn't be coincidence.

Early in the morning, he'd decided to check it out. Unlike the wolf kill site, there was an old overgrown dirt road that led right to the cabin. He pulled his old bike out of the garage. He'd outgrown it a long time ago, but it was too far to go on foot and too rugged for his skateboard, even if the damned thing wasn't still in Carmichael's SUV.

Leg muscles burning from the effort, he tucked his bike under a bush and approached the cabin, looking much less run-down than he'd expected for a place abandoned for years. He got closer, intending to look inside, hoping he'd be able to taunt Carmichael about any discoveries he made.

Stupid of him. He should have told someone, even Carmichael, where he'd been going. Carmichael and Oliver were likely going to check this place out, but it might be too late for him.

Why was the three-day time frame important? Unfortunately, he expected to find out, and soon.

The door creaked open. Adam tried to jump up. And failed. Sweat broke out all over his body. He hadn't anticipated how terrifying this position would be with an unknown behind him.

"Beautiful." A familiar voice spoke in the same reverent tone Carmichael used for that very same word. But it wasn't Carmichael behind him. The solid *thunk* of the door closing made him twitch. He tried to turn his head around but couldn't see his captor. Despite its being familiar, Adam was unable to place the voice. Fear squirmed in his belly.

"Why are you doing this?" Adam squeaked as a man straddled his legs on the bed. Heaving himself up, he tried to thrash around enough to throw off the stranger above him, but the man pressed him forcefully into the bed and moved higher on Adam's body, immobilizing him.

With his hips locked between two incredibly strong thighs and two strong arms holding down his back, Adam began to hyperventilate. The hands stroked along his spine, like a lover's. But this wasn't his lover, and Adam was so far from turned on, it wasn't funny.

"Oh yes. Better than I imagined," the low voice crooned.

Better than he imagined? Who the fuck was this? Adam couldn't stop his frantic breathing, and his vision started to gray at the edges. Damn it. He couldn't black out. Not when some stranger was touching him like...well...like he owned Adam.

The sound of a zipper opening and the unmistakable sensation of a hard cock nestling in the small of Adam's back shocked him enough that he stopped breathing for a moment. This bastard wanted to... he couldn't even form the word in his mind.

When Adam drew in his next breath, the panicky feeling receded, leaving anger. Fuck no! This couldn't happen without a fight.

"Get off me, asshole!" Adam bucked as hard as he could, hoping to move the guy above him enough to get a foot or knee up into his assailant's groin.

Too bad it was like trying to buck a tank off his back. His captor let him flail about, riding him like a bronco, although thankfully with no goddamned penetration, before Adam sank, exhausted, into the mattress.

"Mmmm. A fighter," the voice purred before a tongue sank into his ear. Adam couldn't have prevented the whole-body shudder for a million bucks.

"Who are you?"

"Someone you've never looked at twice."

His voice was so fucking familiar. If he'd speak in a normal tone, not that low voice Adam presumed to be seductive but only succeeded in freezing him to the soul.

"Just let me go. I won't tell anyone about this."

"No. I've waited and watched too long."

Watched? Even worse than *imagined.*

The man astride him huffed near his ear, sniffing him. His captor's hands slid along Adam's biceps before coming to rest on his forearms. The naked skin of his chest pressed against Adam's back, and the sensation of an unwanted erection along Adam's spine made him want to throw up. Revolting. But more importantly, did his captor intend Adam to survive this?

"As much as I want to take you now, it'll be better when you're willing."

"Yeah, right." Adam couldn't stop the derisive words from slipping out of his mouth. He'd never willingly spread for this sick fucker.

"Oh, you'll be willing." The rumble of his captor's words directly in his chest. "In three days, you'll give me whatever I want."

"What happens in three days?" What the fuck was the significance of that? He should have demanded Carmichael tell him the truth.

But the man didn't answer.

Instead the hands holding Adam's arms began to morph right in front of his eyes. Light brown fur sprouted, and the fingers lengthened into claws. Heart trying to escape his chest, Adam was distantly aware of the man—creature—humping against his back, but he found himself unable to focus on anything but the impossibility of a man shifting into a beast. Werewolf? Was that possible? Or was Adam delusional?

Fangs sank into his deltoid, and he screamed from the shock and pain. The mouth gripping him shook back and forth, like it was trying to rip out a chunk of his shoulder. Pain shot out from the bite, radiating throughout his frame. Endless seconds later, the bite eased, and the creature on his back howled as cum sprayed up Adam's back.

Pounding on the door gradually entered Adam's awareness, overcoming his focus on the heated throbbing of the wound on his shoulder and the deadweight of the beast panting on top of him.

"Bill, get the fuck out here! We've got a problem." Adam recognized that voice too, but couldn't identify the owner.

Wait. Bill? No fucking way. Adam didn't know exactly when it had happened, but his captor was human again. Bill lifted himself off the bed.

"Be right out," the man called in his normal voice. It was Bill, that asshole.

"Don't go anywhere." Bill patted Adam's naked ass. "I'll be back later."

The door opened and closed, and Adam was alone again. Fuck if he'd be here later for Bill. No telling what he would do next time. Adam glanced to the left and saw blood smeared across the sheets. That bastard bit him! Adam tugged and pulled at his bonds as hard as he could.

He couldn't fucking get free. No way was he going down like this.

Sobbing in frustration, Adam pulled once more, muscles protesting, and heard a faint *ping*.

TEN

Carmichael tore into Oliver's room, brandishing the blue flyer.

"Oliver, we have to get out there."

Oliver looked up from the equipment. "Hmmm? Oh, you're back. Good. We need to call in a few other teams."

"No! We can't."

"Why not?"

"No time. They've got Adam." Carmichael couldn't remember ever being this agitated.

Oliver rose from his seat. "Calm down. How do you know?"

"He's gone, disappeared. He didn't show up for his shift today." Carmichael didn't want to acknowledge that this was all his fault. If he hadn't freaked about having a relationship with Adam, he would have stayed in bed with Carmichael until it was time for his shift.

"He works in a café; it's not brain surgery. Maybe he's playing hooky."

Carmichael's chest squeezed. Even without knowing about Adam's secrets, he'd known that wasn't like Adam. Why hadn't he let that knowledge guide him? Why had he automatically assumed a skateboard meant Adam was irresponsible?

"He wouldn't do that, Oliver. I know it. And Susie, at the café, says he's never missed a shift before without calling."

"Did you check his home?"

Did Oliver think he was an idiot? He was a trained investigator, despite having missed some very clear signs about Adam that should have made him dig deeper.

"Yes. He's not there, but I found this. I think Adam found it last night or this morning." Carmichael handed over the flyer.

Oliver skimmed the contents. "Shit. This is bad. I was able to get some images on the satellite photos today, blurry as usual because of the portal, but I suspect the pack's at least ten strong."

"Ten? Shit," Carmichael echoed. "And the alpha's either law enforcement or a park ranger, based on this flyer."

Oliver nodded. "Best guess? He's been methodically turning anyone of influence in the town, as needed, which is why we're seeing the different pattern of behavior."

Carmichael filled Oliver in on his suspicions about Adam's parents. Which meant closing the portal might kill them. It could go either way.

"Carmichael, I don't think we have a choice. We can't go after ten werewolves without backup. I can get another team here within forty-eight hours."

"No way. That might be too late. If he's still alive..." Carmichael fought nausea as he tried to convince himself Adam wasn't dead. "If he's still alive, they're going to turn him. You know closing the portal before he's turned will save him. We can't guarantee anything if the transformation's complete."

"It'll be suicide going in there now."

"I don't care!" Carmichael slammed his fist into the wall, sending a framed duck print to the floor and spraying glass shards across the room. "I'm going in after him. Now. I can find the portal and shut it down."

Oliver grabbed his wrist and squeezed, his grip much stronger than Carmichael would have expected, but the pain gave Carmichael something to focus on. "Calm down," Oliver ordered.

Heaving in a deep breath, Carmichael forced himself to relax. Emotions could get him killed, but he couldn't stand the thought of Adam at the mercy of those monsters.

"Sit."

Carmichael obeyed.

"You're sure you can sense the portal well enough to set the charges?"

"Yes." In fact, he realized he'd never stopped feeling it after he'd first noticed the sensation out in the woods with Adam. It was like an aching sickness throbbing at the back of his brain. Without a doubt this was why he'd been recruited for this job, and he could use the sensation to find the nexus of the portal and plant the sonic charges, which were the only reliable means to close a portal before it closed on its own.

"We've got enough charges. I can't—won't—wait until you get another team in here."

Oliver sighed. Stood up. Paced for a few seconds.

"Fine. I'm still calling in the cavalry, because if we both get killed, someone's going to have clear out that nest."

"You don't have to go with me."

"Yes, I do. You're my partner, and I'm not going to let you die if I can help it. I'll create a distraction. Hopefully you'll have enough time to get in, set the charges, and get Adam out. Make sure you take a weapon for him too."

Carmichael stood. "Right, let's go."

"Now?"

"Shit, Oliver, I had my pack portal-ready when I went out there the other day...on the off chance. I'm ready. Grab what you need for a diversion, and you can drop me off partway to the cabin. We'll plan the rest in the car." Adrenaline slid through Carmichael's veins, sharpening his senses, preparing him for the battle to come.

ADAM LOOKED UP, as best he could, searching for the source of the faint noise he'd heard. There it was. His struggles had snapped the welding on one of the metal spokes, leaving a sharp edge. Maneuvering his hands, he began the arduous task of scraping the rope across the piece of metal. With excruciating slowness, the ropes parted. He didn't know how much time had passed, although the frantic babble of voices had long since faded. The voices that sounded like howling? Those he pretended didn't exist. Certain things needed to be ignored, for the sake of his sanity.

When his bonds finally separated, he slumped facedown onto the bed, muscles shaking and spasming from the effort, chest heaving. He had to get away but his body wouldn't obey.

When Adam's muscles stopped spasming, he tumbled out of the bed, almost falling to the floor. Shit. He grabbed at his shoulder. The bite—*the fucking bite*—hurt like that fucker had left his fangs behind in his flesh.

Righting himself, he looked around. No closet, but a wardrobe stood on the wall to the right of the door. He flung open the door and scrabbled through the clothing. All of it was women's clothing, probably been there for years, and too small for him.

Shit, shit, shit. He didn't much relish the thought of trying to escape in the nude, but he'd do what he had to.

He reached up with a gentle touch and pressed his wound. Ow. Fuck. He'd need a damned tetanus shot. Or rabies.

Adam pulled open the bottom drawer and found a pair of sweatpants and nearly burst into relieved tears. They were too short, too snug, and fucking pink, but they covered the important bits without too much vascular constriction.

Next, Adam looked around for a weapon. Not a damned thing in the room, not even under the bed, that would work. Somehow he didn't think a hanger was going to be of much use. Stealth, then, would have to do.

Window or door? Adam considered the choice for all of two seconds before he decided that he was less likely to encounter Bill or any of his friends if he went out the window. He flicked the drapes aside.

Too bad some asshole had barred it. Adam banged his fist against the prison-like grid. Staring out, all he could see were trees. He didn't even have anything to hit Bill over the head with the next time he came through the door. Shit.

Maybe he could use a hanger to pick the lock. He grabbed one of the hangers from the wardrobe and dashed over to the door. On a whim, he tried the knob. It turned in his hand. Bill must have thought there was no way Adam could escape his restraints. Made Adam's life a little easier, though.

Pulling the door open slowly, he peered through the small crack. No one appeared to be in the hall. He opened the door all the way and stepped out, shutting the door behind him.

He assumed he was in the very cabin he'd been spying on. Crazy Mary Winters's place. If so, he knew in which direction to seek help.

He headed to what he hoped was the kitchen, keeping an ear open for Bill's return. Or *anyone's* return.

Oh thank fuck. Knives. If only he had a belt to tuck it in, but a knife in the hand was better than nothing. Now he had to get out of there and out of the clearing around the cabin before he was seen.

Before he got to the door, the smell of smoke reached his nose. Smoke? He'd spent enough time with the rangers to know that smell in the woods was usually a bad thing. A brush fire would complicate his escape. But then, that might be why there wasn't anyone in the cabin to stop him.

The front door burst open, and the first thing Adam saw was a large black gun aimed in his direction. He brandished his knife in front of him, realizing how futile it was but needing to try to protect himself all the same.

"Adam! You're alive."

He looked up to the face of the man holding the gun.

Carmichael. Big, blond, and protective. Adam's muscles sagged in relief, and the knife clattered to the floor.

He wanted to fling himself into those strong arms for comfort, but he didn't dare. They needed to get out of there before Bill—the creature—came back. Carmichael wouldn't be prepared to face that.

"What the fuck did they do to you?" Rage lit up Carmichael's eyes as he looked at the blood smeared on Adam's neck and chest. Adam reached up to touch the tender area again and noticed Carmichael's face get even darker.

"Doesn't matter. We need to get out of here."

"We've got a few minutes. Oliver's creating a diversion."

After tucking the gun back in his holster, Carmichael strode to him and grabbed Adam's hand. He stroked a finger lightly over the raw stripes on Adam's wrists before inspecting the wound on his shoulder.

"Those bastards. Who did this to you? Did you recognize them?"

"Bill. It was Bill."

"Who is Bill?"

"The chief of police."

"As in Chief Sarkovsky?" Carmichael's shock was plain to see.

He couldn't feel more shocked than Adam did, though. How could a lawman act the way he had? Do what he had? Never mind that Adam had known Bill for years. He'd never noticed a whiff of the sick infatuation Bill had hinted at.

"William Sarkovsky, formerly my dad's second in command." Amazed he couldn't see his breath it was so damn cold, tremors rippled through his body. As much as he hated to show Carmichael any weakness, he was helpless against the reaction.

"Hey, it's okay. I've got you." Carmichael wrapped his arms around Adam and squeezed, tight enough that Adam felt safe. Kisses rained gently in his hair. "What the hell is this?" Carmichael asked, bringing one hand away from Adam's back.

Adam looked down and saw dried cum. Shame and humiliation swept through him like a tsunami, the flush so vicious, he was amazed his chest and face hadn't blistered. Adam twisted away from Carmichael, unable to look him in the face.

"Hey. Look at me." Out of the corner of his eye, Adam saw Carmichael wipe his hand on his jeans. Thankfully, he used his other hand to cup Adam's chin, gently coaxing his head up.

"What happened?" There was no pity in Carmichael's gaze, only implacable resolve. This was the soldier Carmichael had been when he was preparing for battle. But there was anger too, on his behalf, and no judgment. "I'm going to kill whoever did this to you. Bill, you say? I just need to know if I'm going to castrate him first. Were you...?" Carmichael was having difficulty saying the word.

Adam had difficulty thinking it.

"No. It...it might have happened if it wasn't for the diversion. But no, it never got that far." He tried to say he was okay, but the lie wouldn't pass his lips. It was an assault all the same, and one he'd have to deal with later, because he was *not* okay.

Carmichael gave a sharp nod and looked as though he were going to kiss Adam, but didn't. Not a good time.

"We're going to have to wrap that good before we leave." Carmichael tipped his face at Adam's shoulder before dragging him toward the kitchen.

"I'll be fine. Can't we get the fuck out of here? It's not safe for either of us." Adam didn't know how to explain Bill's transformation.

Carmichael shook his head. "We don't want them to be able to track you. It'll just take a minute."

Track him? How? The blood had all but dried up.

A couple of minutes later, tea towels were wrapped around his shoulder and under his armpit, and his back had been wiped down with a damp towel.

"Are you happy? Can we go now?"

"Here." Carmichael brandished a weapon similar to the one in his holster, a large gun with a silencer.

"Um, what am I supposed to do with this?"

"Shoot bad guys."

"I'm not much of a shot." His father had tried to teach him how to shoot when he was younger, but to no avail. Adam was hopeless, which had been a little embarrassing as the son of the chief of police. "And these bad guys—they're not normal."

"Don't worry. Aim for the center of the chest. The bullets are silver. Hitting them anywhere will take them down."

Oh. That explained...nothing. Silver bullets? Were they both suffering some sort of mass delusion? The word *werewolf* had whispered through Adam's head during his assault, but he'd convinced himself—mostly—it had been the stress of the situation playing tricks on his mind. Now Carmichael was here, giving him a gun with fucking silver bullets. Adam didn't know what to think.

"I'll explain later. I promise. But we have to get moving. They won't be fooled for long."

Adam nodded and moved to the front door. Exactly what he'd wanted. Once they were out of there, though, Carmichael had some explaining to do.

CARMICHAEL OPENED the door cautiously and peered out, one arm stretched behind him, making sure Adam was within reach. He couldn't see anything in the clearing surrounding the cabin, but one of the creatures could be in the shrubbery beyond, and he might never know. The Umbrae gave their possessed plenty of favorable attack and survival skills.

Gun cocked and ready, he beckoned for Adam to follow him as he stepped out onto the porch. A short sprint took them into the trees, and Carmichael paused for a moment to get his bearings before heading for the place where they would rendezvous with Oliver.

The effects of the open portal oozed into the entire vicinity, and the air itself felt wrong. It made Carmichael's skin itch, like an allergy to malevolence. If others felt even a fraction of the bleakness pulsing at the edge of his awareness, it was no fucking wonder the place had the reputation it did. This had to be a recurring portal, one that had shown up enough times over the years to inspire stories. Even after a good fifteen-minute hike away from the locus of the portal, the effects hadn't dissipated at all. The most unbelievable part of those stories was the fact that Mary Winters had apparently lived in this cabin for decades.

"Ow, fuck," came the muttered curse behind him.

Carmichael stopped and turned to see Adam, torso scratched in various places, tea towels already dirty, limping slightly as he struggled to catch up.

"What's wrong? Did you sprain something?" Carmichael whispered. They weren't far away enough.

"Uh, no, I stepped on something," Adam whispered back, lifting a bare foot to inspect the sole.

Oh shit. Where the fuck were his shoes? Carmichael had been so blinded by the damned bite on Adam's shoulder that he hadn't noticed much else. Fucker had tried to turn Adam. Which wasn't going to happen—assuming Carmichael had set the charges correctly before coming to find him. Carmichael took a closer look at Adam's current state of undress.

"Those aren't your sweatpants, are they?"

Adam shook his head.

"Where are your clothes?"

Another flush swept up Adam's chest, and he shrugged. Carmichael's jaw locked. Between the raw restraint marks on Adam's wrists and the goddamned fucking *cum* on Adam's back, Carmichael was getting a pretty good image of what that bastard Bill had done and intended to do to Carmichael's lover. He was fucking certain Bill wouldn't survive the day, whether or not they could exorcise the Umbrae.

His nostrils flared, and it took some severe willpower not to tighten his fist around the grip of his gun. He wanted to go back there, find Bill, and beat the shit out of him. But he couldn't. Not yet.

While Carmichael was strong and trained in hand-to-hand,

people possessed by the Umbrae were stronger than normal humans. He might be able to hold his own against one of the creatures in combat. Maybe. But it wasn't safe for Adam, and he had to protect Adam.

"God, Adam, I'm sorry. I didn't realize you weren't wearing shoes."

Adam gave him a wry grin. "Me neither. Not until now."

Carmichael took a quick look at the bottoms of Adam's feet. They were scraped and bloody and probably had been for the past few minutes. He wasn't sure if they had time to try to wrap them. It might be a moot point, depending on how long Adam had been leaving a trail the werewolves could track. The scent of smoke in the air, strong even to Carmichael's merely human senses, would confound them, but not enough.

A shrieking howl arrowed through the stillness.

Shhh... Carmichael mouthed the sound at Adam and swept his gaze across the verdant shadows. "Don't move."

Another howl, coming from another direction, rang through the forest. A third howl, closer than the other two, told Carmichael that not everyone had been fooled by Oliver's diversion.

This had all the earmarks of a major goatfuck.

"That doesn't sound like a serial killer." Even with dusk falling, Adam's terror was evident, but thankfully he didn't seem incapacitated by it. Carmichael was so proud of the way Adam was holding up.

Another mournful howl rose up. Fuck. At least one of the werewolves was on their trail. Possession by the Umbrae did not make them stupid animals. Good thing Carmichael had listened to Oliver and brought Adam an extra gun as a precaution. A decent shot between the eyes, well, it didn't matter if the bullet was silver or lead. But silver was crucial to taking down a werewolf with any other type of shot.

"Listen. We're going to slow down, but we're going to keep moving. When I say, we stop and stand back-to-back, got it?" Adam's agreement was immediate and again made Carmichael proud of his strength.

They continued moving through the forest at a much slower pace, the howls getting closer with every minute. The smoke probably confused them some; after the first howl sounded, Carmichael had expected them to be discovered much sooner.

Fuck, fuck, fuck. Adam's life was in danger all because of Carmichael's idiocy. The fight, the lies—all Carmichael's fault. He'd never been so stupid about a piece of ass before. Although to be fair, Adam was the greatest temptation he'd ever come across. Probably because Adam was so, so much more than just a spectacular ass. Against his better judgment, he hadn't warned Adam, because he hadn't wanted Adam to think he was crazy.

He'd wanted Adam's good opinion, even though he'd never returned the sentiment. He'd never thought it would come to this suicide mission to try to save Adam from Carmichael's behavior.

Carmichael could only blame the regular, repeated, and brain-melting orgasms he'd had since he and Adam had started fucking. Allowing them to affect his common sense was inexcusable.

A branch whipped against the side of Carmichael's face, bringing his focus back to the forest.

How many werewolves were on the trail? He didn't have Oliver's experience, and he wished his partner were there to guide him. He was fucking terrified for Adam's safety. Although innocents were never considered expendable, this was the first time Carmichael had a deep, personal *need* to keep one of them alive.

If they got out of this, he would go down on his knees and beg Adam's forgiveness. He had a laundry list of grievances he'd committed against Adam.

A flurry of motion and sound exploded at Carmichael's five o'clock. He spun, but not fast enough. The werewolf, snarling and hairy, knocked Adam flying.

Carmichael heard him grunt as he landed a few feet away, the sudden limpness in his form suggesting he was unconscious.

Or dead.

"No!" Carmichael shouted, drawing the attention of the beast straddling Adam's prone body, teeth bared and claws raised to strike. He aimed the gun at the werewolf's head.

Mulch flew up as the creature dug into the earth to launch itself at Carmichael. He shot, but the werewolf was too fast, plowing him into the ground, flipping the gun out of his grasp.

Carmichael flung the monster off him and dived for the gun. He had to kill it before the noise attracted any others.

His fingers had almost touched the barrel when claws dug into his back. He bucked frantically and rolled, slinging the werewolf off. It bounced back with horrifying swiftness, jaws gaping. At least Carmichael shouldn't have to worry about being bitten. The ability to sense the portals conferred an immunity of sorts.

He managed to get his right hand around the creature's neck when those snapping canines aimed for his throat. Keeping his arm stiff, he was able to hold back the animal. Just because Oliver said he couldn't be transformed by a bite didn't mean he was in any hurry to test the theory.

As he squeezed, claws scraped at his chest and legs, eyes bulging out of the furry face with the elongated snout.

He had to finish this soon, or the bites wouldn't matter. The creature was going to gain enough purchase to disembowel him, and then where would Adam be? Just another nameless corpse dumped miles from here.

Nope. Wasn't going to happen. Carmichael stretched his hand out, feeling one of the clawed appendages digging deeper into his side, and managed to grab the gun. Using his left hand to shoot wasn't ideal, but at this range it shouldn't matter. He lifted the gun and shot his attacker through the heart.

Immediately the snarling, wrestling thing went limp. Carmichael heaved it off, noticing the body reverting to its human form as he did so. The dead man was much smaller than Carmichael. He wondered for a second who the man was, but he wasn't Bill, so Carmichael didn't much care.

Taking quick stock of his injuries, he decided nothing was too serious and stumbled over to Adam, who was still unconscious.

Carefully assessing Adam, Carmichael decided he'd hit his head on the way down. Not that Carmichael was a medic or anything, but the large goose egg on Adam's temple and lack of any other apparent injury supported that hypothesis. Hopefully it wasn't anything more severe than a concussion. Either way, they had to get the fuck out of there.

There were more werewolves near by.

ELEVEN

Carmichael pulled out the knife strapped to his thigh. Cutting strips off his shirt to bind the worst of his injuries, he debated the wisdom of trying to wake Adam up or just carrying him the hell out of there.

Screw it. He could carry Adam far enough to remove them from the immediate vicinity of the dead creature. Then he could try waking him.

Retrieving Adam's gun, he tucked it carefully into the waistband of Adam's sweatpants, put his own into the holster, and tossed Adam over his shoulder in a fireman's carry. He groaned as his abused muscles protested. He wasn't going far, but it took him rather longer than he'd thought, with his added burden.

No hope of hiding where they'd gone, though. A hungover frat boy could track them with the trail they'd left.

Carmichael knelt and gently placed Adam on the ground. If they were being tracked, they were in trouble. Adam had to wake up soon, because they needed to jet. The sonic charges would be detonating at any minute, and they were close enough to feel some negative concussive effects. If the closing portal didn't cure or kill the possessed werewolves, it would drive them insane, making them doubly dangerous.

The sound of growling caught Carmichael's attention. Rising to his feet, hand going to his gun, he stood protectively over Adam. Unable to pinpoint the location of the growling, he spun around.

And kept spinning. The monster had appeared out of nowhere, slamming a fist into Carmichael's head. The gun flew out of his hand as he braced himself for a hard, fast landing.

The world tilted, making Carmichael dizzy. Thankfully the werewolf had curled its claws into a fist, a remnant of the human it had been. Otherwise he'd be dead.

With half-lidded eyes, he watched as the werewolf touched Adam's face before turning to stalk Carmichael. Werewolves were still humanoid. Even with the claws, the excess hair, and the toothy muzzle distorting its face, Carmichael recognized the general build and hair color of the chief of police.

Damn it. He needed to get his shit back together, or he was going to die right here.

The werewolf's—Bill's—elongated jaws opened. "Mine," Bill rasped out, pointing a claw behind him.

Adam? He thought Adam was his? Carmichael hadn't ever known the werewolf muzzle could form words, much less for one to lay claim to people.

"I don't think so." Carmichael launched himself at Bill's midsection.

The beast grunted and staggered back. Carmichael pulled out his knife. If he got out of this alive, he'd get a custom-made KA-BAR that combined silver into the steel of the blade. Iron and silver made the most effective combination by far when facing Umbrae-made creatures.

He'd hoped Bill would fall over, go flying, something other than the quick recovery he demonstrated. Damn him. Carmichael circled, wary of the claws. With those sharp tips, Bill's reach probably exceeded Carmichael's.

They tested each other, both receiving defensive wounds on their forearms. Crimson streaked Bill's arms and chest. Carmichael must look as rough or worse. But at least he didn't have the god-awful snout. The teeth would be handy, though.

Bill growled and lunged, swiping at Carmichael's face. Carmichael ducked, and those damned claws ripped lines of fire down his deltoid. Another couple of inches and they might have snagged his carotid artery.

Grunting, Carmichael knocked Bill's forearm up with his own and blocked the incoming claws from the other hand with his knife. The blade slipped into an opening and caught Bill a glancing blow across the sternum. Carmichael was rewarded by an immediate flow of blood before a clawed hand gripped the wrist of the hand holding the knife. The claws got in the way of the move Bill was trying to execute, bending Carmichael's wrist upward, but the pressure was enough to send piercing pain lancing up to his shoulder.

Not quite a tactical advantage, but Carmichael would take what he could get. With effort, he braced himself and forced the pain away.

Bill drew him closer, jaws gaping, saliva dripping from sharp white fangs.

Hell no.

That fucking asshole wasn't getting a bite of him. Carmichael tried to pull his arms free, but Bill's grip was strong, especially the one on his knife hand. As it was, he could barely feel his fingers.

Letting go of the knife, Carmichael was able to free his left hand and drew it back, aiming a punch for the opened wound on Bill's furry chest.

The blow connected. Bill shrieked and stumbled back.

What the fuck?

The werewolf clutched his fists protectively over his chest. Carmichael turned his fist over. Under the smears of blood, he saw the glint of metal. Adam's ring. Real silver. Perfect.

Carmichael advanced, fist ready to capitalize on his razor-thin edge. Almost faster than Carmichael could track, Bill sprang and grabbed both of Carmichael's fists, sending them both tumbling to the ground, Carmichael pinned below. He couldn't maneuver enough to get the silver in contact with Bill's skin or wounds.

Between Carmichael's blood and Bill's, everything was slippery, and Carmichael wasn't sure how long he'd be able to keep the creature from ripping out his throat. Fuck. If only he'd been able to locate the gun during their grappling.

Muscles straining, he pushed against Bill, fingers interlocking with claws. Bill hissed, heat flaring against Carmichael's skin around the ring. If only Carmichael were able to get the silver in contact with an open wound. Right now, the werewolf might be able to ignore his intolerance to silver long enough to kill Carmichael. In human form, he was a little older, a little smaller, a little less muscular than Carmichael. In human form, Carmichael wouldn't have won easily, but he would have won. With an Umbrae increasing his speed, strength, and healing, Bill had the advantage. Carmichael was no match for him. Concern for Adam's welfare had kept him going this long, but that wouldn't sustain him much longer.

"Mine," Bill growled out again, his obsession clear enough. Carmichael couldn't figure out why Bill hadn't turned Adam sooner if he cared that much.

Movement caught Carmichael's notice, but he didn't dare take his concentration off the creature pressed over him, trying to kill him.

A gunshot, silenced, whispered through the clearing. Bill jerked in his grip before slumping on top of him.

Adam stood over him, gun in hand. "I'm not his, that's for sure. Are you okay?"

Carmichael did a quick mental tally of his assorted contusions and wounds. As long as he didn't have to face any more werewolves without his gun, he'd live.

"I'm okay. How are you?" He pushed Bill off to the side and stood up.

"Head hurts." Adam touched his temple and winced. "But I'll be fine."

Carmichael didn't mention that Adam's wound had reopened from the fall. But the slow seep of blood through the tea towels wasn't enough to worry him and any psychological damage from killing someone would have to wait.

As they watched, Bill reverted to his human form.

"Okay, you need to tell me, now, what the fuck is going on here." Adam stared at Bill's body, anger radiating from every clenched muscle, looking as though he was going to fire more shots into the corpse.

"No time for that now. We need to keep moving."

Staggering, they moved away from Bill's body.

An explosion rocked the forest, throwing them both to their knees.

The tension in Carmichael's head, caused by the open portal, vanished, and he slumped in relief. The sonic charges had worked. Gave them some breathing room, maybe. He could take the time to bind Adam's feet and give him the explanations he deserved. If he waited until they connected with Oliver... Well, the information was still classified, but Adam deserved to know.

SHAKEN BY THE UNEXPECTED EXPLOSION, Adam tightened his finger around the trigger as he fell and the gun recoiled. Carmichael plunked down to the ground beside him and Adam dropped the gun.

"Oh my God. I didn't shoot you, did I?" A miserable bundle of emotions—gratitude, anger, frustration, humiliation—filled Adam, but none of them meant he wanted to shoot Carmichael. Not literally, at any rate.

Carmichael huffed out a small bark of laughter. "No, I'm okay."

Okay? Adam hadn't known it was possible to have that many wounds bleeding and still be conscious.

"Sit down. Let me take care of those feet," Carmichael said.

If that asshole Bill had been wearing shoes, instead of—oh God—claws, Adam would have stripped them right off the body.

"I thought we needed to keep moving."

"The portal's closed. We should be safe." Carmichael didn't have a lot of shirt left after the fight with Bill, but he shredded into strips the cloth that remained.

"The *portal's* closed? *Should be* safe? You need to tell me, now, what's going on. Remember, I'm the one with the gun here." Like Adam could use it to threaten Carmichael. But he could see Carmichael was remembering the much more pleasurable way Adam had demanded something from him. Filthy, aching, wounded, and his cock still twitched at the memory.

As he gazed on the feast that was Carmichael, three little words leaped into his throat, words Carmichael wouldn't want to hear, words Adam never thought he'd say again, never mind feel again. Shit.

"So talk to me," he said instead as he remembered that Carmichael wasn't even interested in a regular fuck buddy. Certainly a relationship with feelings and all was out of the question.

"Fine. Put your feet here." Carmichael patted a thigh. "But first, the other werewolf—"

"The other one?"

"The one that knocked you out."

Oh. Bill wasn't the one that knocked him out. "What about him?"

"Small guy, fifties, dyed black hair. You know him?"

"Bushy unibrow?"

Carmichael nodded.

"Sounds like the mayor. Was the *mayor* one of those things?" Things like this didn't happen in real life, but he had a damned *werewolf* bite on his neck to prove otherwise. He had no choice but to believe.

"Could be. We'll send out a cleanup crew later to retrieve the bodies."

Adam sat down and placed his feet in Carmichael's lap to await both foot tending and storytelling.

"You remember I told you I worked for a secret government agency, right?"

Adam nodded.

"Well, that's true, but we investigate paranormal activity. More precisely, paranormal activity arising from portals opening from other worlds."

After the shit Adam had seen today, that he could believe, as strange as it was.

"So what does MIA stand for, then?"

"Metaphysical Investigative Agency."

"Oh yeah, I can see why you went with an alternate. If I hadn't seen Bill with my own eyes, I might have thought you were a nutcase." Adam couldn't help being sarcastic. If he became too serious, he might lose his shit.

Carmichael grimaced. He must get that a lot. Or not. Depended on how many people Carmichael had tried to tell.

"Anyway, there's a lot we don't know about the portals. We don't know if they all open to a single world or dimension or time, or different ones. We've never been able to pass through ourselves."

"What about probes or something?"

"The portals play holy hell with electronics."

"Oh, I see." Adam remembered all that weird-ass computer equipment in Oliver's room. "Wait..."

With a faint smile, Carmichael held up a hand to forestall Adam's question. "We have equipment that can read *some* information about the portal from a distance, but there was a good reason I didn't bother using the sat phone during our hike until we were much closer to the ranger station."

"Okay, noted. Go on."

"On the other side of the portals are entities MIA calls the

Umbrae. When they cross over, they possess people, turn them into monsters."

"Werewolves, you mean."

"This time, yes. We're not sure how it works, but MIA has seen just about every type of horror-fiction monster develop from possession by the Umbrae. They tap into some primeval part of the brain and pick up on the mythology or legends surrounding the creatures, giving the possessed person many of the creature's strengths and weaknesses."

"Or the legends grew out of what the portals created," Adam suggested, intrigued. It wouldn't be the first time myth grew out of reality.

Carmichael nodded. "That's one theory."

Fucking bizarre. But kind of cool at the same time. "So there could be vampires too? How many are there?"

"No, this nest is likely all werewolves."

"Nest? Not pack?"

"They're all Umbrae. Easier to have a single term. Sometimes we use *den*, though. The first person turned determines the species, and each possessed afterwards becomes the same. The transformation is often precipitated by biting. The bite provides a channel from the portal into the possessed. We don't know for sure how the Umbrae possess the first person they attack, nor what determines the species of the infection. And this is probably the biggest nest we've ever encountered. Oliver thinks there might be up to ten werewolves."

"Holy fuck. Bill bit me!"

"I know. It's okay. The infection needs three days, for some reason. Maybe it takes that long for the Umbrae to stimulate the appropriate physiological changes. We closed the portal long before your three days were up."

Adam exhaled and tried to calm his racing heart. Scary shit. Bill had been trying to turn him into a werewolf. Probably figured Adam would be more...accommodating once he'd been infected too.

"So, the explosion closed the portal. What about those already infected?"

"For some, the shock of the portal closing will stop their hearts. Others will be driven insane, but the physiological changes reverse themselves after a couple of hours. A few will fully recover, with a mild form of amnesia."

Carmichael's phone rang, and he stood to speak. Adam remained silent while Carmichael arranged a pickup with Oliver.

Huh. Rothburg might return to normal. But then, he had had no idea that Bill, a deputy for several years before Adam's father retired, was anything other than normal. He shook his head.

The movement pulled the bite wound on his shoulder, and as he cataloged his aches and pains, sharp, burning anger pulsed in his stomach. Carmichael hadn't trusted him with the truth, lied to him wherever possible, almost gotten him killed, and thought he was a fuckup.

Oh, and let's not forget, he'd also practically been shoved out of bed for thinking Carmichael might want more than a temporary diversion. Why, exactly, was Adam being so accepting? He hadn't even gotten a fucking apology. And he'd still almost told the bastard that he loved him. Apparently Adam didn't have any self-preservation or self-respect.

"What's wrong?" Carmichael held out a hand to help Adam up, but Adam struggled to his feet without assistance.

"Now I've seen all this, this is when you trust me with this information? I could have been killed, and you didn't think a little warning might be in order?" Gaping black sorrow engulfed Adam, making it difficult to remain upright. The man he loved didn't give a shit about him.

Carmichael had the sense to look chagrined. "It was all classified. I couldn't tell you."

"Oh, and it's unclassified now, is it?"

"Well, no, but I felt I owed you—"

"For what?" Adam could feel blood heating his ears. "For

dumping me? For fucking me under false pretenses? For thinking I was a total screwup who couldn't be trusted?"

"No! Shit, Adam, I... It wasn't like that. I'm sorry. I found out about your parents and everything..."

Asshole. He'd found out about Adam's parents—and Adam's schooling too, by the looks of him. Adam wanted to punch someone. Specifically Carmichael. Anger camouflaged everything else. Like with Joel, it was the trappings of Adam's life that mattered to Carmichael, not the person he was inside.

"Is that supposed to make me feel better? Somehow I'm suddenly more reliable or trustworthy?"

"Adam, no, I meant—" Carmichael reached out a hand, but Adam evaded it.

"Save it, Carmichael. I don't care. Oliver said he was meeting us at the end of the old county road, right? It's this way." Adam began hauling through the brush, heedless of the pain in his feet, the stinging wetness in his eyes. Amazingly the sound of his heart shattering didn't echo through the forest. He wasn't going to bother picking up the pieces this time. In the future, he'd be as heartless as Carmichael, feel no remorse.

Carmichael wisely kept silent throughout the trek.

In a surprisingly short time, Adam broke through the brush to a small gaggle of pearlescent, off-white SUVs. If he still had a functioning heart, he might have found amusement in it.

Oliver spotted Adam.

"God, you two look like hell. Kath will get you fixed up in no time."

"How'd you get the other teams here?" Carmichael asked. Adam imagined his voice sounded rusty from disuse, but it hadn't been an hour since he'd told Carmichael to shut up. He risked a glance behind him and noticed Carmichael's heavy limp. Shit. His knee must be acting up. Adam had moved fast, and he hadn't considered Carmichael's injury.

He refused to feel guilty. Carmichael didn't have to keep the same pace. Adam would have been happier if he'd lagged behind. Maybe not happier. Less angry.

"They finished up earlier than expected and were close by when I called in. We're rounding up the last of them. Looks like the two park rangers are going to make it, but most of the others died. I can't tell who the pack leader was, though."

"Probably Bill," Carmichael replied.

"Who is Bill?" Oliver asked. "And what makes you say so?"

"Bill is—or was—the chief of police."

Adam let Carmichael explain because didn't think he'd be able to utter Bill's name without a shudder—ever.

"Oh, of course. Yes, you're right."

Just like that? Carmichael was right? Well, there went Adam's resolve to ignore Carmichael. "How does that make sense to both of you? And which park rangers?"

Oliver gestured to the row of four black body bags. Who were they? Including the two now-dead werewolves he and Carmichael had encountered, that made eight. Was Oliver wrong about how many were in the nest, or were there more corpses waiting to be discovered?

Oliver took his arm and guided him to a woman who Adam assumed was Kath. Adam took a seat in the back of the SUV and allowed her to tend to his wounds, waiting for Oliver to answer his questions.

"You know this is all highly classified, yes?"

Adam nodded. "I'll sign whatever you need me to sign. I just want some answers."

"I've already explained most of it, Oliver," Carmichael said behind him. "We killed two of them, and he watched one revert. I didn't have a choice."

Oliver gave him a wry grin. "Good to know."

Adam waited for Oliver to continue.

"You do realize, though, given the subject matter, you could talk about it all you want. No one would believe you. They'd believe you'd lost your mind."

Uh, yeah. Probably true. Adam hadn't considered that angle. He had no intention of trying to make people believe him, but he had an academic's urge to play the devil's advocate. "But won't there be these poor dead people as proof? What about the bite on my neck?"

Oliver was still smiling, and it looked genuine. "The government will cite some strange disease, food poisoning, something. Your wound could have come from a wild animal. Fever and exposure can make even the most reliable witnesses unhinged."

The stress Oliver placed on the word *reliable* made Adam remember that most of the town shared Carmichael's preconceived notions about his integrity. The government wielded a lot of power, and if Adam had a notion to press it, his rumored instability would adversely affect his life, even at the university.

"Fair enough." Adam conceded the point with good grace since he had no intention of talking about this with anyone. Thinking or talking about it would only remind him of what an idiot he'd been. The sooner this was over, the faster he could forget Carmichael. "What about the park rangers?"

"Most of the possessed had their picture in the paper at one point or another. I recognized all of them, included the editor you spoke of."

"Arthur's in one of those bags? Who else is in there?"

Oliver nodded somberly. "Dr. Ridley, the deputy mayor, and one of the rangers. I suspect the two we're tracking are police deputies."

Holy shit. The Umbrae had possessed the entire police force and all the full-time park rangers? Monstrous. Devastating to the town.

"Which rangers are alive? Where are they?"

"The head ranger, Ranger Goldman, and Cass Harris will recover. They're headed to the hospital right now."

"Ranger Goldman? Smokey was one of those things? Shit. I had no idea."

"No one did. Werewolves are very crafty, very secretive. As I was saying, I recognized everyone. They all held some important role in the town. To ensure the nest could operate in obscurity, the chief of police must have chosen his victims with deliberation and care. Maybe the strongest foothold the Umbrae have made in this world. All because the alpha of the nest was a smart person in a position of power. If the Umbrae are ever able to control the placement of their portals, we could be in some serious trouble."

"How did they get Bill, though?"

"Who knows? Maybe he came out for a call, looking for kids making trouble... In the wrong place at the wrong time."

Adam thought he should be more boggled by this information than he was, but he listened, filed it away, and wanted nothing more than to get back his regular life.

"We done here, Kath?"

"All set, Agent Cardoso." Kath shifted her attention to Carmichael.

"Come on, Adam. I'll drop you at home. The rest of them are capable of finishing up here." Oliver shook his car keys.

"But, Oliver—" Carmichael began.

Oliver shook his head. "No, I need you here."

Adam slid into the SUV Oliver directed him to, without a backward glance at Carmichael. Adam didn't want to look at him. He was tired, cranky, dirty, and the anger had receded, leaving a fragility that wanted only one hangdog look from Carmichael to prompt Adam into doing something brainless like forgiving him.

"CAN YOU GIVE US A MINUTE, KATH?" Carmichael ignored the odd look Kath gave him before she shrugged and moved out of earshot. "I'm okay," Carmichael said to Oliver.

Oliver's skeptical gaze flickered over Carmichael's assorted wounds.

"I'd like to be there."

"I know. You can come back for him." Oliver gave him a look that made Carmichael's stomach lurch. What did he know? How could he know?

"Come back? For who?"

Oliver gave him a sad little smile. Carmichael couldn't think. Didn't want to think. He didn't allow himself to blink, because tears might start falling.

"Okay, then, if that's how you want it. I'm going to run Adam home. After that, we're done here. Wrap this up, and I'll meet you back at the B and B."

Carmichael couldn't speak. He twisted Adam's ring around his middle finger, still tacky with Bill's blood. Adam didn't know he had it. He should return it...but he knew he wasn't going to.

Kath moved back in to provide first aid as soon as Oliver walked away. Her head was down, so Carmichael took a chance and swiped the back of his hand across his eyes.

Oliver got into the driver's side of the SUV and sped away. Carmichael watched until long after the dust from the tires lingered in the air. Adam had been so angry, so withdrawn. Carmichael had lost him before he figured out if he could be open about his desire for Adam. Live out of the closet.

Shit. He couldn't even stop himself from lying to Oliver, when it was obvious to anyone with eyes that Oliver knew something had happened. Carmichael might not be able to read people well, but he did know his partner. This time it wasn't paranoia. Oliver knew and gave him permission to return here, to see Adam. Didn't matter now. Carmichael had fucked up, damaged his chances beyond repair.

He looked down at the silver ring on his hand. A token, a reminder of how stupid he'd been. Maybe next time he wouldn't let his fears get in the way of something special. Next time. Yeah, that'd be a long way off. Though he'd never been involved in a relationship before, he had no doubt that getting over Adam was going to be a long and painful process.

BEFORE THEY REACHED the outskirts of town, Oliver spoke. "There's something I have to tell you."

Oh God. Adam's palms began to sweat. Oliver knew about Adam and Carmichael. Worse, had Oliver ordered Carmichael to seduce him, make him more pliable?

"It's about your parents."

His parents? His parents wouldn't notice or care if Adam had been fucking Carmichael on the kitchen table. "What about them?"

"Their illness started a little over a year ago, correct?"

"Yes." Adam was aware of the surliness in his tone. Too much had been thrown at him today. And he'd hit his head pretty fucking hard. What the hell was Oliver getting at?

"Sometimes aborted or incomplete possessions can manifest as neurological conditions such as Alzheimer's."

All of a sudden there wasn't enough air in the world to fill Adam's lungs. At the edges of his consciousness, he noted that Oliver had pulled into his parents' driveway and parked the SUV.

"You need to prepare yourself."

"Are they dead?"

"I believe so." Oliver stretched out a hand, placing it comfortingly on Adam's arm. "I have to go in with you. If I'm right, they'll need to be part of the cover story the agency is creating. Their condition may be the reason the doctor was turned."

For all that Oliver's words were cold and matter-of-fact, Adam saw sympathy in his eyes.

No sense in putting it off. Adam unbuckled and got out. In front of the door, he paused for a moment before opening it.

"Honey, I'm glad you're home." Jennifer hugged him. "I've been trying to page Doc Ridley for the past hour."

"I..." Adam didn't know what to say. Announcing Doc Ridley's death was not his responsibility.

"Who's your friend?"

"This is Oliver."

"He treat you better than that other one?" Jennifer nodded a greeting in Oliver's direction.

Adam blinked at Jennifer, amazed that she could think about his love life at a time like this. "My parents?"

"Oh, honey, your parents, I can't believe it."

Tears welled up in his eyes, and he sniffled.

"Are you catching a cold? Your parents may appear much better, but they're still weak. Don't you go getting them sick, now."

"What?" Adam looked back at Oliver, who was smiling. He hadn't noticed, until it was gone, how tense Oliver had been. "What are you talking about?"

"I can't begin to explain it," Jennifer said. "You're going to have to get the doctor to check them out, but I haven't seen them this lucid in the entire year I've worked for you."

"Can I see them?"

"They're asleep again. Wait, honey, what happened to you?" Jennifer seemed to see him for the first time. "You need some rest too, from the look of you."

"Skateboard accident," Oliver said. "I drove him home."

Jennifer tsked. "I'm going to make you some tea. Then I'm ordering you to bed. I'm a nurse, I know what I'm talking about."

"Fine, thanks. I'll just walk Oliver out."

The second the door shut behind them, Adam turned on Oliver. "What the fuck is going on?"

"I didn't want to get your hopes up, but rare cases like your parents' end the same way as everyone else possessed by the Umbrae —insane, dead, or recovered."

Relief. Happiness. Adam's eyes welled up again, for a different reason. He hugged Oliver, pleased to feel Oliver's arms tighten around him. Made him feel almost as safe as being in Carmichael's arms. He'd gone through a terrifying, life-altering experience, but he'd do it all over without any hesitation if the end result were his parents' recovery.

"Thank you," he whispered in Oliver's ear.

"Get inside. Your nurse is right. You need some rest. Act amazed at your parents' miraculous recovery. Play dumb about the cause. It'll all work out."

A debilitating lassitude crept through Adam's body. Rest, real rest, sounded like the best idea anyone had had in a long time.

THE NEXT DAY, after a happy reunion with parents Adam had resigned himself to losing, the news exploded with stories of a bizarre case of food poisoning that affected brain tissue and neurological function, killing several prominent citizens of Rothburg.

Adam went to the B and B to congratulate Oliver on a cover story well executed—and not to see Carmichael, nope. All he found was his skateboard in the care of Gladys at the front desk. A dark cloud shadowed the happiness he'd been feeling. The two MIA agents were gone as if they'd never been, without even a note.

A clean break. Enforced by no forwarding address.

TWELVE

Just over two months later, Adam stood amongst a pile of boxes in his tiny new apartment near the college. Desperate for a distraction in between intensive therapy sessions and self-defense classes to help him deal with his assault, Adam was able to arrange for a January return to his degree program. His parents had made a miraculously swift recovery, and with so many of Rothburg's town leaders dead from the virulent "food poisoning" incident, his dad had been rehired as chief of police and his mother elected as interim mayor. In a blink, Adam's crushing debt load had been substantially reduced.

Having his parents returned to him, whole and sane, had been a gift and he treasured spending the holiday season with them. But without a word or text from Carmichael the entire time made Christmas bittersweet. Then he'd rung in the New Year without a boyfriend, yet again. Every text, every phone call, every time the door opened at the café during his shift, gave him a tiny spurt of hope, which was quickly smothered under the crush of disappointment.

In a matter of days, he'd have research and papers and classes to keep him busy but the only distraction he had right now was unpacking.

The apartment was part of a large, old house cut up into small, oddly proportioned living spaces. Adam had hoped he'd eventually find it charming, but now, without any enthusiasm or energy for unpacking even the bare necessities, it was simply depressing. There hadn't been much to choose from, and while he didn't enjoy the musty smell, it didn't have cockroaches and it was close to campus. January was a shitty time to resume school but he couldn't bear to wait until the fall.

A far cry from the slick, modern apartment he'd shared with Joel what seemed like a hundred years ago. Now his bedroom, living room, and kitchen were all one room. He could practically cook dinner without getting out of his futon. As long as dinner only required two functional burners.

A knock at the door interrupted his complete and utter lack of progress. He jumped for the door, trying to suppress the leap of his heart, and opened it.

"Joel."

"Don't sound so thrilled, Adam." Joel pushed past him into the apartment. A tiny sneer of distaste appeared as he inspected his surroundings.

"What are you doing here?"

"You're the one who texted me the address."

"Ah, yes. My mistake."

Joel giggled like Adam was teasing him, and not stating a cold hard truth.

Adam sighed. The proximity to campus had him feeling nostalgic, and he'd stupidly texted Joel this morning, letting him know he was returning to his doctoral program.

Joel shared some superficial similarities with Carmichael, but he was an older, less buff, more faded version. Apparently Adam had a physical type, but the two men couldn't be more different, personality-wise. Joel was a shallow, appearances-obsessed English professor desperately trying to regain his youth from the other side of thirty-five. Aside from his struggle against aging, he'd never had to fight for anything in his life. He was the spoiled only child of wealthy parents and if he'd wanted to be a cat wrangler or cupcake baker or investment banker, his parents would have made it happen.

Even without knowing Carmichael's past, Carmichael's strength of character and protective nature had been self-evident. In comparison, the only laudable aspect of Joel's character was his desire to be a professor, although Adam suspected even that was the result of intellectual snobbery.

"As you can see, Joel, I have a lot of work to do." There was zero chance Joel would offer to help, and Adam hoped that would convince him to leave again.

"I wanted to see you."

Adam narrowed his eyes at his ex. If he'd wanted to see Adam, all it would have taken was a ninety-minute drive in his swank Beemer to Rothburg. But Joel hadn't made the trip once. Joel hadn't called or texted, not even to check on Adam's state of mind or wellbeing in the entire year he'd lived back home.

"Why?"

Joel's eyes widened at Adam's antagonistic tone. Adam almost never snapped at Joel when they'd been together, because the resulting sulk was just not worth it. Now, he didn't understand why he'd even gotten involved with Joel in the first place.

"Don't you miss how we were together? I miss you. We could start again. Fresh."

"I'm sorry, but you want to get back together? Why?" Six months ago, he would have said yes, no questions asked. But the feelings he'd had for Joel when they been together were nothing compared to what Carmichael had managed to make him feel after only a few days. The difference between a light bulb and the sun. And the pain of losing both men? A paper cut versus a near mortal wound. Carmichael had scourged his soul of all romantic feelings for Joel.

"I don't think that's a good idea."

"Of course it's a good idea." Joel moved close and tried to wrap his arms around Adam.

Adam stepped neatly away, a minor miracle given how little floor space he had in which to maneuver. "You dumped me. Remember? My family emergency was an inconvenience for you."

"And I'm sorry. I should have stuck by you. But I can spend the rest of our lives making it up to you."

"Oh, no I don't think so." If there was a hell on Earth, it might just be enduring Joel for the next several decades.

"But we were so good together. So hot." Joel made another grab for him, and Adam made use of a self defense technique to keep him at bay.

Adam let out a relieved breath. No panic attack. After his assault, he wasn't sure how he'd react to an unwanted advance, especially from someone larger than him. Therapy plus a distinct lack of werewolf both played their part.

Joel backed off, pouting. Adam should have known Joel was horny and assumed Adam would be a low-effort booty call.

"Please leave."

"Just think about it, okay?"

"Nothing to think about, Joel. We're done. I met someone else." Even if they weren't together, it had changed him. MIA had barreled into his world and turned it upside down.

"Oh. I see. Well, we can still be friends."

"Sure thing, Joel. I'm super busy but we can catch up later." As soon as he got Joel out of here, he was blocking his number and all social media. He was certain Joel thought being "friends" meant there the possibility of sex was still an option. It wasn't. Adam would rather be alone the rest of his life.

He all but shoved Joel out the door and locked it behind him. His apartment seemed a lot more homey and welcoming now, without Joel in it.

Adam took a box of toiletries to the bathroom and started unpacking colognes. Once, the scents made him think longingly of Joel. No longer. They made him smell damned good, and that was all that mattered. And one day, he'd recover from Carmichael. However long that took.

He couldn't hate Carmichael, though. No one had promised him anything. It was his own fault for falling so hard, so fast. He emptied the box and escaped the confines of his minuscule bathroom, all while avoiding his reflection. He looked tired and didn't need any reminders. He wasn't vain, but gaunt was not a good look for him.

After all this time, how could he still have such strong feelings for Carmichael? What kind of idiot held on to a torch for so long? Especially when the "relationship" numbered in days and the other party considered him little more than a hookup. An idiot like Adam Farelli, obviously.

Adam opened another box. Great. Condoms. But no lube. He'd not needed either of those since Carmichael, but surely they both should have ended up in the same box. Probably he should just trash them, because he had no interest in an anonymous hook-up, and every time he tried to jerk off, the only image that came to mind was Carmichael. Which made him lose all enthusiasm for the sport, damn Carmichael anyway. Fucking ruined him, Carmichael had, with his brand of hit-and-run sex. Yet another thing to blame him for.

Carmichael had done a lot for Adam's family. It wasn't that he wasn't grateful. He was. But a whole slew of less favorable emotions tainted his warmer feelings, and fuck if Adam knew how to shut them off.

A knock sounded at the door. He rolled his eyes. Not Joel again. The man could be irritatingly single-minded at times. He threw the condoms in a drawer beside his futon, where they could rot.

Another knock sounded, more rapid and impatient than the previous one. How many times did he need to tell Joel there was no chance of reviving what they'd had?

He unlocked the door and flung it open as he spoke. "What do you want now, Joel?"

Carmichael.

A kaleidoscope of butterflies came to life in Adam's belly. Was this a dream?

Nope. Carmichael stood in Adam's doorway, looking as edible as ever. He gave Adam a bashful, shamefaced smile.

"Well, I'd like to know who Joel is, but I'm not sure I have the right to ask."

Too fucking right. Carmichael's stunning blue gaze, brighter than Adam remembered, kept flicking over Adam's form but didn't stay in any one place long, and he seemed reluctant to meet Adam's eyes.

Adam sternly told his dick—and the butterflies—to behave. No way was he letting this man tie him up in knots again. Or still. More? Whatever.

"What I should have said was: what do you want, Carmichael?" Adam's tone was less exasperated than before, but if Carmichael thought he could show up on Adam's doorstop whenever he wanted, looking for a bit of easy tail, well, he'd come to the wrong place.

"Can I come in? I'd like to talk to you."

After more than two months? Stupidly, he stepped out of the doorway and swept his arm out, gesturing for Carmichael to enter. He'd have to check later if there was supposed to be a full moon tonight.

"Can I get you something to drink?" Unlike Joel, he wanted Carmichael to stick around, but he couldn't bear it if Carmichael knew how much he'd been hurt by the man's abrupt departure from Rothburg and subsequent radio silence. "Beer? Water?"

"Beer would be great." Carmichael followed Adam into the kitchen and leaned against the counter, which was small enough that Carmichael's large frame obscured most of it.

Could he really feel Carmichael's body heat? Surely not. Just in case, though, he leaned farther into the fridge than necessary, hoping to armor himself as best he could.

Unable to put it off any longer, he swung away from the fridge and handed Carmichael one of the two beers he'd grabbed.

"It's good to see you, Adam."

Well, at least he hadn't said Adam looked good. Because that would have been a big, fat lie. Carmichael looked great, though. A little tired, maybe, but great. Not that Adam was going to tell him.

"I'm glad you stopped by." Adam strove for nonchalance. "I never got a chance to thank you."

"I don't want your fucking gratitude," Carmichael snarled.

Whoa. Adam waited a moment while Carmichael breathed deeply and closed his eyes. When he opened them, Adam could see he was calm again. Calmer, at any rate.

"What do you want, Carmichael?" Not that he was going to get it. Letting Carmichael fuck him again was only going to make it harder to get over him. "And how did you know where to find me?"

"Government agent, remember?" Carmichael pointed at himself with a cute smile. No. Not cute. Adam couldn't think like that. It was dangerous. "Besides, Joel knew you were here."

"Yes, well, I told Joel I was here. You…I didn't. If I'd wanted to, I didn't even have an e-mail address for you. So why are you here?" Anger overshadowed other, less welcome emotions. Anger was safer for his heart.

The bluster drained out of Carmichael, and if Adam wasn't mistaken, he looked nervous.

Carmichael set down his untouched, unopened beer on the counter and moved the couple of steps to look out Adam's kitchen window—a painful reminder of Carmichael in this exact pose in the dreadful Manx Room. His heart ached and Carmichael didn't give a damn.

"I've missed you."

Uh-huh. Booty call. His pheromone game was *banging* today. His dick, of course, didn't care. It was poised and ready for more of the best sex he'd ever had. But his dick didn't make the decisions around here.

"Look, whatever impression you formed about me, I'm not some easy lay. You think you can waltz back here after nine weeks without a word, an e-mail, nothing? No government office would even admit your agency existed." Oops. He hadn't intended to let Carmichael know he'd tried to contact him. Or that he'd been counting weeks. Shit.

"You think after that, I'm going to spread for you, just because you ask nicely?" With supreme effort, he said those words without shouting.

Carmichael colored a dusky pink under his tanned cheeks. His hair looked blonder too. Hope he had a good time at whatever tropical destination he'd been vacationing in. *Dick.*

Then Adam noticed the shadows under Carmichael's eyes. Looked a lot like the ones Adam sported. And he didn't look at all relaxed either.

"It's not like that, I swear. I'm sorry." Carmichael's voice trailed off, and those gorgeous, erection-inducing eyes gave him such a doleful look that Adam almost said, *To hell with it,* and leaped into Carmichael's arms. Almost.

Self-respect. Dignity. *Remember those, Adam?* Was a time he had 'em—a time before Carmichael, obviously.

"I'm sorry," Carmichael said again.

"For what?"

Carmichael stared at him, like he couldn't believe Adam wanted him to be specific. But a blanket apology wasn't going to cut it.

"I'm doing this all wrong. And that's one of many things I'm sorry for. But please, let me say what I came to say. Please."

Adam wasn't sure he wanted to hear it. He couldn't get any words past the sudden constriction in his throat, though.

"Yes, I miss the sex. Of course I miss the sex. It was fucking unbelievable."

A sliver of pride slid through Adam, defrosting some of the coldness settled in his belly.

"But more than that, I miss you, Adam. You know I've never had a relationship before. I joined the military as soon as I could, and a relationship wasn't prudent. I don't know how... I've never... Look, I know I fucked up. Bad. I know you think I didn't trust you, respect you, and you think I deliberately put you in danger. But..." Carmichael seemed to be at a loss about how to go on. Adam stayed silent, wondering what the point of this was.

After several seconds, Carmichael nodded, as though he'd come to a decision after a fierce internal debate.

"Okay, first. I was trying to do my job. Without getting fired. Which could have happened after everything I told you."

Remembering everything Carmichael had told him, classified information he was sure Oliver wouldn't have shared, it was as though their weeks of separation had never occurred.

"But in reality, when it sounded like you wanted something long-term, I panicked. And in doing so, I failed to take the proper precautions to keep you safe. You're right to blame me for that. As for not respecting you... I never told you why I dislike my first name, did I?"

No. Adam had wanted to coerce it out of him, maybe the same pleasurable way he'd wrung Carmichael's name out of him, but the Umbrae had intervened.

"I've never met my father. I don't think my mother knows who he is."

Adam's eyes widened. Whatever the reason for Carmichael's avoidance of his first name, he hadn't thought the story would start like that.

"My mother was sixteen when she had me. A high school dropout, she cared more for drugs and booze than she did for me. She was in and out of jail during my childhood, and my grandfather raised me. His name was Lachlan too. My grandfather was also a drunk, and he spent his days drinking and out of work. He'd work a few low-wage jobs, but the booze and the inability to control his tongue got him repeatedly fired. His..."

Carmichael clenched his fists, knuckles turning white.

"Did he hit you?" God, Adam had never expected this.

"Yes. And the booze made him meaner."

"Your mother didn't stop him?"

"My mother was never home enough to notice. Even if she had, where else would she get free child care? As soon as I turned eighteen, I enlisted. The army saved me. My grandfather died while I was in basic, and my mother killed the clerk of a convenience store she'd been robbing shortly thereafter. She's still in prison."

Carmichael looked him in the eye again, but Adam could almost see the expectation of a blow. Like Adam would ever do that.

"I'm sorry. I had no idea."

Carmichael shrugged, as if it meant nothing. Adam wasn't fooled.

"That's why I had such a negative reaction to what I saw as your life choices. Please believe me, though. Before I'd gone to your house, before I found out what an exceptional person you truly are..."

Adam felt a blush equal to Carmichael's rise up his neck.

"I'd stopped caring," Carmichael said. "About that. You were nothing like my family, I could tell. All I knew was that I wanted you safe and in my life as long as I could have you. Whatever job you wanted to have."

What? Adam forgot to breathe. He couldn't have heard that right.

"Why did you..." Adam's shock had stolen his words.

"Leave? I thought it best. You were so angry. So cold. I thought you hated me. I thought a clean break was best. But—" Carmichael's voice became broken, anguished. "I can't stop thinking about you. I can't sleep. I can't eat. I can't function..."

Were those tears shining in his eyes? Shit, how many times had Adam dreamed of Carmichael coming back, begging for forgiveness? Now he was doing it, and Adam was torn. It was the most beautiful thing anyone had ever said to him. It was everything he wanted, and he couldn't quite bring himself to believe it was happening.

"Oliver thinks I'm an idiot for not coming sooner."

"Oliver knows?" Carmichael was out of the closet? Long dead hope stirred to life in Adam's chest, even though he wasn't sure hope was a good idea.

"What do you want from me, Carmichael?" Adam leaned back against the counter. He needed more. Carmichael had broken his heart and stomped on the shards. He needed to know exactly where he stood with Carmichael.

Carmichael dropped to his knees in front of him. "I'm sorry," he whispered and pressed a kiss on Adam's fly. No mistaking the bulge there for anything else. No matter what his dick thought, Adam was still angry and hurt. Carmichael opened Adam's jeans, yanked them halfway down his thighs, and sucked his cock into that warm, talented mouth before Adam could process what was happening.

With a groan, Carmichael closed his eyes and pressed the heel of his hand to the impressive erection under his cargo pants. Oh shit. How could Adam think with those sexy lips wrapped around him?

Frantic suction and frenzied tongue action, focused on the pulsing tip, dragged Adam to the edge faster than anything he could remember. He reached up and grabbed the handle of the cupboard door to steady himself, his other hand going to Carmichael's blond head.

"Oh fuck... So good."

Carmichael moaned his response around the mouthful of cock, the vibrations causing little shivers of ecstasy to ripple up Adam's spine. He couldn't help himself; he began thrusting into that wet mouth, holding Carmichael's head where he wanted it. Carmichael could break the hold if he wanted, but the hands clutching Adam's hips indicated he was more than happy with Adam's attentions. Dimly Adam heard a *crack*, but his attention was focused on nothing but his dick and Carmichael's tongue.

One hand released its grip on Adam to slide into his crease. A finger pressed dry into Adam's opening, and without warning, his orgasm erupted from his balls, firing volley after volley into Carmichael's greedy mouth.

Carmichael crawled up his body and pressed his lips to Adam's neck. God, he smelled so good, so right. But the orgasm had cleared his mind. He still wasn't sure what Carmichael wanted. If it was occasional sexual relief, he wasn't interested. Despite what had just happened. He pushed at Carmichael, wanted to look at him.

Carmichael hadn't gotten off, but right now he wasn't concerned about that.

"What's wrong?" Carmichael asked.

"I don't know if I can do this." Carmichael was out, at least to Oliver, but that didn't mean he wanted what Adam did.

Carmichael's eyes widened, and Adam saw, clear as day, pain in that beautiful blue gaze.

"I think I love you." Carmichael flushed before looking away.

Oh God. From anyone else, Adam would have considered that a half-assed declaration, but he sensed the power behind words he knew Carmichael had never said to anyone else. An inner warmth, like he was filled with sunshine, burned away the icy fog of his anger and upset. The peace and contentment left behind were better than anything he could have imagined, and Adam took a moment to savor it, to bask in the realization that this wasn't merely a spectacular dream.

"I'm sorry to have bothered you. I'll just let myself out." Carmichael angled himself to move around Adam, gaze still on the floor.

"No!" Adam closed the gap between them and cupped Carmichael's smooth-shaven cheeks with his palms. "I love you too," he said softly before he tilted Carmichael's—Lachlan's—face down for a kiss, mouth still flavored with Adam's cum. For a fraction of a second, the kiss remained sweet, gentle, a beautiful expression of love. Then it transformed into a hotter, fiercer, sensual expression of loving passion.

Panting, frantic, they roughly stripped clothes from each other's bodies. The clean scent of soap and male skin hit Adam's nose, making him salivate. He was damned glad he'd had a shower that morning. Adam was desperate to have naked skin-on-skin contact after months of longing, and Lachlan seemed just as desperate.

He grabbed Adam by the waist and turned them, stretching Adam out on the futon. With a smile, he swept fingertips along the length of Adam's body, as if assuring himself Adam was really there.

Then he straddled Adam, taking his lips again in a sweet kiss, while his fat, drooling dick rubbed against Adam's renewed erection.

Overwhelming joy flooded him. He was making love for the first time in his life, and he squirmed in anticipation.

"In me, now," Adam demanded.

"Lube?" Lachlan panted in his ear, fingers clutching Adam's hips hard enough that Adam knew he was going to bruise. Knowing he'd be wearing Lachlan's marks made him even more excited.

Fucking hell. One of those unpacked boxes held the prize. Then Adam looked up and saw a bottle of olive oil. "There." He pointed. He hadn't known when he unpacked it that it was going to become a necessity as required as breathing, because he'd put the actual lube somewhere stupid.

Lachlan leaped up, grabbed the bottle, and returned to Adam.

"Oh fuck." Lachlan whimpered. With shaking hands, he opened the oil and smeared some along Adam's crease. Adam couldn't help him; he was too busy relearning the hardened planes and dips of Lachlan's chest. The bottle dropped from Carmichael's hand, and he nudged Adam's legs farther apart.

A blunt head pressed against his hole, and Adam spread his legs wider, drawing his knees up, knowing he was going to blow any minute.

Carmichael stopped, arms shaking with strain.

"What?" Adam hissed, twisting his hips but unable to get enough leverage to impale himself. There'd been no stretching, and he didn't want any. He wanted to feel every solid inch of Carmichael's fat cock sliding into him, and he wanted it now.

"No condom." Lachlan's voice was strained. "I... didn't think you'd forgive me."

When the drumbeat in his cock ceased demanding satisfaction, Adam would be charmed that Lachlan truly hadn't sought him out for a booty call.

"The drawer. I have some."

Carmichael grabbed the condoms and quickly covered himself.

"Now fuck me. Love me." Adam knew in his heart he wasn't making a mistake putting his trust in this man. Going bareback for the first time in his life with the man he loved, and who loved him, was symbolic. And hotter than hell.

"Love." Carmichael pressed his hips forward, Adam meeting the thrust with one of his own.

Adam wailed, the pleasure more intense than anything he'd ever felt. Carmichael groaned, and his hips snapped back and forth. The futon moved a couple of inches, and Adam heard it banging against the wall in time with Carmichael's strokes.

Ohgod, ohgod, ohgod.

"So fucking good," Adam heard whispered in his ear.

"More," he ordered.

Carmichael pulled his left hand free from Adam's hip, shifted slightly, and then grabbed Adam's dick, rigorous strokes matching rhythm to the cock pistoning in and out of Adam's ass.

The feel of metal on his overheated dick made Adam look down. When he realized what he was looking at, his urgent need to come was superseded by his need to know something else.

"Is that my ring?"

Carmichael's hips didn't pause. "I took it. When I was trying to find you." Lachlan's breath heaved out in pants between the words.

The notion that Carmichael had taken something of his, kept it all this time... All traces of doubt evaporated. Carmichael had meant every word he'd said. Adam's balls hitched up against his body.

Lachlan shifted again, nailed his gland, and Adam screamed Lachlan's name, cock pulsing, spraying cum everywhere. Lachlan yelled and bucked, his dick flexing in Adam's channel.

One day, they'd do this without the condoms. Adam had no doubt of that.

Lachlan slumped on top of him, panting. Adam had difficulty getting his own breath back, but he wouldn't have moved Lachlan's solid weight for anything.

Arms curled around Carmichael's sweat-slicked back, fingers

stroking along his spine, Adam surveyed the mess. The futon had battered a hole in the drywall. Oil covered the kitchen floor and had splashed on the wall, leaving large, greasy stains by the baseboard. He looked up and saw he'd managed to get cum on the wall above his head. Go, him. Did jizz stain paint? He had no idea but guessed he would find out. He tilted his head and noticed the cupboard door he'd been holding on to during the blowjob had pulled partly away from its hinges.

Huh. Probably wouldn't get his security deposit back.

Years later, or so it felt, Lachlan lifted himself from Adam and gently disengaged, drawing Adam's attention back to where it belonged. In no rush to leave the comfort of Lachlan's arms, Adam curled into the warm body next to him, pressing their chests together.

"I love you." Carmichael's blue, blue gaze met his, soft and sincere. Nothing else mattered, nothing but what they shared between them. "Move in with me, please."

Adam nodded and kissed those pink, swollen lips.

Fuck the security deposit.

ABOUT THE AUTHOR

KC Burn is a Canadian transplanted to California who writes happy-ever-afters about men loving men, whether they're psychics, space travelers, aliens, professors, construction workers, cops, amateur sleuths... you name it, she'll probably write it. She's got a pair of black cats, aka muses/nuisances, and a supportive, understanding hubby.

ALSO BY KC BURN

Contemporary

Cop Out (Toronto Tales #1)

Cover Up (Toronto Tales #2)

Cast Off (Toronto Tales #3)

Tartan Candy (Fabric Hearts #1)

Plaid versus Paisley (Fabric Hearts #2)

Just Add Argyle (Fabric Hearts #3)

Banded Together

Tea or Consequences

Rainbow Blues

Pen Name - Doctor Chicken

First Time, Forever

Set Ablaze

Sci-Fi

Spice 'n' Solace (Galactic Alliance #1)

Alien 'n' Outlaw (Galactic Alliance #2)

Voodoo 'n' Vice (Galactic Alliance #3)

Union of the Snake

Paranormal

Wolfsbane (MIA Case Files #1)

Blood Relations (MIA Case Files #2)

Craving (MIA Case Files #3)

Illusion of Life

North on Drummond

Holiday

A Cowboy's Christmas Luck

Heirlooms, Junk, and Christmas Luck

Three Dates of Christmas

www.ingramcontent.com/pod-product-compliance
Lightning Source LLC
Chambersburg PA
CBHW021032130626
46552CB00005B/1801